M

"I am your wife."

"Ah, but are you my woman?" he said and bent his head to nuzzle her hair. "Do you know what it means to be a woman? My woman?" He breathed close to her ear and shivers of excitement darted through her. "Sally, you're so beautiful. Do you know what you do to me? Let me love you. Let me make you a woman."

"Luke, you are drunk," she said shakily. She was excited and yet scared—he was so different from usual, so strong, so suddenly demanding, as though he'd unleashed the power and wildness normally kept under such tight control.

Sarah was not at all sure that this Luke would not hurt her...

Also by Lisa Gregory

Bonds of Love
*Before the Dawn**
*Solitaire**
*The Rainbow Promise**

***Published by**
WARNER BOOKS

The Rainbow Season

LISA GREGORY

A Warner Communications Company

WARNER BOOKS EDITION

This Warner Books Edition is published by arrangement with the author.

Cover art by Max Ginsburg

Warner Books, Inc.
666 Fifth Avenue
New York, N.Y. 10103

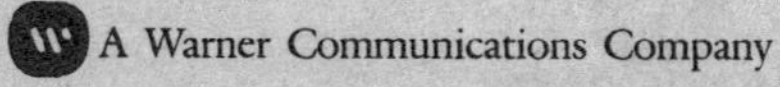
A Warner Communications Company

Printed in the United States of America

First Warner Books Printing: September, 1989

10 9 8 7 6 5 4 3 2 1

Chapter I

IT was all over town: Digger Turner was back.

Mary Beth Hewlin heard it when she stopped by the millinery shop, and she could hardly wait to rush home and tell all her neighbors. There was nothing she liked better than to be the carrier of news. She tried her neighbor to the east first, but she was not at home. So, almost bursting with her load of gossip, she slipped through her back yard and up to the back door of the Harpers' house. There, she knew, she would have a bigger audience, since Jennifer Harper's sister Sarah had been staying with her since the baby was born.

Sure enough, both the sisters were sitting at the kitchen table, chopping up vegetables for the evening stew. They were amazingly similar, the two sisters, yet so different, the one a poor reproduction of the other, or the first attempt of a later, perfected product. They were of the same stature, small without being fragile, firm and fine figured. Both had wide, intelligent foreheads and delicately triangular faces, with large expressive eyes and vulnerable little mouths. And if they spoke from another room, where one could not see them, even Jennifer's husband was sometimes unsure whether it was his wife calling him or her sister, so similar were their voices.

But looking at them, none would ever have mistaken the two. Alone, Sarah was a pretty girl, but beside Jennifer, she could go almost unnoticed. Though their hair was identical in color, Jennifer's shone with a luster lacking in Sarah's; Sarah's skin did not have the glow of Jennifer's; and Jennifer's long-lashed eyes were a bright, deep-emerald green, while Sarah's were a light hazel color that looked brown from a distance. But the major difference was, as their father once said of them, "Sarah glows, but Jennifer sparkles." Jennifer was possessed of a vivacity, a freshness that rarely visited Sarah. When Jenny spoke, her eyes flashed, her dimples jumped in and out, her soft curls bounced, her ear bobs danced. Her personality reached out like a magnet and drew people to her.

They looked up at Mary Beth's knock and smiled to see her round, eager face peering through the glass pane of the door.

"Well, she has obviously got something to tell," Sarah said laughingly.

"Come on in, Mary Beth," Jennifer called.

Sarah poured three cups of coffee from the pot that always sat on the stove. Soon, when the weather got warmer, the women's chats would be enlivened with iced tea or cold lemonade in huge glasses bedewed with drops of moisture.

''You know, I am really going to miss this when I go back to the farm,'' Sarah said as Mary Beth bustled in.

''That's the nicest thing about town,'' Jennifer agreed, ''being close enough to your friends to visit nearly every afternoon.''

It came easily to them, almost without thinking, this way they spoke, conveying to a mere acquaintance that she was welcomed, appreciated, a friend, without the direct compliment that always left one wondering if it was sincere or just polite. There was an intrinsic kindness and diplomacy in them that people felt rather than realized. It was simply pleasant to be around them, and everyone could express the feeling only as, ''Those McGowan girls are the *sweetest* things.''

It was obvious that Mary Beth was bursting with her news. Her fair skin was flushed and she clutched the skirts of her calico dress as if she had to contain something.

''Guess what?''

''What?'' they chorused and leaned in over the table, intrigued by her manner.

''That Turner boy is back.''

''Who?'' Jennifer asked vaguely, and Sarah suppressed a smile at the other woman's crestfallen face.

"Oh, you remember, Jenny," Sarah prompted. "Luke Turner. Everybody called him Digger, for some reason. Isn't that who you're talking about, Mary Beth?"

Mary Beth nodded emphatically and Jennifer said, "Oh, you mean the boy who was tried for—" Her voice trailed off delicately.

"Exactly. And now he has come back, bold as brass."

"But why is he out of prison? It was only three or four years ago, wasn't it?" Sarah asked.

"Five," Mary Beth corrected. "But they didn't give him a long sentence, not like he deserved. Why, I'd have given him twenty years."

"Oh, but, Mary Beth, he was so young," Jennifer protested. "Only eighteen or so."

"He was young, but he had the soul of a devil," Mary Beth declared dramatically.

"Surely, now, you can't mean that," Sarah joined her sister. "He was a wild boy, but—"

"Wild? Huh! He was more than wild. Drunk as a fiddler all the time, and lazy and shiftless, just like his father. And womanizing—wasn't a woman in town safe from him."

"Well, he kept some pretty loose company, but I never heard of him accosting any other girl except Tessa Jackson," Jennifer said.

"If you want my opinion," Sarah stuck in, "I don't think he accosted her, either. I never heard of anyone having to force Tessa. Why would he rape her when everyone knows he could have had her voluntarily, any time, like everybody else?''

Jennifer blushed at her sister's bluntness and their neighbor gasped, ''Sarah!''

''Well, I don't care!'' Sarah said defiantly. ''I didn't believe it then and I still don't. And I think nobody more than half-believed it or he wouldn't have gotten such a light sentence. I think that Tessa hadn't any idea who the father was and she was scared to death of her father, so she said she was forced and named a boy she knew everyone would believe capable of it. He got railroaded into it just because he was Digger Turner.''

''Well, personally, I feel sorry for him,'' Jennifer said, to divert Mary Beth from launching into an argument with Sarah.

''Sorry for him!'' Her neighbor stared at her. ''Whatever for?''

''He never had much of a chance, with that drunken father of his and no mother and growing up in that dirty little shack.''

''People always *expected* him to be bad, just because he was Turner's boy,'' Sarah put in, to prove her point.

''Although, you have to admit,'' Jennifer sought to maintain a middle course, ''that he never tried to make people think any differently of him, always playing pranks and getting into trouble.''

''Remember the way he acted at the Fourth of July picnic?'' Mary Beth reminded them.

Sarah remembered. It had been the most excitement at a Fourth of July picnic ever. She could still see Digger, staggering drunk, his face flushed and defiant, his pale eyes glittering. He had disrupted everything, insulted people, made lewd comments to girls, and finally beat up Jimmy Banks right in the middle of the dance. Oh, he was mean and wild, all right, not the sort you would care to be associated with.

"Well, I wouldn't say I would like for him to come calling on me," Sarah said dryly and they all three laughed. "I just don't think he did what he got sent to jail for."

"I wonder what he's going to do." Jennifer firmly steered the conversation in another direction.

"He can't farm. Old Man Turner lost his land and just lies around drinking all day."

"Digger will probably join him."

"I, for one, won't get a decent night's rest as long as he is in town," Mary Beth declared.

Sarah shot a glance at Jennifer and saw mirrored in her eyes a furtive amusement at the unconscious double entendre of Mary Beth's statement. Not that Jennifer would ever mention it, even to her. Sometimes Sarah wished she had a friend a little freer and easier in her speech, someone she could comment to on such a statement, someone who would listen to her roiling jealousy and hurt and love without condemning her. Not much likelihood of that. She was doomed to live like this, mired in the turmoil of her own emotions, never letting on.

The real difference between Jennifer and herself, Sarah thought, was not that her sister was effervescent and she quiet and placid; rather it was more that Jenny's personality was all light, but her own had a dark side. Jennifer loved everyone, was never cross and rarely troubled, and found enthusiasm in little things. But Sarah, though she knew she was kind and pleasant, was often bored or angry or jealous. There was a flat realism, almost cynicism, to her thoughts and speech, and her humor came out wry and almost sad at times.

Sometimes, like now, she was amused by really rather indelicate things, or felt a wicked desire to prick the balloon of people's pride or self-satisfaction. Sarah felt a sort of kinship to outlaw types like Digger Turner. There were times when she, too, felt excluded and looked down upon, overshadowed as she had always been by her sister. Somehow she felt that she had never quite lived up to what was expected of her, that she always managed to fall short of the mark.

She loved and admired her sister, and alone with Jenny, she laughed and talked and loved her without measure, but when others were around—her parents, friends, the children—she felt stabs of envy at Jennifer's success. Often she struggled with her parents, much as she loved them, and wished she were free of them. And many times despondency or loneliness fell upon her out of nowhere, and she could not shake the blue feeling.

The women were interrupted by the arrival of Jennifer's husband Stu. Jennifer's face lit up, and she leaped to her feet.

"Stu! Why, darling, what are you doing home so early?" she cried, her voice vibrant with delight.

Stu Harper smiled down at his wife lovingly. He was a handsome, well-built man, with thick black hair, a wide-boned face, and strong, white teeth. His adoration of his pert, charming wife was obvious.

"Why, to see you and my new son, of course. I wanted to make sure you weren't tiring yourself by doing too much too soon," he answered her.

Mary Beth Hewlin quickly took her leave; there was never any room for a good gossip once a man was in the house. Besides, she had many more people to spread her news to, and she needed to be on her way. When she had gone, Stu held out his arms to his wife, and she quickly slipped into his embrace. Neither noticed that Jennifer's sister quietly stood and left the room. Once she reached the parlor, out of the couple's sight, she stopped and drew a deep breath. Her pulse had leaped and her face flushed at Stu's unexpected arrival. Thank heavens no one had noticed. Usually she had more control that that; it must have been that the surprise jolted her from her carefully-schooled indifference.

Sarah loved her sister's husband, had loved him from

the moment she saw him, when he came to call the first time on Jennifer. It had been hopeless, of course; she had known that from the start. Sarah was sixteen years old, shy and awkward, her prettiness just beginning to develop. Jennifer, at eighteen, was the beauty of the county and completely overshadowed her sister.

For a brief moment, Sarah had felt a flicker of hope; Jennifer had always discarded, eventually, the many men who came to call on her—perhaps she would not want Stu either. But when he dismounted his horse with fluid, casual grace and stepped into their parlor, Sarah saw the way Jennifer glowed at the sight of him. Then she knew she had no chance; Jennifer wanted him.

Because it would have been unseemly for the courting couple to sit on the porch or in the parlor by themselves, Sarah was often forced into the role of chaperone and passed many evenings with Stu and Jenny. Continued proximity to Stu did nothing to cool her ardor. With all the hopeless passion of a sixteen-year-old, she savored every precious moment she spent around him. She laughed at his witticisms, listened with near awe to his opinions, and memorized his gestures. He was always courteous and friendly; he always smiled at her and teased her gently. Sarah never revealed her feelings about him; her mother had raised her to be a lady who bore her problems silently and never embarrassed herself or others by expressing unseemly emotions.

A year later, he married Jenny, and Sarah lost both her

sister and the man she loved. She had continued to love him, still nursed that queer little ache in her chest. She visited them in town for a few days now and then, saw them on Sundays when they came to the McGowan house for the midday meal, and had gone to keep the house and nurse Jennifer when she had given birth to her two girls and now the new baby, Jonathan. She was an accepted and loved member of their family; dearest aunt, sister, sister-in-law, always there, ever ready to sacrifice herself, eternally loving.

Although the world saw only that picture of her—the virtuous aunt and sister—Sarah knew that she coveted her sister's husband and children. She yearned after Jenny's two big-eyed, beautiful, dainty little girls with a fierce, possessive love, and inside her burned a futile, hungry longing for Stu, a steady little fire within her that she managed to bank but could never put out. So she could sympathize with sinners like Luke Turner. Others might think she was steadfast and virtuous; she knew better.

The most wrenching thing was that she could not stop, could not tear herself away from them, would not if she could. She loved each so dearly. The girls were her own children in her heart, and she loved them like a mother separated from her children. She yearned for Stu, ached for him. But she loved her sister also, and she could not even dream of ever having Stu and the girls because the dream would have to be built on Jennifer's death. She wanted to be with them, was frantically happy when she was, and yet at the same time was miserable at seeing daily what she would never possess.

No one knew; she never allowed herself to reveal a hint that she was enamored of Stu. Her only visible reaction to him was that she was a little quieter and stiffer around him. Everyone saw her only as a very devoted sister and aunt. Some people said she was almost too devoted to her family, and that was why she had never married. Others said she was simply too choosy. No man had ever asked her to marry him because her indifference toward all her suitors was so clear from the beginning that they dropped out of the pursuit long before the proposal stage. So she had moved into spinsterhood; at twenty-five years old, she was close to being a full-fledged old maid. And she couldn't see much hope of ever changing that.

''Sarah? What are you dreaming about in here?'' Stu's voice, hearty and cheerful, cut into her thoughts.

Carefully she arranged her features into a pleasant smile and turned to face him. ''Nothing, really. I was just thinking that it's time to go back to the farm, that's all.''

''Nonsense! Why, we'd all miss you terribly. Jennifer and I have been talking, and we think it's time you spent a few weeks with us without working and taking care of Jenny the whole time.''

''Oh, no, I really couldn't,'' Sarah said, horrified by his suggestion. Although she had mentioned leaving only to hide her real thoughts, she knew that she must get back to the farm. The longer she was around her brother-in-law, the greater her love for him grew. Her nature was an intensely loyal one, and once her affections were fixed, she was not inclined to change them; certainly no man she had ever met was capable of jarring her from her love for Stu. But even so, time and separation tended to dull her feelings for him until sometimes she thought she might get over him. However, every time she visited them, her emotions fed once more upon the sight of him.

He was so good, so kind, so handsome, so capable. At every turn she saw signs of the admirable qualities that made him worthy of her love. But just as often she saw his overwhelming devotion to Jennifer, and she felt the bitter anguish of jealousy. And somehow it seemed those wicked, roiling emotions fed the fires of her passion as much as did the presence of Stu himself.

''Why not?'' Stu argued with her now, his kind entreaties pleasing her even as they filled her with anxiety. ''You rarely come to town. And you should be here in town, where you can have some fun, some life of your own. You shouldn't be stuck way out there on the farm, never seeing anybody or doing anything.''

''But I can't stay here forever. It will be spring soon and there'll be so much work to do on the farm. Mother and Daddy will need me. There'll be spring cleaning and canning and preserving and all that. I really think I had best go back with Daddy when he comes to town Saturday.''

''All that won't be for awhile yet, Sarah. It's still

winter, really. Your parents can get along without you for a time. Besides, I know someone who would be awfully glad to see you stay in town,'' Stu said, his brown eyes twinkling. It was his opinion that Sarah had never married because her parents kept her too much on the farm; they simply did not want to lose her. But Stu was very fond of his wife's younger sister and wanted to see her happily married. She had caught the eye of a good friend of his, and he hoped to have a hand in a little match-making.

''Who?'' Sarah asked, her breath coming a little faster with the idea that maybe, just maybe, he was going to express some affection for her.

''Grady Snowden.''

''Oh.'' Sarah knew he was a friend of Stu's, so she carefully did not express her opinion of Mr. Snowden. But she certainly would give no indication that she wanted Stu to go on with the subject.

Stu moved closer to her and put his hand upon her shoulder. Her heart began to pound violently at his nearness. For one brief moment, she imagined that he loved her, that it was she he called ''darling'' and ''my love.'' It was her warm, cozy home, her girls upstairs playing, her baby quietly sleeping in his crib. Most of all, Stu was her husband, and she was the center of his life. His hand upon her shoulder was an expression of his love. In that one sweet instant of fantasy, Sarah felt the glow of happiness and security, the comfort of one's own safe, loving little world, a world like the one Jenny reigned over.

Then Jennifer entered the room, and her sparkling voice shattered Sarah's dream. She looked at her sister and abruptly came back to reality.

"Jenny, I've decided to go back to the farm Saturday when Daddy comes to town," Sarah said. "It's really best that I return."

And Jennifer gave in with a smile, as she always did, never hearing the touch of despair in her sister's voice.

Chapter II

EDNA McGowan attacked the potatoes determinedly, mashing them in firm, quick strokes that emphasized her words. "Well, if you want my opinion, you are wasting your life away."

"Mama, really, you make it sound as if I do nothing," her daughter replied, carefully setting the table with the china plates. It was Sunday dinner and company best was used, even though the only guests today were family: Jenny and Stu and the children.

"No, I don't mean you don't work. I can testify that you do your fair share of the work around here. And these past couple of months, running Jennifer's house, you've no doubt worked your fingers to the bone. What I mean is: you don't have a life of your own."

"Oh, Mama—"

"Don't 'oh, Mama' me, my girl." Mrs. McGowan

paused to push back a stray lock of hair and looked at Sarah meaningfully. She was a small, plump woman, still pleasant to look at though time and toil had marred the fresh prettiness she had had as a girl. Not a stern woman, she was nevertheless imbued with definite ideas of right and wrong and how the world should go, and she could be unyielding in following those ideas. However, her daughter could be equally stubborn and they had battled to a standstill countless times on this same issue.

"You should get married, have children of your own. Here you are, twenty-five years old, pretty daisy, and all primed to run a house. And yet you just sit, whiling away your time in your parents' house."

"Would you like for me to leave?" Sarah's voice was chilly.

"Don't be any sillier than you already are. You know your father and I love having you here. If we thought only about our own comfort, we would keep you with us always. But we want you to be happy."

"I am happy."

Her mother snorted in disbelief and opened the oven to check the roast which had been put in to bake early that morning before they had gone to church. She spooned its juices over the meat and prepared for her next assault on her daughter's defenses. Jennifer had always given her the greater joy, and if she had been forced to choose, Jenny was mostly her favorite. But she loved Sarah deeply as well and often found her the more comfortable daughter to be around because of the flat practicality that ran through Sarah's nature as it did through her own. Because she loved her, she wanted her to be happy; and because she felt they were similar, she was sure she knew what would make the girl happy.

"I love living here with you and Daddy." Sarah felt forced by her mother's silence to repeat her assurance. "I have plenty to do and I'm surrounded by people who love me. And I have Melissa and Penny and Jonathan."

"No, you do not!" Mrs. McGowan slammed the roast back into the oven. "Melissa and Penny and the baby belong to Jennifer."

Stung, Sarah picked up the pitcher and began ladling in water from the bucket, keeping her back to her mother to hide the hurt her words had caused. Why did she have to remind her constantly that she had no claim to Jenny's children, that she poured out her love to children to whom she would never be more than an aunt? At times she thought her mother liked to hurt her. Or was it that she was defending Jennifer's territory, disliking Sarah for daring to intrude on the other daughter's possessions? Sarah knew her mother loved her, but she had long believed that Edna favored her older daughter, and she often construed her mother's statements to be an expression of favoritism, even when rationally she knew better.

Edna, not seeing the hurt, continued. "You can't live through your sister. I know you love her and the children, but you simply cannot sacrifice yourself to them."

"They need me," Sarah said stubbornly, setting her jaw. "What do you think I should have done—refused to go help Jennifer when she had her baby?"

"I didn't say that. You are a fine and loving girl to do what you did. But she has a mother and a husband, a mother-in-law, two sisters-in-law, and an aunt in town with her. She could have gotten by without having you there all the time."

"She wanted me!"

"Of course she did, but that's beside the point. The point is, you ought to be married and have children of your own, not be at Jenny's beck and call!"

"What do you suggest I do, go out and lasso a husband?"

"There's that perfectly nice young lawyer who comes calling on you."

"Oh, Grady Snowden," Sarah said slightingly.

"What's wrong with him, may I ask?"

"I don't love him, for one thing, and for another, he treats me as if I were a child and—"

Fortunately, the sound of a surrey pulling up outside interrupted Sarah before she could get fully wound up over the liabilities of Mr. Grady Snowden as a husband. Edna McGowan, who had not seen her older daughter or grandchildren in two weeks, abandoned her opposition and flew to open the door to greet them. Sarah sighed and began to carry the food to the table.

"Aunt Sarah!" Her nieces running in engulfed her

joyously, as if they had not seen her for months, instead of only the day before.

"Careful, let me set down the butter," Sarah warned and discharged her load, then bent and swept the girls into her arms. "Mmm, I love you," she said and felt like crying; every other Sunday was not enough.

"Sarah." It was Stu's voice, very jovial. "Already we're at our wit's end without you."

"Oh, I imagine you will manage," she said lightly, looking up at him. It struck her anew, as it did every time she saw him, how handsome he was, with his crisp, curling black hair and bright black eyes and clear-cut features. Yet her voice revealed nothing except mild affection; she had schooled herself for too many years ever to make a slip.

"Sarah, you simply must return!" Now Jenny entered, one arm around her mother's waist, vibrant and laughing. Sarah suppressed a pang of envy and laughed and went to hug her sister.

Dinner was the usual Sunday feast. The table was loaded with steaming meat, potatoes, peas, rolls, corn, fresh milk and butter, and cream for the rich black coffee. The heavy bowls were in constant movement, and a steady stream of chatter ran through the eating. Stu described the business of his store that week; Jennifer made an amusing tale of baby Jonathan's nocturnal habits; the men discussed the weather and its effect on the approaching planting season, while the women discussed Tilah Harrison's latest in a long list of physical complaints. And throughout, the girls piped in with their own childish observations.

The noise was such that they almost failed to hear the quiet tap at the kitchen door.

"Now, who could that be?" Mrs. McGowan said in surprise.

"I'll go see. No, sit down, Mama; I've finished anyway." Sarah stood and went into the kitchen to open the door.

A man was standing on the porch steps, on the verge of leaving. He turned as the door opened and looked up at her. The man was of medium height and too thin, but his leanness was tough and sinewy. He wore no coat, only a grimy shirt and trousers, and he shivered a little in the chill of the wind. His hands were jammed into his pockets and he stood with his shoulders hunched, a stance somehow defiant and unsure at the same time. He was bareheaded and his thick blond hair was tousled and unruly, falling over his forehead and almost obscuring his eyes. His thin face was young, yet etched with a look of bitter experience that aged him far past his years. But it was his eyes that caught and held her; they were a pale, bright blue, chilling in their intensity and yet somehow flat and blank.

Digger Turner. Digger Turner, back from jail, five years older, prison pale and thin, more subdued, and with that funny old look that sat so poorly on a young man of twenty-three. Yet still there was that aura of wildness to him, the touch of sin and violence, an almost tangible animalism. Despite her protestations of his innocence, Sarah felt an involuntary clutch of fear.

''Ma'am?'' He shifted uneasily at her silence, glancing at her, then down at the porch, then up again at her.

Her momentary paralysis vanished at his nervousness, and he seemed suddenly only dirty and cold and rather vulnerable.

''Hello, Luke,'' she said, her voice calm and even. She had always disliked his nickname, for it seemed to her tinged with contempt, and she made an effort to call him by his given name. ''It's nice to see you.''

His eyes registered a faint surprise at her statement and he looked quickly back at his feet. ''Uh, is your pa home, ma'am? I'd—that is, could I talk to him?''

''Why, of course. Come on in.'' She opened the screen door and again he looked a little startled, but he came up the steps and through the door, halting just inside.

Sarah realized that it probably would not be considered proper to let him in like that, but she could hardly leave him out on the porch in the cold, especially coatless and hatless as he was. She hurried back into the dining room, anxious to hand the problem over to her father.

''Daddy, Luke Turner's here to see you,'' she said, and watched eyebrows shoot up all around the table.

Her father, a heavy, placid man, lumbered to his feet, his face as surprised as the others.

"Luke Turner? Why?" Edna exclaimed.

Mr. McGowan shrugged and went into the kitchen. Behind him at the table, the family sat still, looking at each other in pantomimed bewilderment, and straining their ears to hear the conversation in the adjoining room.

"Digger," McGowan greeted the boy who still stood just inside the door, looking ill at ease.

"Afternoon, Mr. McGowan."

McGowan noted that the boy was as wild and unkempt looking as ever. Somehow he always looked as if he had just hastily left a lust-filled bed or returned from a night of drinking. Turner also apparently still talked in that annoying mumble he affected with adults.

The boy cast a look of embarrassment toward the doorway to the dining room, obviously aware of the highly interested ears in the next room. Mr. McGowan felt a flash of pity for him: it would be a hard thing to know your every movement was examined as if through a magnifying glass and saved to pass around the rumor circuit.

"Why don't we step out on the porch?" he suggested, and Turner sent him a look of gratitude.

Outside Digger spoke up, clear and without the mumble, but in a rush and with his eyes fixed on some object out in the yard. "Sir, they told me sometimes you hired a helper during the planting season. I would—that is, do you think you might could use me?''

The older man stared at him in astonishment. A Turner wanting to work? ''Well, I don't have a son to help out,'' he said, buying time to think, ''and sometimes I have to get a hired hand.''

Turner's whole body was taut, and the cords stood out on his neck. McGowan realized how much it cost the lad to speak. ''I know you probably don't think much of me, sir, but I'm a good hand. When Pa was still share-cropping that land, it was me that worked it. I ain't real big, but I am strong, and I can work from sunup to sundown. I sure—I sure could use the job, sir.''

Henry McGowan was a kind and just man, and he believed that Digger was innocent of rape as strongly as his younger daughter did. His first reaction was to give the boy a chance. He felt sorry for him: the kid had always been on the bottom, loaded down with a drunken bum of a father and sneered at by all the respectable citizens. Digger was thin and pale and poor, and he needed the job. Henry admired the pride he glimpsed in him. But, after all, McGowan thought, he had to consider the fact that he had a wife and daughter. Even if Luke Turner was not guilty of rape, he wasn't the sort you wanted near your daughter. And he could not help but remember that peach tree of Harrison's that the boy had torn up, or the times that he had seen him drunk on the street, or the way he had beaten up the Banks boy.

At his silence, Turner relaxed and his eyes became perfectly blank. He mumbled something and moved down the steps.

"Wait a minute, boy," McGowan said. "If you want to work for me, you can't be so all-fired jumpy. I always like to think things over. I think I would be willing to hire you on."

Digger stared at him, stunned. He wet his lips and tried to think of something to say, but nothing came.

"You can start tomorrow. I'm in the fields about six o'clock."

"I'll be there."

"Well, good, then." McGowan now felt awkward, too.

The boy broke away and began to walk rapidly toward the road. McGowan stared after him, wondering whether he had made a mistake. Suddenly he grinned—he could just hear Edna when he told her the news.

"Luke Turner! Have you gone daft?"

They all stared at him in shock, and he had to hide his smile—his wife's reaction was just what he had expected.

"You hired that Turner boy on? Henry McGowan, you must have taken leave of your senses!"

"Mr. McGowan," Stu said earnestly, "you can't mean to let him hang around, with Sarah and Mrs. McGowan here. Why, the boy is—"

"Stu," Jennifer warned and nodded meaningfully at

their daughters, who were listening with wide-eyed attention. "Melissa, Penny, I think you are through with dinner now. Why don't you run outside and play?"

"But, Mommy, the blueberry pie. We haven't had pie yet," Melissa protested.

"Later. We will all have some after a while. Run along now."

The girls left the table reluctantly, and the adults sat silent and as if poised for action, until they heard the door close behind the children. Then, as one body, they swung toward Mr. McGowan and began to jabber.

"Wait! Wait!" he cried, flinging up his hands in mock horror. "Now, if you will just all be quiet, and let me explain. The boy needs the work, and I thought I would give him a chance. What harm can it do?"

"What harm!" Stu echoed disbelievingly. He was an upright, protective, conservative soul and very fond of his mother-in-law and sister-in-law. It shocked him that McGowan could be so careless of their safety. "But Sarah and—"

"Now, really, Stu, do you think the boy would try anything with Edna or Sarah, with me right here?"

"But, Daddy, he's so wild," Jenny said, trying to find a middle ground between her husband and her father.

"He was a boy, Jenny. Lots of sixteen-year-old boys are wild like that, but later they settle down."

"*All* the Turners are lazy, shiftless, good-for-nothings," Edna said authoritatively. "You will never get a decent day's work from him, and you'll be lucky if he doesn't steal everything right out from under your nose."

"That's right, Mr. McGowan," Stu chimed in. "Look at old Jake Turner—couldn't even hold on to that farm he was sharecropping. He's dead drunk all the time, living in that ramshackle cabin with the kid's grandmother, who's crazy as a loon. And remember his brother Earl?"

"Left town two steps ahead of the sheriff," Edna sniffed. "And look at his sister—what is that girl's name?—married one of those Dobson boys from down by Cold Springs, and in a mighty big hurry, too, if you ask me."

Sarah felt warmed by Stu's concern, but she was her father's daughter; it was his standards of morality that she had grown up by. Foremost in his scheme of values—and hers—were fairness, open-mindedness, and Christian charity, and so she felt compelled to take issue with Stu.

"But we can't blame him for what the other people in his family do. Perhaps he is different."

Stu smiled at her indulgently. "You are a tenderhearted girl, Sarah, and that is a fine thing in a woman. Heaven knows, we are always in need of a little forgiveness. But what is a fine thing in a home," he patted his wife's hand, "is dangerous in the outside world. You just cannot take a chance like that."

Sarah felt a spurt of anger at his patronizing air: men could be obnoxiously superior sometimes. "I am not being naive, Stu. Luke never stole anything like his brother, and I certainly don't think we need to be concerned about his getting in the family way like his sister."

"Sarah!" Edna exclaimed. "A little propriety, please."

Henry laughed and said, "Well, I am with my Sally here. You cannot taint a man with other's misdeeds. How do you think you would have done, Stu, if you had grown up in a tarpaper shack instead of that nice house your parents own? Or if you had had a drunken loafer for a father instead of a respected citizen and store owner?"

"For heaven's sake, it isn't worth quarreling over, is it?" Jenny interjected, feeling trapped between the two men.

"Of course not," Henry said and smiled at her. "I am just saying that I don't think the boy has ever had a chance and I think I ought to give him one. He looks to me like prison sobered him up some. And, after all, if he turns out lazy, I don't have to keep him."

Edna made a disbelieving sound in her throat, but did not say anything, just stood and began to clear off the table. No use sitting here arguing and Stu and Henry getting mad at each other about it. Not that her husband was going to get off so easily: she would have a thing or two to tell him later tonight.

Luke sent a stone skimming over the pond and instinctively counted the number of touches it made before it sank. He was good at skimming stones—why not, since it was about all he had learned at school. That and the way to throw up that hard, defiant sneer to protect yourself. They had got the jump on him, the teachers, because they had had Earl and were prepared for him. All he had to do to be in the wrong was to walk in the door. Well, he had learned quick enough, and before he quit school forever at thirteen, he had made more than one teacher rue the day she had ever seen him.

He shrugged, as if putting them behind him once again, and squatted down, his arms resting on his legs, and began to tear a blade of grass into strips while he thought about McGowan. The bitter taste of gall and the sweet taste of success mingled in his mouth: he didn't know how to feel. The way the old man and his daughter had stared at him rankled, taking in his ragged clothes, the uneasiness showing in their eyes, like they half expected him to bare his teeth and start growling like an animal. He got the same look everywhere, usually worse, but he could take it. He had taken it all his life, hadn't he, and spit right back at them? Only it still made his stomach turn to jelly, made him want to slink away and hide in a bottle, like Pa. Having to beg for work like that, knowing that McGowan hated his guts, like everybody else did, knowing McGowan would go back to his family and recount what he had done and they would tear him to bits all over again.

Sighing, he stood up and started again toward his shack. You could never shake it, that sick fear in your stomach, the wanting to hide, until it boiled in you and then you started slamming things—and people—around. Living was hell, always had been, and that trial and jail had been a special hell. Nothing could make him go back to prison; he could not stand to think of it. Even being back here in Willow Springs was worse than before. Pa did not have the farm anymore, and everyone was more contemptuous of him than ever. You would think he was dirt, the way they drew back from him. He snorted. Well, maybe he was. Look at his clothes; at least Julie had used to keep him clean and mended. Now she was married to that bastard Dobson, and Luke went untended. Worse than that, his sister had been the only one who loved him. Now there was no one.

His dream was to leave Willow Springs; maybe he would even leave Texas altogether—go out to New Mexico, maybe, or Arizona. Anywhere, as long as it was away from here. He could homestead; that didn't cost anything. But still he would need money to get there and to buy supplies. That was why he had tried to hire out. Tried was the word; nobody would take him. They just looked at him, scared or scornful or mad, until he wanted to smash their faces. Only McGowan had hired him.

That was the thing; that was what made him feel all mixed up inside. McGowan had said yes and had looked at him with a sort of kindness. And that daughter of his had called him Luke. Why had she done that? He had been called Digger for so many years, he hardly knew he had another name. But somehow it was surprisingly pleasant to be called Luke, like she thought he was a person. Inviting him into the kitchen, that was unexpected, too—you didn't ask Digger Turner inside your house. After all, he might steal the silver and run. Or throw some woman around down on the floor and rape her. But she had asked him in, and McGowan had said yes. He had a job, and he could touch the earth again and sweat and broil in the sun and work until he ached, and that would be good. It had been a long time. So what if the place wasn't his? Neither had Pa's land been his. He doubted if he would ever have land of his own. Now at least he had something.

He cut across the corner of Benton's land to reach his house. Pa was sitting on the steps, half drunk already. He raised his bottle in salute to his son.

"The prodigal son." His eyes were sly and drunken. Luke made a disgusted noise and shoved past him.

The old woman was in her corner, as always, rocking, her arthritic hands idle in her lap. She looked ancient, but her eyes were bright and, when they looked at her grandson, bitter.

"I need some clothes washed," he said to her. She merely shrugged and held up her hands. His mouth twisted. "I noticed you can manage to do for yourself; somehow your hands don't hurt so much then."

"Won't none of your fancy women wash your shirts for you?"

"What fancy women? I never had one that wasn't ordinary. Haven't even got *them* now."

She kept on rocking and did not reply.

He tried again, "Grandma, I got a job, and I'd like to look decent."

"Why try to look like what you aren't?" she said sarcastically.

His face closed down and he grinned insolently. "I know, I know, I've heard it before. I am a drunk and a rapist and a convict and I have been a shame to you all my life." He left her and picked up a bucket from the kitchen and headed for the cistern.

Luke drew up water from the cistern and filled the bucket. Then he stripped off his shirt despite the cold and dunked it in the water. He wondered if there was any soap in the house. Julie used to make soap when she was here, but he doubted that his grandmother had. Crazy old bitch. He drew up more water and doused his head and chest. Probably he would catch pneumonia, but he did not want to have to build a fire in the stove to heat the water.

He went back inside to get out of the cold and dry off. Then he explored the cluttered kitchen and found three rolls of cornbread and some unheated black-eyed peas. While he ate, he thought about the McGowan girl. A pretty thing. Not the kind to make you catch your breath, like her sister, the one that married Harper, but still pretty enough to set you thinking. He wondered what she was still doing at home. She ought to be married by now; he knew she was a couple of years older than he, maybe more. 'Course, the men around here had never been exactly bright, but surely it didn't take much brains to see the advantages of having her to warm your bed. He thought of her small firm body in his arms, pressing against him, and he felt a flood of desire. Damn it, he couldn't even look at her or she would cry rape. He was almost afraid to think about a woman anymore.

Tessa Jackson. What a laugh. As if anyone would have to rape Tessa; she would spread her legs for anybody. Only he could have managed to get locked up for raping Tessa. Damn the bitch; and damn that wild-eyed father of hers for beating her until she came up with a name and an excuse for her baby. Damn the world, in fact, for being what it was.

It was still early enough in the year that there was a tiny layer of frost on the grass in the morning when you got up, so wet and melting it was almost dew. Sarah gathered herself against the cold, then leaped from bed to grab her clothes and dash down to the kitchen. Her mother always got up first and started the fire going in the stove, so that by the time Sarah and her father came down, the room was already warm. Sarah hurried into her clothes and splashed her face with water from the tank attached to the stove. The water was warm and her mother dipped some of it into a pitcher to take up to

Henry for shaving. Neither Sarah nor her mother thought twice about the way Edna came down first in the pre-dawn chill to warm the kitchen for her family or the way she then heated water and carried it upstairs to her husband. Such pampering was simply accepted as things a wife and mother did.

Sarah put on her coat and went out to the chicken coop to gather the eggs. She liked the task, even in winter when it was colder than this; the warmth, the pungent odor, the familiar sound and feel, all combined to make her feel good, like when she was a little girl and she and Jenny used to come out here to gather the eggs. It made her smile to think about it.

When she got back, the coffee was ready and the bacon was sliced and already beginning to sizzle in the pan. She poured herself a cup of coffee and began to break the eggs into a bowl. Her father came down, hearty and warm and smelling of shaving soap.

"How's my Sally?" he said, calling her by the nickname only he ever used—and he only rarely.

"Good morning, Daddy. Breakfast will be ready soon," she said, as she did every morning.

Mrs. McGowan was still in a huff from their argument over Luke Turner, and she did not greet him. He slipped into his coat and picked up the milking pail. He winked at his daughter and smiled as he went out the door. Sarah smiled, too. They were used to Mama's silences and knew they did not mean anything. She would set the table heavily, as she was doing now, and later slam the pots and pans when she washed the dishes, and then her anger would be gone.

The bacon was done, but Sarah waited until her father returned before scrambling the eggs. Otherwise, they might be cold when he was ready to eat. By the time he did return, it was turning lighter outside; the sky was the deep gray it became just before the sun really brightened things. As she put the egg pan in the sink to soak, she looked out the window and saw a dim figure under the tree beyond the barn. She jumped in fright, then recognized the pale cap of hair.

"Daddy, Luke Turner's already here, down by the chinaberry tree."

Her father refrained from pointing out his employee's better-than-promptness to Edna, and just said, "Well, maybe you better offer him some coffee while I finish eating."

"Early as he is, do you suppose he had time to eat?"

Edna sighed and said, "Oh, for land's sakes, child, offer him some breakfast. Even if he had time, who'd have made it for him? Not that daft, crippled old woman."

Sarah suppressed a smile. A hungry boy was too much even for Mama's righteous wrath. She stepped out on the little back porch and called to him, cupping her hands around her mouth to make her voice carry. He came toward her in a lope and she noted that again he was without coat or hat; he must be freezing.

''Ma'am?''

''Come on in. It's cold out here.'' She stepped back inside, and he hesitated for a moment and then followed her.

''Have you had breakfast? We were just about to eat. Wouldn't you like some?''

''Oh, no, thank you, ma'am. I've already had breakfast,'' he lied, feeling that same funny, sick confusion he had felt the day before. In fact, he had not eaten anything except a piece of bread, but somehow pride demanded that he not admit it, just as it made him reluctant to enter the light and warmth of the kitchen that he had been enviously watching from under the tree.

''Well, at least a cup of coffee, then, to warm you up.'' Sarah did not really believe him, not with the way his eyes strayed to the table in the next room, but she did not know how to force him to accept it.

He mumbled something in reply and Sarah had to ask him to repeat it. ''Uh, the coffee would be fine, ma'am. Nice.''

She poured a cup for him, noting that today at least his shirt was clean, though terribly wrinkled. There was a little tear in it below the collar that needed mending.

''Come on in and sit down,'' she urged. ''Surely you could at least have a biscuit, couldn't you? Mama's biscuits are very good.''

''Oh, no, ma'am, I'll just stay right here. But you go on back in now, before your breakfast gets cold.''

For a moment she hung there, undecided, then went into the dining room. Turner leaned against the counter sipping the hot black coffee and watching the family at the table. It warmed him: the coffee sliding down his throat and his being on the inside of the lit-up windows. Sitting at the table with them would have been too much; he would have felt awkward and conspicuously bad. But here, on the edge of it, close, but not close enough to be compared to them, he felt better than he had in years—since before the trial, before Julie got married.

Chapter III

LUKE awakened slowly, foggily; the light was streaming in the window, and for a second he froze, thinking he was late, but then he remembered and relaxed. No, it was Sunday, and he did not have to go to work. He let himself sink back into the painful mist of a hangover. His head ached and the sound of his father's drunken snoring over on the mattress by the door irritated him and made his head worse. The left side of his face hurt and he touched it gingerly; it was puffy and tender. He thought about the fight and almost smiled; it had been good, swinging into someone like that. Made him feel better, even if it did hurt like hell the next day.

He had gotten drunk with the Sloan boys last night and they had visited that whore over by Pecan Ridge. Trust himself to spend his first week's pay drinking and whoring;

saving for that homestead was just a dream and he had known it all along. Still, it was worth it to feel a woman underneath him again, even if he was just a job to her. It would not have taken much to please him, it had been so long, but she had been talented, and when she found out he had just gotten out of prison, she had let him do it again for nothing.

He closed his eyes, remembering the things she had done to him, and drifted into imagining it was McGowan's girl doing them, her mouth and tongue running wild over his chest and stomach, her hand between his legs, caressing, teasing. Now they were in her barn, in the loft, and she was looking at him in the hot way Emmy or Tessa used to look at him. He unbuttoned her dress, could feel her quivering beneath his hand. Her mouth was soft and sweet against his, and he kissed her for a long, long time, his tongue exploring, claiming her mouth, until little whimpers rose from her throat. And then they were lying in the hay and she was naked and so was he, and his hands roamed her soft pale body, arousing her, arousing him. He was in her, thrusting, and she clutched at his back and moaned into his ear, saying, "Luke, Luke."

He groaned and turned on his side. Damn fool thing to do, exciting himself over her this way. As if he would ever do anything to McGowan's daughter. Oh, she was pretty, and he would like to take her. Not to mention the fact that he had always wondered what one of those

Sunday school girls would be like in bed. And sometimes when she looked at him as if he were some strange form of animal life, he wanted to scare her, shove her down and crush her with his masculine power, hurt her, make her admit he was a man. But he would never touch her. Not after the way McGowan had treated him, letting him work there, never insulting him, talking to him just as if he was a regular human being.

The girl was all right, too. Sarah. The name did not suit her; her smile was too quick and light for such a Biblical name. If she were his, he would call her Sally and make her smile more to banish the kind of sad look in her eyes. She did not look at him so often like she was scared of him or like he was a snake or something, as other women did. Oh, sometimes that look was there, and she sure kept a safe distance between them, but not as bad as others. Like her mother, for instance, who brought their lunch out to them every day so he would not contaminate her table. Sarah was kind, a little like her father. Every morning she invited him in out of the cold and offered him breakfast and then a cup of coffee when he refused the meal. No, he would not touch her, for her sake as well as her father's. And for his own sake, too, for he would hate to see the revulsion in her eyes if he did.

He should not even think about her; she might see it sometime in his eyes. He felt a flash of resentment towards her—what made her so much better than him, that she should feel sullied because he had a yearning for her? Bitch, he thought irrationally and eased off his mattress onto the floor, searching for the bottle he had discarded last night. A little drink would make the hangover more bearable. He found it down by the foot of the mattress and took a swig. The liquor burned and his stomach lurched in protest, but then it settled down and he felt a little better.

The day stretched out in front of him, empty because he did not go to work on Sunday. He looked around the little room; it disgusted him, messy and poor, with no beds, just mattresses on the floor, and his pig of a father snoring away. He sat back on the bed and took a longer pull on the bottle.

Reverend Carson clasped her hand firmly, sending her a worried, meaningful look. Inwardly Sarah sighed, but she smiled pleasantly and moved out of the doorway of the church, her mother just behind her. Kate Harwell pounced upon them, placing a firm hand on one arm of each. She leaned in secretively and lowered her voice.

''Are you two all right?''

Edna stared at her blankly and said, ''Of course. Why shouldn't we be?''

''That Turner boy.''

Edna raised her eyebrows. She might disagree with her husband, but she certainly was not about to let Kate

Harwell know that. "He seems to be a very good worker."

"He's always there at the crack of dawn," Sarah said, hoping Kate would remember that when her boy Rob had worked for the McGowans one summer, he had never arrived until long after sunrise.

"But, Edna, do you think it's safe? I mean with Sarah there and all."

"I think Mr. McGowan is capable of protecting us," Edna said dryly.

Sarah suppressed a smile. Luke had worked for them a week now, and in that time he had never come within three feet of her except when she handed him a cup of coffee. There was a closed, surly look to his face and he mumbled so you never knew what he said, but he was certainly not at all offensive in the way Mrs. Harwell meant. She rather thought he disliked her; he would hardly even look at her—she could not imagine him touching her. Even if he had such thoughts, her mother was a more than effective barrier. Before Luke's arrival, both women had taken Henry's lunch to him in the fields, so he would not have to return to the house; they had sat with him while he ate it. Or sometimes Sarah alone had taken it. Now, however, Edna took the lunch basket down herself, adamantly refusing to let Sarah even accompany her. Amused, Sarah asked her what she thought Luke would do right there in front of her father.

Edna compressed her lips and said that the less temptation thrown in his path, the better.

The two women pulled away from Mrs. Harwell and went to join Mr. McGowan, who was already standing by the buggy, impatiently waiting for them.

"Old busybody," Mrs. McGowan muttered under her breath, and Sarah giggled.

The ride home from church was pleasant, the three of them feeling united against the disapproval of the world. Mrs. McGowan was more pleased than Sarah, however, for she was buoyed by the idea that Grady Snowden was coming out to eat dinner with them. That idea only detracted from Sarah's enjoyment. Grady was a perfectly nice young man, a respectable, intelligent lawyer with a good future ahead of him. He was nice looking, though not handsome, and had a steady, likeable personality. If only he were not so persistent in calling on her, Sarah would have liked him well enough. But he did call on her, had been calling on her regularly for six months now, and her indifference had not shaken him. She had the uneasy feeling that before long he would ask her to marry him, and she did not want that.

Her mother's argument that she needed a family of her own was a valid one, she knew, but she could not bring herself to marry Grady for that reason alone. Her life with him would not be a bad one, for he was pleasant and mild-tempered, but she did not love him and she simply could not face the idea of engaging in the intimacies of marriage with a man she did not love. Being a farm girl, she had a fair idea of the essential act of sex, and it seemed to her a rather embarrassing thing to embark on without the impetus of love. Nor did she share many interests with him. He talked of torts and equities and political and social issues; she was more concerned with the price of cotton or a breed of milch cows or the best method of making sweet pickles. Also, she felt it would be highly unfair to him to enter a marriage in which he loved her, but she did not love him. She knew that she must refuse him, but still she would find it hard to do so. It would be so much easier if Mama did not encourage him by inviting him out to Sunday dinner.

The meal this Sunday was much larger than last, as they had invited her father's cousin, Andy Davis, and his family, as well as Mr. Snowden. Two fried chickens and a ham, as well as various vegetables weighed down the table, with apple cobbler and chocolate cake waiting on the sideboard. The Davis family had three teen-aged sons, and that meant a huge amount of food would be put away.

The brunt of the conversation was carried by Grady Snowden, for the Davis men tended to concentrate on eating rather than talking and both Henry and Sarah were bored stiff by his remarks. After the meal, Edna refused to allow Sarah to help with the dishes and insisted that she and Grady take a little walk around the place. Inwardly chagrined, Sarah smiled politely and agreed.

They walked down toward Crooked Creek, which split the farm in half, to see how it was rising, now that spring was almost here.

As they walked, Snowden talked of his plans for the future—the books he would add to his legal library, what sort of house he wished to have, when he would run for mayor and when for state senate. Watching his earnest face, Sarah felt close to panic. Soon he would be smoothly sliding into the qualities he was seeking in a wife and how he would raise his children. It was with great relief that she saw Luke Turner emerging from the little pecan grove and cutting across south.

"Luke!" she cried, as if overjoyed to see him, and waved to catch his attention. "Luke Turner!"

Almost warily he approached them, puzzled by the enthusiasm of her greeting. Beside her, Sarah sensed Grady stiffening, no doubt preparing to protect her.

"Really, Sarah, you should not encourage him," he admonished and she stared at him open-mouthed. "I cannot imagine what possessed your father to allow him to work here, so close to you."

"He hired him because my father believes that everyone deserves fair treatment, which is more than your 'law' gave Luke."

He smiled stiffly. "Sarah, being a well brought up young lady, you are no doubt unaware of the exact nature of his crime. Nor do you realize how the sight of a lovely, innocent young girl such as yourself would enflame a man of his sort. But your father should certainly be aware, and the blame must fall on him for—''

''I am perfectly well aware of what he was convicted for,'' Sarah cut in on him, furious at his indulgent, superior air and the slight directed at her father. ''Rape, which is taking by force what everyone knows Tess Jackson gave away to anyone who asked.''

''Hello, Miss McGowan,'' Luke said as he drew near, and nodded at the man with her. Now that he was close, he could see the angry flush to her face and her snapping eyes, and he wondered what the man had done to put her in such a snit. He had the feeling she had called him over in order to somehow put the man in his place. Judging from the slight shock on the fellow's face, she was doing just that.

''Luke!'' Sarah cried out in real concern when she saw his face. ''Whatever happened to you?'' She went up to him and stood on tiptoe to inspect his bruises, firmly taking his chin in her hand to turn his face down toward her.

He liked the feel of her cool, steady hand and the concern was enjoyable, too, but he felt uncomfortable under the other man's stare. ''Oh, it's nothing. Don't bother.''

''Nothing? Why, you have a black eye, and, look, your lip is split, and there's a cut right here. Oh, and your knuckles! They're all scraped and raw. You must come back to the house and let me doctor that.''

"Oh, no, ma'am," he said, genuinely embarrassed now. "I can't disturb your Sunday afternoon. I just didn't have anything to do and I was going to set in some of those fenceposts down on the south fence."

"Don't you know that Sunday is a day of rest?" she said teasingly, now that she could see his wounds were not as serious as they had first appeared.

He grinned, and behind her the man said in a warning tone, "Sarah."

Turner looked over at him; he did not like the way the man spoke to her, as if he had some right over her and could tell her how to act.

"What, Grady?" Sarah's voice was cool; she had not liked the tone either.

"I think it's about time we started back, don't you?" His voice hinted at command.

"Yes, it is; we must get Luke all fixed up. Come on, Luke, I insist."

Luke fell in with her because it made the man angry. Who the hell did he think he was, anyway? She walked back with a hand on each man's arm, which amused Luke. She was out to shake the man, get back at him or arouse his jealousy or something, Luke wasn't sure what. Luke didn't mind being her weapon; he had taken an instant dislike to the man, and he thought Sarah's air of innocence, which rested on solid anger, was charming. Besides, he liked the feel of her small hand on his arm.

Sarah kept up a cool babble as they walked. "Luke,

do you know Grady? This is Grady Snowden; he is an attorney in Willow Springs. Grady, this is Luke Turner; he works for Daddy."

Luke grimaced. No wonder he had disliked Snowden on sight; he hated anybody who had anything to do with the legal system, from the sheriff clear through to the judge. Neither man spoke to the other.

"When do you think you all will begin plowing?" Sarah went on, blithely.

"Well, pretty soon, your Pa says. Tomorrow, after we finish stringing the fence, I think we'll probably start to get all the equipment cleaned up. And then we'll break the soil, depending on the weather, of course. He's taking a couple of the hogs to auction Thursday, I think, but I'll keep plowing."

"Well, don't you let him forget Mama's field."

"What?"

"He always gets all carried away with the cotton and corn fields and it is absolute murder sometimes to get him to plow our vegetable garden. You know, potatoes and carrots and peas and all that. Of course, he would be fit to be tied if we turned up some year without any vegetables on our table."

Luke laughed, enjoying the light way she talked, the sting of criticism removed by her amusement. That voice, he thought, would be able to take a lot of pain out of things. He wondered if the lawyer was courting her; if so, he was not doing so well at the moment, getting stiffer and stiffer, in fact. Luke hoped they were not engaged; he would hate to see Sarah stuck with a fossil like that. Before many years had passed, he would have dried her up, too.

"I promise that I will plow it myself, ma'am."

Sarah, looking up at him, was startled. Why, when he really smiled and his eyes crinkled up like that, the bitterness fell away and he looked downright handsome. No, not handsome, exactly, but somehow appealing, like a devilish little boy. He should laugh more often. And so she launched into an amusing tale about three summers ago, when Daddy had delayed so planting the garden that one morning her mother had bolted the doors behind him and declared he was not going to get back in the house until he plowed her vegetable garden. Sarah did not have her sister's sparkle, but she could turn an ordinary event or even an angry one into one that was humanly funny and somehow both critical and loving of the people involved. Snowden was rather taken aback at her revelation of a family quarrel to a relative stranger, but Luke laughed with affection at her father, and the story even raised Edna a little in his esteem.

Mrs. McGowan was more than a little upset to see that Sarah and her beau had returned from their walk with Digger Turner in tow, particularly since Snowden's face looked like a thundercloud and he immediately took his leave of them. But she could hardly vent her anger in front of the other women, whose number had swelled as two more families had dropped in for a Sunday visit, and so she blandly brought out her medicines for Sarah to use on him.

Luke felt like a fool, standing there with all those women watching as Sarah carefully washed off his cuts, then daubed them with a liquid that stung like fire. The touch of her capable fingers on his face and lip and the way she leaned toward his face to see stirred him, but there was a disdainful look in her eyes that killed the feeling. No doubt she smelled the whiskey on his breath and he knew she thought he was an animal for fighting. And he was, he guessed, lambasting Dick Sloan like that for no reason except that he was drunk and itching for a fight to release the turmoil within him. It was just that sometimes he had to hit something or he would go crazy.

"Thank you," he said—almost inaudibly, for they were words he never spoke—and edged out the kitchen door.

However, he was not able to make good his escape, for Mr. McGowan rounded the corner of the house just then and saw him.

"Why, Luke, what are you doing here? Say, what happened to your face?"

"Got in a fight. I just came to put in some posts down on the south fence, only your daughter saw me and made me let her doctor me up."

"That's Sarah—always had a soft spot for the sick and injured. But say, no reason for you to be working on those posts. It's Sunday. Come on down to the corral with me. We're just all standing around talking, playing some games."

Luke demurred, trying to slip away, but Henry would not take no for an answer and pulled him off toward the others. When he approached, he saw the other men's eyes stare right through him, then skitter away only to return to him with that same cold look. He felt that they all leaned away from him, though no one said anything since he was clearly there under Henry's auspices. Nobody spoke to him as he stood and watched. Their "games" on horseback were contests to see who could reach down from the saddle of a running horse and pick up a hat or who could stay longest on a cinched-up bucking horse or do the fanciest trick riding. Henry asked him if he wanted to join, but he declined. He was not good on horseback, had never really been able to afford a good riding horse, and after five years in prison, his ability was almost nil.

When the talk drifted from horses to guns, however, he was more in his element, and when Henry brought out a rifle and shells for a little target shooting, he did not refuse. They lined bottles up on the top rail of the corral, then fired at them. Luke quickly, efficiently sent the entire row flying, even after they moved him farther back. He had always had to hunt for meat for their table, and he was a good shot. He looked around at their faces when he finished; it wasn't such a bad thing, he guessed, to let them know he was not a man to cross. He handed the rifle back to Henry and left, moving unhurriedly across the field.

"That boy is a menace," Jim Ferguson said and shook his head.

"Good worker," Henry defended him.

"Well, he's always had a grudge against the world, and if you ask me, I'll lay odds he'll be back in prison within a year," Andy Davis chimed in.

"What I can't understand is why you tolerate him around here."

McGowan shrugged.

After breakfast, Sarah began making bread—the usual Monday and Thursday chore—while her mother separated the cream and milk and put them in the cool icebox and then churned the butter. When Sarah had finally finished the mixing and kneading and flouring and rolling and had patted three loaves into shape, she set them aside, covered, to rise. Then she and Edna attacked the breakfast dishes, working in the smooth, efficient coordination that came from years of practice. As they worked, they talked. Edna filled her in on all the news gleaned from the visitors the day before while Sarah had been out walking. Then they speculated on the cause of the fight Luke had engaged in, hinting at dark, evil things without knowing exactly what they could be. Then their topics widened to more general things, often discussed: the stupidity of this person, the gentleness of that one, the intelligence and beauty of Jenny's children and the impossibility of comparing them to anyone else's.

Sarah popped the bread in the oven and then mixed a batch of sugar cookies and one of oatmeal cookies while her mother went upstairs to make the beds. By then it was time for lunch, and they sliced bread and ham for the men's sandwiches and prepared the basket to take to them: six sandwiches, hot black coffee, a small jar of pickled beets, cold potato salad, and two thick slices left from Sunday's chocolate cake.

"Why don't you take the basket today?" Edna asked her, and the girl tried to keep from staring in astonishment. After her daughter had come traipsing in with Turner the day before, Mrs. McGowan had decided to give up trying to keep her isolated from him. Obviously Sarah would run into him, despite her efforts. Besides, Edna was getting tired of having to carry the lunch to the men every day; it was a better chore for a young girl. She could not, after all, raise her daughter alone, and if Henry insisted on bringing Sarah together with scoundrels, there was no way she could combat it by herself.

Sarah was glad to take the basket. Aside from the fact that the task had been forbidden for a week and was therefore desirable, she enjoyed the walk down to the south fence where they were working. The day had turned warm, so warm that she did not even need a shawl around her shoulders. She could almost feel the budding trees popping their shells in the heat. Soon it would be really and truly spring and the thought made her happy.

The two men were working at a post as she approached, and did not see her. Luke stood behind the fence, facing her; he pulled the wire taut and wrapped it around the post. Her father, squatting before the post with his back to her, hammered the heavy fence staple into place over the wire. Luke, heated by the day's unaccustomed warmth and his own exertions, had discarded his shirt and stood barechested, and Sarah found herself staring at him in fascination. It was rare that she saw a man's naked chest. Luke was thin, too thin—his ribs showed—but the network of muscles across his chest and shoulders and down his arms were hard and strong. She watched the play of his muscles as he moved the wire and pulled it tight again. It sent funny little darts of feeling through her stomach, not pain exactly, but not exactly pleasure, either. She wanted to avert her eyes and at the same time wanted to watch much longer.

Luke looked up and saw her; his face was startled for an instant, then he flushed and reached hastily for his shirt. McGowan turned and greeted her with surprise.

''Why, Sarah, how nice!''

''Hello, Daddy. Luke.'' She could not hide the amusement in her voice. The dangerous Luke Turner, indeed—blushing and scrabbling for his shirt because a lady had seen him barechested.

Her father and Turner dived into the lunch, and for a

while they sat in complete silence. Sarah found herself thinking of Luke's naked chest and his flat, muscled stomach. She remembered the feel of his skin under her hand yesterday when she fixed up his cuts and bruises and wondered if the skin of his chest felt the same way. Suddenly she thought of Tessa Jackson and what he had done to her. Sarah did not believe he had raped her, but surely he had lain with her. He had always had a reputation for promiscuity and so had Tessa. Had Tessa seen him completely naked? Touched him, kissed him?

She glanced at him sideways, ashamed of her thoughts. It was wicked, just as it was wicked for her to try to picture Jenny and Stu in bed together or imagine how Stu's lips would feel against hers. Thinking that, she began to wonder how Luke's lips would feel. She looked at his mouth; it was wide and sensual but set in bitter lines. Feeling her gaze, he looked up at her with that bright blue stare of his, and she quickly looked away, embarrassed. What would he think if he knew what she had been imagining? He might sneer—or he might satisfy her curiosity. The idea was scary, but exciting; it sent a little shiver through her. She had never been kissed full on the mouth, and she often wished she could experience it without having to have a steady beau. It was sinful, she knew, the way she was always thinking about being kissed by different men, even the dirty, dissolute Turner boy (who was younger than she, to boot). She tried to bring her mind back to propriety by reminding herself of his brutishness, the way he had gotten into a fight Saturday night and the whiskey smell on his breath, on a Sunday afternoon!

Her father, once his appetite was somewhat assuaged, began to talk to her while they finished lunch, but Digger said nothing, just sat apart from them and ate and watched. The girl had surprised him; he could hardly believe her dragon of a mother would allow her to come so close to him. No doubt she had been horrified at finding him shirtless and he felt all kinds of a fool for showing his surprise and embarrassment. He could tell she had been laughing at him from the way the corners of her mouth twitched and her eyes sparkled. He felt awkward eating in front of her, particularly since she kept looking at him. He knew she must be staring at some crass behavior of his, but he did not know how to correct it. Damn her; she had no right to come here and look down her nose at him, and then no doubt dissect him later with her mother. He felt a perverse desire to frighten her, to act like the animal she thought he was, as if that would somehow punish her. And so the next time she looked at him, he set his hot, insolent gaze on her and was both gratified and enraged to see a twinge of fright cross her face.

When he finished eating, he immediately went back to work to avoid being near Sarah. McGowan gave him a puzzled look, since they usually rested in the shade for a while after lunch, but then tossed his napkin back in the basket and joined him. Sarah picked up the basket and left, calling back her ritual warning not to work too hard. Watching her retreating figure, Luke thought how her mother always said the same thing and felt an empty ache for the years of family closeness and love and comfort that lay beneath their habits, and for the lack of them in his life. Oh, there were customs in his family, too, like Pa's knocking Julia halfway across the room or lighting into him with his belt, until Luke got big enough to stop him from doing either. Or Grandma telling him he was a drunken bum and a shame to her all her life, worse even than Earl or his sluttish sister. Or Earl's sly laughter: "Boy, are you dumb, killing yourself plowing the fields for the old son of a bitch, when there's money just lying there for the taking." Yes, he had some fine family customs himself.

Casually, McGowan said, "You know, Digger, I won't kill you for speaking to Sarah."

"What?" His stomach tightened.

"What I mean is, you don't have to try to pretend you don't exist when my girl's around. I don't think you raped George Jackson's daughter, and I have no expectations of your trying to hurt Sarah."

Confused, Luke retreated behind a sullen mask. Uneasily, he sensed a trap was being laid for him. "I don't have to answer to you."

McGowan sighed in exasperation, "I'm not asking you

to. I'm just trying to tell you I'm not sitting around waiting to pounce on you for talking to Sarah.''

Luke shrugged. ''Nothing to say.''

The older man smiled. ''My Sarah's not exactly the kind of girl to make a man tongue-tied, like Jennifer does. And when a boy's been in prison for five years and doesn't want to look at a pretty girl or get close to her or say a word to her, it isn't natural.''

''What're you saying?'' He lowered his head in his mulish way, hands on hips, glaring at the post before him.

''Just that I trust you and know that your talking to her or looking at her like any young man would doesn't mean you're about to attack her.''

Luke swallowed, but could say nothing around the lump in his throat. Instead, he set to work furiously. The older man looked at him, then smiled and shook his head in amused bafflement.

Suddenly, Luke broke the silence. ''I'm scared to death of her.''

''Of Sarah?'' McGowan's voice rose in astonishment.

''She's the nicest lady I ever met, and I—it—I'm afraid I'll do something or say something that will make her hate me like everybody else does.'' He flushed in embarrassment at having blurted his feelings out like that. He had not even realized how he felt until the words tumbled out of his mouth. But at least he had refrained from adding that sometimes he wanted to scare her so she *would* hate him and he would not have to wait and worry anymore.

Henry felt a burst of pity for Turner, for the poor opinion of himself the boy had. "I think you misjudge Sarah."

Luke shrugged, closing the subject, and the two men worked in silence. McGowan hoped to himself that the lad was not falling in love with his daughter. Surely Digger realized how hopeless it would be. Besides the obvious disparities in their temperaments, backgrounds and positions in the community, Sarah seemed to have some aversion to men. She had ignored far more eligible prospects than Digger Turner. He saw little hope for him, and certainly Henry would oppose the match if he thought Sarah was developing any feeling for Turner. Digger was not as bad as others thought, but hardly the sort for his quiet, sweet, virtuous daughter.

By the middle of the afternoon, the men had finished the fence and returned to the tool shed to clean the plows and cultivator and other equipment. It was almost dinnertime when Edna, stirring the black-eyed peas, happened to glance out the open kitchen door to see Luke and Henry moving slowly toward the house, their bodies hunched closely together. Fear froze her and it was a moment before she realized that Henry was the one supporting and Luke the one hobbling and leaning on the other man.

Relief washed over her, and then she was out the door, hurrying to help.

"Mama, what is it?" Sarah asked as her mother left, then followed to the door to see. With a little cry, she too went rushing out.

Luke, who had kept up a steady stream of cursing, stopped at the approach of the women. His face was white with pain, but his expression betokened more anger than hurt.

"What happened?" Edna cried.

"Hammer fell off the shelf and landed on his foot. I'm afraid it may be broken."

Edna took charge. "Sarah, go fill a big pan with cool water and put in some ice and get out the bandages. Henry, take him into the kitchen. I'll get a chair for him."

Henry eased Luke down into the chair his wife placed in the kitchen, and Edna knelt to take off his shoe. Luke's foot had swollen so much already that it was difficult to get it off. When Sarah brought the water, chilled with ice from the icebox, Edna put Luke's foot in the pan to soak. Gingerly she felt the injured foot, and Luke bit his lips to hold back the pain that even her gentle touch brought.

"I think a bone or two are broken. I've seen worse, though."

"Shall I ride for the doc?" her husband asked.

"Oh, I think I can handle it. Unless you want the doctor, boy?"

Luke shook his head.

"We'll just soak it for a while and then I'll bind it up. You stay off your foot and keep it propped up, and you'll be okay in a few days."

Luke wanted to scream in helpless rage. Damn his luck; only to him would this happen—a hammer chancing to fall off a shelf and cripple him just when plowing was about to begin. He was useless to McGowan now, unable to walk the field behind a plow. Hell, in this condition, he would be lucky to make it home. McGowan would have to get a new man and there went his start at a brand new life.

"I'm sorry, Mr. McGowan," he said shakily, "I don't know how I managed to do this."

"Come on, now, it was an accident. The hammer was too close to the edge. It doesn't look too bad; you'll be up in no time."

"The plowing—I can't—"

"For heaven's sake, boy, don't worry about that."

"But I can't do my work, I can't. You'll have to get someone else. God, I'm sorry."

"Don't get all wrought up about it. We can work it out. We haven't finished clearing yet; that'll take another day. Then I can start the plowing, and you can do my chores here—slop the hogs, milk the cows, clean the barn. You can chop a good-sized supply of firewood, so we won't have to do that chore for a while. And if I know Mrs. McGowan, she'll be starting her spring cleaning soon, and she could use your help with heavy things. You're young, and your bones will mend fast. You'll be back in the fields before you know it. Why, I probably won't even have finished breaking the ground."

McGowan paused, apparently deep in thought, while Luke stared at him in astonishment. " 'Course you won't be able to walk home," he continued after a moment, "but we've got a place out in the barn where the hired hand slept last year. Sarah! Go out and fix up that room in the barn for Digger here. And do you remember where we put Gran's old cane?"

"In the attic, I think. Over by the trunk where Mama's wedding gown is. I'll get it. Just a minute."

Luke relaxed in his chair, belief slowly spreading through him. It was not all lost. McGowan had not fired him; he was even allowing him to stay here, sending Sarah out to clean up a room for him and fetch him a cane. He closed his eyes, luxuriating in the warm smell of the cooking dinner and the bread and cookies baked there that afternoon. In the next room, he could hear the clatter of dishes as Edna set the table; now Sarah's light tread as she came through on her way to the barn, stopping to hand McGowan the cane. He smiled, floating in the comfort of the sounds.

"Well, I'll be damned," McGowan said, "I think he's fallen asleep."

"Henry, your language, please!"

He dozed through the bustle of dinner preparation, but not through the bandaging of his foot. The pain brought him bolt upright, a vivid curse escaping him before he realized where he was.

"Excuse me, ma'am," he managed to gasp and Edna laughed, sounding almost friendly.

"You should have heard Henry last year when I had to pull four big splinters out of his foot. There now, you're all fixed up. Here, put your foot up in this chair and eat this food." She shoved a full plate into his hands. "And then you go on down to the barn and sleep; you need some rest. Sarah ought to have it fixed up by now."

He ate quickly, hungrily, and immediately felt better. Then, with McGowan's help and the cane, he hobbled down to the barn. A door on the side facing the house led into a small room which contained a bed, table, chair, and dresser. As Luke stepped in, Sarah turned from the bed where she had been tucking in the quilt.

"Oh, there you are. You came just in time; I'm finished now. How are you feeling?"

"All right." He found it difficult to speak. The room was cramped, the furniture old and the mattress only straw, but Sarah had quickly scrubbed and cleaned it, even swept the floor, and the mattress was on a real bed and covered with fresh sheets and a bright quilt. In the glow of the kerosene light, the room looked beautifully cozy and warm, and he felt a sudden rush of emotion. He was unaccustomed to gratitude, but he forced himself to say "thank you" to Sarah.

"Oh, it's nothing," she replied airily and left with her father.

Luke shut the door and eased himself down onto the bed. Maybe it was nothing to her, but it seemed a lot to him. Even when Julie had been home and struggling to keep the place clean, he had never had a room all to himself or a bedstead or a fine quilt and sheets such as these. During the years in prison he had lived in filth, packed in with all the other prisoners, and now his home, with his sister gone, was little better—neglected, dirty, decaying. Just the simple, sweet cleanness of the little room touched him with pleasure, but the thought of Sarah's presence there, working to make it clean for him, doubled his happiness with the place. He remembered the sight of her in the gentle glow of the lamp, standing by his bed and smiling at him.

Slowly, tiredly he undressed, blew out the light and crept between the sheets, luxuriating in the feel of the smooth ironed linen against his naked skin. For once, his stomach was full, and the room wrapped around him, comforting as the womb. He began to tremble from the aftermath of pain and tension and relief and from the conflicting emotions invading his body. He imagined Sarah there, soft and tender, wrapping her arms around him and holding him to her breast until the shaking stopped; and slowly he drifted into sleep.

* * *

Sarah and her father strolled back to the house in the cool evening air. She felt happy and at ease with him, as she always did.

"That Luke is a sad boy," Henry McGowan said. "Never seen anyone with such a poor opinion of himself."

"He doesn't seem nearly as bad as other people say," Sarah commented.

"Yeah, folks like Stu don't have any notion what it's like for Luke Turner. They just can't forgive him for not doing things the way they would."

"Oh, Papa, Stu's not like that!" Sarah came hotly to her beloved's defense. "He was just concerned for our safety, because of Luke's reputation, that's all. But Stu's not the type to judge a man without knowing him or dislike him just because he's different. That sounds like Grady Snowden, not Stu."

Her father shot her a quizzical glance. Was even his sweet, sensible Sarah bedazzled by Harper's good looks? It seemed as though all women were. Not that he had anything against his son-in-law; Stu was hardworking, a good provider, an exemplary husband and father. He was intelligent and interesting to talk to and even capable of a jest now and then. But if he had been asked, Henry would have said that Stu was very much *like* Grady Snowden—rather rigid and strait-laced and intolerant of other people's failings. Funny that Sarah did not seem to recognize that; she was usually so perceptive.

When they reached the side porch, Henry McGowan went inside, but his daughter sat down on the railing to watch the stars. They blazed white in the clear Texas sky. The night was still and warmly enveloping, a good night to stargaze and dream. Sarah dreamed, as she always did, of Stu.

She never imagined Stu and herself in a real setting, for that would entail getting rid of Jenny somehow. Instead, she placed them in a different time, a different place. Often he was a Rebel soldier and she a Southern belle. Or maybe he was a knight, and she was a medieval lady in need of a champion—like Rebecca in *Ivanhoe*, one of her favorite novels. Tonight she envisioned them in revolutionary America, where he was a brave patriot soldier—wounded, perhaps, at some battle. She had stumbled upon him, and although she was from a loyalist family she could not bear to let him be captured by the British soldiers or die out there in the fields. So she took him in and nursed him back to health and hid him from his enemies, and naturally they fell in love, despite the fact that they were on opposite sides. He rescued her from many dangers, and then at last, they were married.

Sarah was in general a very practical, down-to-earth woman. But there existed in her a romantic, passionate person who had no place in the dry Methodist farming community that was her life. The only outlet for that part of her was a richly romantic fantasy world, where she could win the man she loved and pour out the wealth of emotion inside her in a safe way. So she daydreamed, and in her dreams love bloomed for her, as it never did in her reality.

With a sigh, Sarah shook herself out of her dream. Why, she wondered disconsolately, could she never have any of that in her actual life? Must she live in dreams forever, and never taste the real love of a man? Unbidden, tears came into her eyes, and she blinked them back. She turned and went inside to join her parents.

Chapter IV

HE awoke and stared around him, for a moment unsure of where he was. The soft tap at the door was repeated, and then cautiously the door opened and Sarah stuck her head inside.

"Luke?"

"Miss McGowan," he said, startled and suddenly very aware of the fact that he was completely naked beneath the sheet.

"Good morning." She entered, smiling, carrying a tray. "How are you this morning? I brought your breakfast."

"I'm fine."

She came over and stood at his bedside, while he felt more and more ridiculous, lying there looking up at her, trapped by his nude state. "Can you sit up so I can give you your tray?" she asked, and he was forced to pull himself to a sitting position, awkwardly trying to keep the sheet from sliding down. She leaned down and placed the tray on his lap. The nearness of her, the slight scent of lavender soap that emanated from her, her placing the tray on the most intimate part of his body, separated from her by only a sheet, all combined to make desire begin to throb in him. He was thankful for the concealment of the tray.

Sarah sat down to wait until he had finished, so that she could take the tray back. She had not meant to, but somehow she could not pull herself away. She was drawn by the sight of his bare chest and arms, the line of his legs beneath the cover and the suspicion that he wore nothing under that sheet. The sleepy look of his pale blue eyes, and his heavy, tousled blond hair excited her, even though they also made her feel as if the walls were closing in on her, crushing out her breath, and she longed to break loose and run. A heady sense of power swept over her at his obvious embarrassment, and she felt a strange desire to tease him by lingering. Her stomach danced with excitement as she sat watching him with apparent calm.

Why didn't she leave, Luke thought desperately, awash with confused emotions: fright, lust, embarrassment, humiliation that they felt he was too inferior to eat with them, gratitude for their unusual kindness, anger at himself for getting into this position, and resentment at his own humble gratitude and their holy generosity.

"'Ain't your ma scared to send you out here alone?" he sneered.

"No." Her answer was calm, despite her suddenly pounding heart. "Why should she be?"

His eyes burned into her. "Don't you know what I might do to you?"

Her breath caught in her throat and she searched for words to cut him off. "I think I could outrun you, since you have a smashed foot."

He flushed and set to eating his food in silence, mentally calling her every name he knew.

After a few moments, Sarah broke the silence. "Daddy thinks you should rest today."

"What?"

"He thinks you ought to stay here and rest and keep your foot up and not walk any."

"But my work—"

"One day won't hurt."

"I'm not helpless," he protested angrily. "I won't stay here and let your father do the work he hired me to do."

"Don't be silly, Luke. You have to take care of your foot."

He set his jaw stubbornly and his eyes turned blank and remote. "I promised him I would work and I will."

"But why?"

"I don't break my word. I'm not shiftless. I'm not—" he broke off suddenly and shoved the tray at her. "Here, take this."

"But you haven't finished your food."

"I don't want any more," he lied, for it was the best breakfast he had ever tasted, but he was seized by the sudden conviction that he must hurry to his job before it was somehow snatched from him.

"Luke Turner," Sarah said as she grabbed the tray from him, "you are just being foolish and stubborn. Everything will be there tomorrow, just the same. The farm is not going to run away, you know. You could at least finish your breakfast."

"I am getting up," he said doggedly. "And since I ain't got a stitch on, I suggest you leave—"

Sarah's eyes widened at his rough tone and she swept out of the room, thinking angrily that she could understand why everyone disliked him so.

Luke worked steadily all day long, and after his initial protest, Henry did not try to induce him to stop. He could see that the boy was driven and that it would be useless to argue. What a switch that was: a Turner who refused *not* to work. By the time Edna called to them that supper was ready and they quit their repair of the plow, the boy was pale with pain and fatigue, though he would not admit it.

"You go straight to bed now," McGowan said. "I'll have Sarah bring your supper out to you. You don't need to do any extra walking."

Luke swallowed against the bitter taste flooding his

throat at this further reminder that he was not fit to sit at their table, despite the kindly way the older man tried to conceal it. He shrugged. What did he care? He did not want to have to sit there with them staring at him, judging him. Let her put herself to the bother of bringing him down a tray. He pulled himself to his feet and limped back to his room.

This time Sarah left the tray and did not wait for it, but returned after supper to fetch it. Neither said much, though Luke would have liked her to stay and let him look at her and hear her voice. But he could think of nothing to say—what did you say to a nice girl like that? Certainly not the soft, seductive things he said to the girls he knew. Nor the hard, masculine talk of hunting and drinking and whoring that he was accustomed to with boys like the Sloans. So he kept quiet and watched her leave and then went to bed, exhausted and alone.

Once in bed though, he could not sleep, and lay troubled by his thoughts. It seemed to him that he had always been alone, always lonely. At home, in school, in prison, even out carousing with his friends or lying in a girl's arms. The righteous people of the town would not associate with him. His friends and lovers were "trash" like him, but with them he was locked into certain patterns of speech and action—you flirted with and seduced the girls and were rowdy and wild with the boys—and he felt separated from them by the things he felt and thought that never occurred to them. To none of them could he confide his innermost dreams and fears and emotions, and so with them he always felt a certain separateness, aloneness. His father hated him and Grandma, too, just for being born, for his birth had sent his frail, beautiful blond mother to her death. If anything, the rift between them widened as he grew older, his father resenting the way Luke showed him up by working hard, and his grandmother deploring his wild, shameful ways. Julie loved him and always stuck with him, but loaded as she was with housework from childhood, his sister had never had time to be a companion to him. And since she had married, through the trial, prison, his return, the loneliness had consumed him. Every moment alone, as if there were a stone wall encircling him.

Most of the time he accepted it, hardly noticed his isolation, but sometimes, like now, it rushed upon him, beating at him like the wings of a great dark bird. Usually a drink helped, but he had no liquor here. He could only lie huddled up and wait it out; only endure it.

Sarah went down the kitchen steps with her basket of laundry to be hung on the line. From the clothesline she could see Luke chopping wood, going at it as if his life depended on it. He was a madman, she reflected; nothing else could explain this frenzy of his for work. This morning he had done all her father's barnyard chores and was now chopping enough wood to last for weeks. He was a peculiar boy, not at all what he was said to be. The despoiler of women—who blushed with embarrassment when she saw him only partially dressed. The insolent, wild rebel—who meticulously called her "ma'am" and her father "sir" and jumped at Daddy's every wish. The lazy, shiftless Turner—who worked like a demon. It simply did not make sense. Had prison changed him that much? Or was it that all those people who talked about him did not really know him, just as none of them really knew her? Only her situation was reversed, for everyone thought she was sweet and good and it was the wicked inner Sarah that they did not know.

She thought of the way she worked so hard at Jennifer's, harder than at home; she felt sometimes as if she did it to punish herself, to make up for her jealousy of her sister. As though if she worked hard enough, it would raise her to the level of other people. She watched Luke hobble across the yard with an armload of wood for the woodbox—he had to make twice as many trips as normal, because he could carry only a small load—and she wondered if he too worked so hard in order to punish himself for the opinion others held of him.

"I have to be so much better than other people because I am so much worse," she murmured, then caught herself, startled. She smiled; imagine what Mama would say, hearing her ponder the similarities between herself and Digger Turner.

Sarah shook herself and returned to pinning the sheets on the line. Wednesday was wash day, just as Monday and Thursday were bread days and Tuesday and Saturday were heavy cleaning days and Friday was ironing day. Her mother scrubbed the clothes on the washboard and tossed them into the rinse tub, then Sarah wrung them out and hung them on the line to dry. Hers was the easier job of the two, for she was able to move around whereas Edna had to remain bent over the washboard the entire time. Still, after hours of bending to wring out the clothes and stretching to hang them up, she was tired and her back ached. She paused at her task, standing with her hand against the small of her back in the age-old feminine gesture of weariness, and watched Luke Turner for a moment.

He never seemed to tire; he was like a machine, his axe rising and falling rhythmically, ceaselessly. He had not taken off his shirt in the heat—she guessed because he was so close to the house—but he had unbuttoned it, so that his chest was partly visible. Looking at him, she was reminded of Monday when she had watched the ripple of his muscles beneath his smooth, almost hairless chest; and then yesterday morning crept into her mind. He had been naked beneath the sheet; she remembered the clean, hard line of his legs against the cloth. Her throat seemed to close at the thought and it was difficult to breathe.

Sarah left the clothesline and went rapidly to the cistern to pull up a bucket of water. Her mouth felt parched and she needed a drink. She poured water into the dipper, sloshed it around to clean the container and poured it on the ground, then poured more into the dipper and drank it eagerly. The crackle of twigs behind her startled her and she turned quickly to find Turner standing a few feet away.

"Hello, Luke," she said, sounding more self-assured than she felt.

"Ma'am."

"Would you like some water?" she asked, holding out the dipper to him.

He took the dipper but first splashed water on his hot head and face. Then he filled the dipper and tilted back his head and drank long and thirstily. She was intensely aware of his open shirt and glanced surreptitiously at his chest as he drank. His skin glistened with sweat and she watched two drops converge and lazily trickle down his breastbone and across the flat plain of his stomach until they vanished, absorbed by the cloth of his trousers. She felt a strange, wild urge to follow their path with her fingers; instead, she clasped her hands firmly behind her back.

Finally he stopped drinking, hung back the dipper and began to run the bucket down. It occurred to Sarah that it was silly of her to just stand there, watching him; she had no reason for hanging around there.

"How is your foot?" she inquired to give herself a reason.

He shrugged. "All-right, I guess."

They stood facing each other awkwardly.

Sarah tried again. "You know, I've been thinking: your parents must be getting worried, with you not coming home for two days. Maybe you ought to take Mexico and ride over there and tell them what happened."

"Worried?" He laughed shortly. "I never had a Ma, just Pa and Grandma, and no doubt they're sitting over there hoping against hope that I've died."

"Digger!" In her shock, the nickname slipped out of her mouth. "That can't be true!"

"Can't it!" His face was closed, bitter. "Lady, you don't know the first thing about people. You've been wrapped up in cotton batting all your life, protected from the world by your parents." He regretted the harsh words as soon as they were out. He had not intended to offend her; he had seen her at the well and hurried over because he wanted to talk to her, be near her. Why did he do this, trying to drive her away when what he wanted was for her to stay?

Sarah felt pained by his words—but for him, not for herself. "You don't really believe what you're saying, do you? A father loves his children; sometimes he loves one more than another, but still he loves each one. You must be mistaken."

"You talk like a child."

"No, you're the one who talks like a child. Only children think things are always so extreme. Black-white, up-down, right-wrong."

For a moment something flared in his eyes, then vanished. "Sometimes things are extreme."

"You certainly seem to enjoy keeping all your old wounds open," she retorted, feeling sorry for him and angry at the same time.

That stung him—she thought he was like some old sob sister, always recounting his misfortunes in the hopes of getting pity. "I don't. I never talked about it before."

"Then maybe you should. Talk about it and then forget it. Sometimes it hurts to have to keep it all inside you," she said, thinking that at least she was an authority on that subject.

He grimaced. Did she think he was so without pride that he would talk about his father's beatings or vilifications of him? That was like admitting that it hurt or that what the old man said was true. She wanted him to tell her, so she could poke and pry, thrust the probing finger of her curiosity into all his gaping wounds. He stared at the ground, torn between a desire to tell and feel the release and maybe, maybe, be comforted, and an equally strong urge to shield his shame.

Suddenly, surprising both of them, he spoke in a low voice that sounded like a muffled cry. "I ain't so bad! I never did that—what they said. I never forced Tessa to—I wouldn't—" He stopped and clenched his jaw, the muscles in his cheek jumping, until he regained some control of his voice. "I would never hurt a woman, I swear. Not anything weak or small or helpless; I know how that feels.''

Sarah felt that for an instant she had had a glimpse of his soul, bright and strong and straight, before it got all covered-up and warped and twisted around by his life, and she wanted to cry out for the loss of it, for the way they had wrecked what could have been a good person.

''I believe you,'' she said and tentatively touched his sleeve. His head shot up in disbelief. ''I never thought that you—violated Tessa Jackson. It was wrong.'' Her voice rose earnestly. ''The whole trial was wrong. I know you were innocent; I always knew it.''

He stared at her, his face confused and full of conflicting emotions, and then suddenly turned and left her, almost running, as if afraid of her belief, or perhaps afraid to believe in her belief. Sarah watched him go in amazement. Be nice to him and he ran like a rabbit. She felt that had she been unkind, he would have stood his ground. There was no understanding the man.

At first his only thought was that he could never face her again; he had acted like a fool, revealed his stupid, weak inner self. He was too chagrined to even glance at her hanging out the clothes, as he had been doing all day. But gradually he relaxed and let himself think about what she had said. She believed him, had thought him innocent all along. How strange to think that out there in all that concerted hatred, there had been one stranger who had not hated him, who had believed him. No, two, for

McGowan had said he did not believe Luke had raped Tess, either. It made him feel all mixed up and shaky inside, bursting with surprised happiness and yet scared to death of believing her. He did not know how to react to kindness, had never learned the pattern of it. How should he act now? Polite? Friendly? Humble? Stiff? Relaxed? What he wanted to do was throw his arms around her and hug her till her ribs cracked or lift her up and whirl her around and around. But of all he did not know, at least he knew that was not what he should do. His uncertainty was punctuated with moments of awed joy. *She believed him.* She did not hate him or fear him; she believed him. Each time he thought it, he immediately told himself it could not be true; there was a catch in it somewhere. But why should she lie? She must have meant it. Of course, he reminded himself, that did not mean she had a good opinion of him. No doubt she still thought he was lazy, dirty, drunken white trash. Still—he could not keep his spirits from rising—still, at least she did not think he was a vicious maniac. At least she was not scared of him.

"Luke!" He raised his head at Sarah's voice. She was standing on the back porch, one hand shading her eyes against the sun, the other on her hip. The wind whipped her skirts around her legs and tugged at little tendrils of her hair. "Luke, supper's almost ready. Better stop and get cleaned up." When he continued to stare without saying anything, she said teasingly, "Or have you gotten so spoiled having your food brought to you on a tray that you don't intend to come to the table?''

He had to grin. ''No, ma'am. I'll quit right now.''

Her teasing disconcerted him. The whole thing disconcerted him. Why had they suddenly decided to let him eat with them? It never occurred to him that they had brought his food to him as a favor, out of a desire to keep him from walking on his bad foot.

Suddenly he was seized with an attack of nerves. How was he to act? They would stare at him and judge him, despise his lack of manners, and when he was gone, shake their heads and tut-tut over his commonness. He quickly hung the axe in the tool shed and then hurried to the cistern to wash up. So anxious was he to obliterate the dirt that he pulled off his shirt and poured the whole bucketful of water over his chest and head. He scrubbed away at the sweat and grime, wishing for some soap, and despaired of ever getting his nails thoroughly clean. He smoothed his wet hair into some semblance of order and put his shirt back on and tucked it in. It now clung damply to him and he was overwhelmingly certain that he looked a fool. For an instant he thought of running away, then laughed at the absurdity of it—hell, he couldn't even walk, let alone run. Besides, he didn't run for nothing or nobody. He had taken a lot of hell from *them* for years and always given back as good as he got, hadn't he? No reason to turn coward now. He could remember once when he was little, old Mr. Harper, Jennifer's father-in-law, had leaned over the counter at his store, holding out a licorice stick like he always gave the kids who came in. Luke had shaken his head stubbornly though he ached to grab the candy, and the old man had heaved an exasperated sigh and said, "Boy, you have got a chip on your shoulder a yard wide." Well, so what if he did? It kept them all away from him, didn't it? He braced himself and headed for the house.

It was not so bad at all, he discovered. Sarah and Mrs. McGowan were so busy dishing food up and slapping it down on the table that they paid no attention to him except to point out the chair where he was to sit. Mr. McGowan was already there at his place at the head of the table, and he immediately engaged in a nonstop monologue on the vagaries of his team of mules and the problems he had had with the plow that day. The women joined them, Sarah sitting across from Luke and her mother at the other end. Luke watched Edna out of the corner of his eye; she disapproved of him being there, he could tell. But no one noted, or at least did not remark, his uncertainty when they said grace, and no one stared at him while he ate. Gradually he relaxed; it was almost like he was not there. There was no need for him to talk, even to explain or defend himself.

And later, after dinner was over and he had awkwardly excused himself and gone to his room, there was a light tap on the door and Mrs. McGowan entered, carrying a wash basin and pitcher, towels, and a bar of soap.

"I saw you washing up out at the well," she said. "So I brought you these. Heaven knows why Sarah forgot to put them in here. I don't know what I'm going to do about that girl. Sarah would forget her head if it wasn't attached to her." Her voice was severe, but he sensed an unbending, a kindness in it.

"Thank you," he stammered, astonished. He could hardly believe that she would put herself to any trouble for him.

Suddenly she smiled, and he realized that she looked like Sarah. She turned to leave, then stopped and said hesitantly, "I knew your Ma. I saw her now and then at church. She was a pretty little thing. I'm sorry." Then she hurried out into the night.

Luke watched her cross the yard, wishing he could call her back and ask her questions about his mother. She disappeared into the well-lit house, and he shrugged and picked up the pitcher to go fill it with water.

The days slipped by, and his foot healed quickly, though not as quickly as he would have the McGowans believe. He used it as soon and as much as he could, determined to get back to the fields, suppressing the pain. He did not realize that it showed in the evening in the lines of pain and fatigue in his pale face; the others knew, but forbore to mention it. Luke would have been astonished to hear that they admired his determination.

Even Edna would now admit that "there is more to that boy than meets the eye."

The rest of the week he helped around the house, repairing the broken railing on the front porch, cleaning the gutters, moving the heavy furniture for the women's spring cleaning, putting up the screens on the windows for summer, replacing a broken hinge on one of the kitchen cabinets. Then came Sunday, a day of blessed rest, marred only by having to endure a Sunday dinner eaten under the distrustful gaze of Stu Harper. (Although that was almost made up for by the chance to look for an hour at the beautiful Jennifer. Strange how the usually pretty Sarah dimmed beside her sister.) Monday he went to plow with Mr. McGowan, though the other man insisted that he quit at noon. Tuesday he stuck it out the whole day, and by Saturday his foot hardly hurt at all. It was then that he realized that soon he would have to return home; when his foot had healed, he would have no excuse for staying at the McGowans' farm.

He spent Saturday evening contemplating the fact that he must leave soon. He looked around his tiny room, savoring its aloneness, its belonging to him, its quiet, neat cleanliness. He realized that he was more attached to it than to any place in his life. And the food! It was delicious; he was embarrassed sometimes at the huge amount he ate—though his ability to eat seemed to be the one quality Mrs. McGowan admired in him, for she was constantly urging second and third helpings on him and beaming when he took them. He had even gotten to where he felt almost normal sitting at the table with them.

The worst thing of leaving, though, was returning home: leaving the comfort of Sarah's and McGowan's easy, gentle friendliness and returning to that pigsty inhabited by his drunken father and soured grandmother. The thought of going back smothered him.

"Hey, boy, what're you doing here?"

Luke looked up to see the lanky, lounging form of Zach Sloan.

"Zach!" he exclaimed, welcoming the diversion. "What are *you* doing here?"

Zach laughed and entered the room. "Looking for you, that's what. Went by your place tonight to see if you wanted a little fun. Your pa said you musta taken off—hadn't seen you in two weeks."

Luke shrugged and said, "I hurt my foot, couldn't make it back home."

Zach grinned, "Well, that don't sound too bad, lying around here watching that pretty little piece of tail up at the house yonder."

Zach Sloan was a good buddy, maybe his best friend, always light and easygoing and ready for a good time, but suddenly Luke wanted to smash his fist into Zach's face to wipe off the leer. He controlled himself, making a noncommittal grunt. Damn fool way to feel, considering the fact that his own thoughts about Sarah for the past three weeks had been rather less than pure. It disturbed him, though; she should be out of the reach of Zach's mind—or his.

Sloan, unaware of the other's thoughts, cheerfully pulled a bottle out of his hip pocket and extended it to Luke, his eyebrows raised in questioning invitation. Luke took a swig; the liquid burst fiercely in his throat. Zach settled his long frame on the floor and they talked and drank quietly. Before long, Sloan tired of the restful scene and went to join his brothers, but he left the bottle behind him, declaring that it would be more comfort to Digger than to him.

Luke agreed: it helped to keep the world at bay.

When Sarah came down to the kitchen Thursday morning she was brought up short by the sight of her mother's face. Edna looked like a thundercloud.

"Mama, what's the matter?"

"Matter? Should something be the matter? Only that your father has gone stark staring mad. They ought to lock that man up, I swear, before he does himself harm."

Sarah carefully kept a straight face. "What now, Mama?"

"Do you know what he said to me last night? 'Edna,' he says, 'how would you like to take a little trip to Dallas next week?' "

"Why, Mama, how wonderful!"

"Wonderful, my eye; you have no more sense than *he* does. He wants to go to an auction and buy a brood mare. A brood mare—all we need around here is trying to raise horses!"

"Oh, Mama, for heaven's sakes. Here you are getting to go to Dallas, getting to look at it all and go window shopping and maybe buy something. Mama, just think, you can buy a hat or a blouse or gloves or something and then you'll have something from Dallas to wear. Why, you'll get to spend the night there, I bet, 'cause it will take all day to get there, practically; maybe two nights, even. Just think, three days with no work to do!"

"That is just the point. I said as much to your father: 'Henry, that would mean two nights away from here, and what about Sarah? We can't let her stay out here all by herself. What if something should happen to her?' And do you know what he said?"

"Good heavens, Mama, don't worry about that! I can take care of myself. I am a grown woman, you know—twenty-five years old, after all. And I will lock all the doors and windows and be perfectly safe."

"He said—" Edna continued heatedly, ignoring the interruption, "he said, 'Oh, I thought of that, Edna. Today young Turner said he guessed he would start going home again to sleep, but I persuaded him to stay until next Sunday when we will get back from Dallas. So Digger will be here to protect her.' " The woman stopped, her breast heaving with indignation. " 'Digger will protect her,' " she mimicked sarcastically.

"Well, he can, Mama. That sounds like a fine idea to me."

"That's because you are an innocent, just like Henry. How a grown man could have no more gumption than a child is beyond me! Good Lord, girl, who do you think you need protection *from*, if not men like Digger Turner?"

"You're being unfair," the girl cried. "You know as well as I do that Luke never—"

"Tessa Jackson is beside the point. Even if he was not guilty—and, mind you, I say *if*—he always had a bad reputation. Why, think of the way he came here two or three weeks ago, with that black eye from some brawl and stinking of whiskey!"

"Well, I can remember even Daddy coming home late and smelling of whiskey a couple of Saturday nights."

"How can you compare your father to that shiftless—"

"*And,*" Sarah continued doggedly, "I should think his being in a fight would show you he would jump in and rescue me if something happened to me."

Her mother met that remark with an icy stare. "Don't be frivolous."

"Oh, Mama, even you have gotten to like Luke. Surely you can't think he would hurt me."

"I feel sorry for the boy is all, and I don't think he's as bad as people say," her mother retorted. "That does not mean that I would entrust my daughter to him. Sarah, that man has been in prison; he grew up with one of the worst men in the county. His brother is a thief, and his sister had to get married. Digger has been in trouble all his life over one thing or another."

"Are you still carrying on about that?" came Henry's voice from the doorway. "You know good and well that boy would not hurt Sarah."

"I know nothing of the sort. And even if he didn't, just think how it would look. Sarah alone here with Digger Turner! It would ruin her reputation."

"Don't be silly, Mama," Sarah said. "Who's to know? Besides, I believe my reputation is sufficiently good to withstand spending one or two nights in the same vicinity as Luke Turner."

"I already told him about it," McGowan said. "If you refuse to go, he will realize why."

"You can't do that to him, Mama. He needs to be trusted, I think."

"I am more concerned with your safety than Digger's hurt feelings," Edna said and turned back to the stove.

"Edna, you are being a fool. I insist that you go," Henry said firmly, his voice so determined that his wife stared at him. "I mean it, Edna. I won't let you hurt his pride like that for one of your whims."

"Whims!" Mrs. McGowan gasped, but in a voice less sure than before. After a moment, she said, "Well, perhaps Sarah could go in to stay with Jenny."

"And I leave the house untended for two or three days? And no one to fix Digger's meals? Or take care of the chickens? No, I am going to stay right here," Sarah refused. Earnestly, she drew close to her mother. "I think this is important, Mama. Please don't fuss about it."

Mrs. McGowan looked from her daughter to her husband and back again. She sighed. "I shan't have a moment's rest in Dallas for worrying about you."

Sarah and her father smiled at each other; they knew they had won. And when Digger entered the kitchen later and Sarah saw the new confidence in his walk, she felt pleased and sure that she had done the right thing.

She felt less sure Saturday night, when she was roused from her sleep by a loud noise outside and crept to the window to see Luke leaning against the small side porch, obviously far gone in drink. As she watched, he reached in his hip pocket and brought out a bottle which he uncapped and tilted back his head to drink, his movements slow and unsteady. He replaced the bottle, shaking his head and laughing at some private amusement.

Sarah sighed in exasperation. As soon as they had shown they trusted him, he had had to show his irresponsibility by going out and getting blind drunk. She wondered where he had been—with that Sloan boy who had come by last week? With some loose woman? Had he gotten into another fight? Or had he lain out in the woods on the spring-smelling soil, wrapped in the arms of some girl? Sarah imagined him with some unknown beautiful slut, kissing her, holding her, rolling with her in the soft black earth.

She pulled her thoughts away from that image and hastily pulled on her wrapper and tied its belt. She had better get down there and get him away from the house, she thought, before he woke up her parents, too, and Mama saw him and refused to go to Dallas. Softly Sarah slipped down the stairs in the dark and out onto the porch, easing the door to behind her.

"Luke Turner!" she hissed down at him, and he turned. The moonlight turned his hair silver, but his face was pale and featureless, his eyes pools of darkness.

"Miss McGowan," he said, baring his teeth in a smile, "I am honored." He swept her a bow, stumbling as he straightened."

"Are you mad?" she berated him in a stage whisper. "Do you know what Mama will do if you wake her up and she finds you in this condition?"

Turner scowled at Sarah, swaying slightly as he stood in silence. Damn the girl, she had no understanding of the wonderful, awful burden placed on him by their trust. His pride was equalled by the fear of failing in his new responsibility; a fear that made him drink to get away from it, made him almost hope that her mother would see him drunk. Finally he shrugged and assumed his hard, insolent expression, looking her up and down in her light wrapper.

Suddenly Sarah was conscious of being clothed only in her nightgown and robe in the middle of the night with

Luke Turner just a few feet away. She suppressed a desire to pull the wrapper more tightly around her.

"You better get back to the barn, Luke, before they hear you."

Luke saw the look of disgust and fear on her face and it made him writhe inside. He came up the stairs toward her and involuntarily she backed up against the railing. He stopped inches away from her, so close she could feel the heat of his body and smell the young male scent of him and the reek of whiskey. She forced herself to look up into his face, determined not to let her fear show, feeling somehow that drunks were like animals and would back down before an absence of fear. His face was blank, his eyes pale and glittering in the dead light of the moon. She felt a strange pull from him, a crazy wish to move forward into his hard body instead of away. Unconsciously she caught her lower lip with her teeth and a sudden tremor shook him.

"Sarah," he said, his voice rasping, unsteady. "Girl, don't you know it ain't safe to be out here alone with me in the middle of the night?"

She wanted to snap out a calm, cool retort, but her voice seemed to have left her. She could not think, only sense the enveloping nearness of his body, the warmth and strength and animal fascination of him, and wonder how his lips would feel against her mouth.

He leaned down into her face. "I am not your slave. What I do on Saturday night is none of your concern. If I want to get drunk, I will, and your mother be damned. And don't you come out here preaching at me, or I might have to take you down a peg.''

Now he was going to kiss her, she thought, and she felt a little pang of disappointment as he moved back from her. He turned and went down the steps and across the yard toward the barn. Suddenly her knees felt weak and she leaned against the railing for support, her brain whirling in confusion. Oh, she had been wrong to trust him—what would he do when her parents were gone? But, no, what he said was true: she really had no right to condemn him. Only, she had not meant it that way; she just wanted him to escape her mother's detection. That was the only reason she had come down here, wasn't it? Why had he not kissed her? And why, oh, why, was she so wicked as to wish that he had?

Quietly, cautiously she re-entered the house; it would never do for her to wake up Mama and get Luke into trouble. She dared not look in the direction of the barn and so did not see Luke standing by his door, watching her.

The next morning neither Luke nor Sarah gave any indication that anything had happened Saturday night, except for a reluctance to meet the other's eye. After church, Jennifer and Stu and the children came for dinner and Luke went home to visit instead of eating with the family. Sarah suspected he was avoiding Stu, and she could hardly blame him. Stu was everything that Luke was not; no doubt he stirred up envy in Luke's heart just as the sight of him made her churn with love and despair and jealousy.

She wished Luke had stayed, however, for then Stu would not have been able to try to dissuade her parents from going to Dallas.

"You can't be serious!" he had exclaimed, disturbing her dreamy contemplation of his standing close to her as Luke had done last night. "You cannot mean to allow Sarah to stay here alone with that—"

"Oh, no, Sarah must come stay with us while you are gone," Jennifer said.

"Oh, yes," her daughters agreed, and Sarah felt a sudden rush of desire to do so—to be with Jenny and the girls again, to play with baby Jonathan, to be near Stu and hear his voice and see his face. Why not go? The house would not fall apart if she was gone for three days. And Digger could feed the chickens and get his own meals and—no. Firmly she braked her rushing thoughts. No, Luke would misinterpret it, think she was scared of him because of last night. She knew that it would eat at his confidence, and surely she was not selfish enough to hurt that poor, strange man just to satisfy her own desire to pine after Stu.

"No, I simply cannot leave the house; I have too much to do. I am perfectly safe; really I am. Luke Turner simply is not the evil person everyone thinks."

"Well, the children and I will come stay with you then," Jenny decided.

Sarah wavered at that, but Stu said, "Absolutely not. I will not have you exposing yourself to danger, too. No, I think it would be best if you came into town, Sarah."

Unreasonably Sarah felt a spurt of anger. Why did he have to take away her chance to be with her sister without feeling the guilt of wanting him? And who was he to take that commanding tone with her? "I believe not, Stu," she said crisply, almost rudely.

He looked surprised, and she immediately felt guilty. How could she have unkind thoughts about her dear, beloved Stu? Especially when he was just concerned about her.

"I—I'm sorry, Stu, but I really do not think—" she floundered helplessly, unable to explain why Luke would feel betrayed or why his feelings even mattered.

"Don't think what?" Stu asked, puzzled.

"I don't think it would be a good idea," Sarah concluded lamely.

"I agree with Sarah. She is needed here and there is absolutely no reason for her to go into town," Henry said.

"I fail to understand this fascination with Digger Turner!" Stu said almost angrily. "The boy is nothing but trouble, always has been."

Henry leaned back and regarded Stu, one eyebrow cocked in amusement. "You know your problem, Stu?"

he said lazily, humorously. "You have always been so darned perfect that you can't understand a boy like Luke. You can't sympathize with him because you have never been lonely or abused or scared or disliked. But Sarah and me, well, sometimes we have felt like that—oh, not like Digger feels, but a taste of it, enough to want to help him, enough not to be scared of him."

Stu looked chagrined at McGowan's assessment of him, and Edna hurriedly changed the subject. The subject of Sarah's coming into town to stay was not raised again.

Chapter V

THEY left for Dallas in the rain. It had started raining during the night, a steady, gentle spring rain, and by the time breakfast was over and her parents had gotten into the buggy, the ground was already slickly muddy. Sarah waved to them from the side porch; her mother looked back at her, her face hesitant, worried.

The rain continued all day. It was too wet to plow and Luke was forced to occupy himself with chores around the yard and barn. Sarah, busy in the house with the full load of chores, smiled to herself—if this rain kept up, however would Digger manage to find enough things to keep himself at an obviously safe distance from her? He was such an odd man, like two or three different people, at one moment surly, the next scary, the next aloof and silent, and then suddenly miserable and desperate for your good opinion. A person never knew what to make of him or how to treat him.

She called him to lunch and he came running across the yard, sidestepping the puddles and keeping his head down in a vain attempt to keep the rain out of his face. He shook himself off on the porch, brushing the fat drops off his dampened hair. She noted that his hair looked darker when it was wet, more gold than the almost white color it usually was.

They sat down to the table in silence, taking their accustomed places on either side. It seemed strange and awkward not to have her parents there, seated at the head and foot. Edna was the chief instigator of conversation at their meals; Sarah and her father spoke mostly in reply to her, and Luke sat silently and listened. With Edna gone, the silence was encompassing, embarrassing. Luke wolfed his food down and kept his eyes on his plate. Sarah wondered why he was avoiding looking at her and why he never said anything, and why, for that matter, she could think of nothing to say to break the oppressive quiet. She gazed at him; already in the warmth of the kitchen and dining room, his hair was drying, no longer the color of wet hay, but its usual silver gilt. Corn silk, that was it, she realized; his hair was the color and texture of the soft, fine silk that lay between kernel and husk. Not quite gold, not quite silver, not quite white; a glimmering color all its own. He felt her gaze and looked up at her uneasily. She felt the color flooding her face at being caught staring.

"Your hair has dried," she said and immediately thought she must sound like an idiot.

"Just get wet again." He shrugged. "I gotta get up and clean out the gutters. Something's clogging them on the north side of the house."

That sounded unpleasant, she thought, climbing a ladder in the rain to slip around on the roof and clean the rain gutters. "You better wear a slicker then. And a hat, too."

He shrugged again and she felt hot with embarrassment—he didn't have them, of course.

"You can wear one of Daddy's old hats. And I'm sure he left his slicker here." Better embarrassment than pneumonia. She left the table to find a hat and slicker before he could protest.

Her father was a big man and the slicker hung ludicrously on Luke. She smiled at the sight of him crossing the yard in the bright yellow garb, the too-big hat pulled forward to shield his face from the rain. He looked like a child playing grown up. She tried to remember him as a child; she could not really recall him before he was about fourteen or fifteen. She must have seen him around the school, even though he was a couple of years behind her. He would have been a real towhead, of course; surely she would remember that white-blond hair, no doubt much lighter than it was now, and those intense blue eyes.

Dimly she could remember his sister, who was only a

couple of years younger than she. A thin girl with dark blond hair and wary eyes, whose clothes were always poorly mended (the clumsy stitches of a child, not a woman). Sarah frowned. Why had the girl had to mend them herself? Mama said their mother had died when they were little, but their grandmother lived with them; surely she could have kept them neat and clean. Suddenly an image popped into her mind: the three of them walking into the schoolyard, their clothes ragged and faded, their hair too long and unkempt, Earl swaggering in front and prodding at the ground with a stick, the girl a few steps behind him, and beside her, clutching her hand, a white-haired, thin-faced little boy. That must have been Luke. She could not remember when the scene took place; she had still been in the lower grades, so he could not have been more than eight or so. Maybe only six—the way he was holding onto his sister's hand. Perhaps it had been his first day at school.

Sarah frowned. What *was* the girl's name, anyhow? Janet? Something like that. She was the kind it was hard to remember, quiet and unobtrusive. Sarah could not remember when she had stopped coming to school, her absence had aroused so little notice. It was long before Sarah graduated. Her mother claimed the girl had had to get married; somehow that did not seem to fit with her character. Tess Jackson, of course, one expected it from, or one of the Sloan girls, or Emma Whitehead. She remembered being surprised to hear the rumors when the

Turner girl married. Of course, rumors did not make it so; people always hinted at pregnancy when one of the girls from a trashy family got married.

Now, the rumors about Earl she firmly believed. He had been only a year ahead of her at school and since the school had been too small for each grade to have a separate classroom, they had been in the same class. She knew him to be a sly, thieving boy. One of her most vivid memories of childhood was of Earl getting whipped with a switch before the class for one of his tricks or smart remarks or defiances; no doubt she remembered it well because it had happened so often. She remembered his set face, the determination incongruous on his freckled, pug-nosed countenance, his teeth biting into his lip to hold back the sound. She had felt an admiration for his stubborn pride, mingled with disgust at his mean nature and the obnoxious way he had of pulling her hair. Always when it was over and he walked stiffly back to his desk, the backs of his legs red from the stinging switch, he would make a face at her to show how little he was affected by the whole thing. She never had been quite sure why he singled her out for that.

Her Aunt Betty, who was a teacher, said that Luke was just as bad in school as Earl, if not worse. He made everyone's life miserable, she said, always fighting the other children—even the boys who were older than he—forever sassing his teachers or sullenly refusing to listen to them or tormenting them with some trick or other. Of course, Aunt Betty was a teacher in the high school, not in the elementary school, and so she did not speak from personal experience. She merely recounted what she had heard from the other teachers, no doubt magnified with each retelling.

The sound of the ladder against the house shook her out of her reverie. What nonsense! Here she was lost in memories, with the afternoon slipping away and the noon dishes not even cleared off the table yet. She set to work with gusto, determined to have the house in as good a shape when Mama returned as it would have been with Mama there. Better, maybe.

Supper was late, but at least she knew she would get no gripes from Luke. She was right about that; he came when she called, obviously cleaned up and sure to have been waiting for some time, but he did not mention her tardiness. In gratitude for his kindness, Sarah was determined to set him at ease and conduct a real conversation over the meal.

"It's been a real wet spring, hasn't it?" she began brightly.

He nodded and mumbled something. She felt exasperated; she thought he had stopped that annoying mumbling of his.

"Excuse me?" she inquired politely.

"I said, Crooked Creek is clear up over its banks. And the river's up almost two feet above usual."

"Well, I hope it stops soon so we can get the corn planted."

"Yes'm," he replied, again concentrating on his plate, and another silence fell upon them.

He felt a fool. Here she was, trying to be nice, even after the way he had acted the other night, and he seemed to have lost all powers of thought and speech. Surreptitiously he stole a glance at her. She looked pretty in that pink dress; it added color to her cheeks and emphasized her breasts. But that was not exactly the sort of thing she would welcome his saying. He thought about the way she had looked the other night, clad only in her gown and wrapper, with her thick braid of hair hanging loosely down her back, and something tightened in his chest. He had almost kissed her then; only some hidden remnant of good sense had kept him from it.

And now here he was sitting at the table with her and like an idiot, wanting to unpin that thick coil of hair at the nape of her neck and let the heavy braid slide softly through his hands. He could almost feel his fingers sinking into her hair, unbraiding it, winding it around his fingers. Hastily he pulled his eyes from her hair and studied her face. How delicate it was, the fragility emphasized by those huge hazel eyes. There was a light sprinkling of freckles across her nose and under her eyes; he had never noticed them before, and now he ached to touch them with his fingers, then lips and tongue. He wondered what she would do—probably slap his face and then kick him out.

"Luke, what's your sister's name?" Her voice pulled him roughly from his dreams.

"Why do you want to know?" He looked at her suspiciously, his face closed against her.

She looked at him in amazement. "Why do I want to know?" she repeated, then said sarcastically, "Is she going about incognito or something?"

His voice was sullen. "I don't know what that means."

"Hiding her true identity."

"Of course not."

"So what is the big secret about her name?"

"There's no secret. Her name is Julia." His eyes sparked a little, but he said nothing more.

"Julia. Of course. All I could think of was Janet. I was trying to remember you all when we were children."

"Well, I'm sure you and Julie never exactly ran in the same circle," he sneered.

He laid down his fork, his appetite suddenly gone. Let her say it, he thought, let her say one snide thing about Julie, and I'll walk out of here and let her look out for herself.

"No, I guess not. We weren't the same age, either. I remember your brother Earl, though. He was in my class at school."

"Not for long, I'm sure," he said shortly, still tensed for an attack.

"He used to pull my pigtails, but he quit after a few months."

"You must not have yelled enough."

"Oh, I never yelled. I was afraid of getting in trouble."

"You getting in trouble?" he said in disbelief, but his attitude softened a trifle.

"Well, I didn't want to get him in trouble because he was always—I mean—anyway, mostly I did not want to get myself in trouble."

"But you hadn't done anything. Believe me, they would have just gotten Earl."

"Oh, I realize that now. But then I was never too sure what they would think; maybe that I was guilty, too. I was terrified of being punished—you know, being embarrassed in front of the class."

He grinned. "Oh, you get used to it."

She smiled back. "I guess so. I remember I had a sneaking admiration for your brother because he wouldn't cry. He would do the strangest thing. When he would walk back to his seat, he would make this face at me."

"To show he didn't give a damn. Oh, excuse me, ma'am."

"But why me?" she said, ignoring both his swearing and the apology for it.

"Probably thought you were worth impressing 'cause you wouldn't holler when he hurt you." He thought it was wise not to mention what it was about her that had impressed Earl when he grew older. "Earl never respected anybody unless they stood up to him. He used to bully me all the time, hated me, until I hit him over the head with a board. After that he liked me well enough."

Immediately he wished he could recall the words—

what a thing to be telling a lady! But she laughed, and he felt a warmth permeating him at the sound of her laughter. He wished he could think of something else to make her laugh.

"And were you a terror, too?" She sounded amused.

"Kind of."

"Why?"

He moved uneasily in his chair. "What do you mean?"

"I mean, why did you play those pranks and get in trouble and fight all the time?"

His eyes went blank and hard. " 'Cause I'm a Turner, I guess."

"Oh, pooh, I never heard of Julia doing anything bad like that and she is a Turner."

He looked at her steadily, and then she remembered the rumors about Julia and a flush rose up her neck and into her face. He smiled grimly when he saw the blush.

"Yeah, remember? Old Julia jumped the gun, didn't she?" Suddenly fury contorted his face and he slammed his fist onto the table. "Goddamn you!"

"Luke! My God, it isn't that terrible. Or that unusual."

"Oh, no, not at all unusual for a girl like her, is it? Not for 'poor white trash.' "

"For anybody," she said mulishly.

He stood up so suddenly that his chair went flying back and turned over with a clatter. Sarah felt a little thrill of fear at the wild, piercing blueness of his eyes.

"For a Turner girl. You think Jimmy Banks would

have come crawling around here trying to get in your skirts, taking you out into the trees and—"

"Jimmy Banks!" She gaped.

"Sure, Jimmy Banks. Why do you think I beat the hell out of him? Julie full of his kid and him up there dancing with a *good* girl!"

"But I thought—"

"Oh, yeah, she married Will Dobson, saddled herself with that son of a bitch for the rest of her life so her kid at least wouldn't have to be a bastard. But the father is Jimmy Banks. He knew he could have her; she was easy 'cause she was trash. With you he would have had to be a good boy, behave himself, but with Julie Turner, hell, she ought to feel honored that he turned his attentions on her."

"Perhaps," Sarah said levelly, "the reason Jimmy Banks never tried to lure me out into the woods at night was because I had a father at home who could stop him if he tried anything. And perhaps he could succeed with Julie because both he and she knew she didn't have a father or brother there to protect her because they were out taking some other girl into the trees."

He went white, as if she had hit him in the stomach, then turned and slammed out into the dark rain. Sarah remained in her chair; she felt slightly ill. Shakily she stood and began to clean off the table. His plate was still half-full. Suddenly tears welled in her eyes and spilled down her cheeks.

* * *

Sarah washed the dishes listlessly and then began to prepare to go to bed. Somehow she did not feel like sitting up to read tonight. Just as she was about to go up to bed there was a thunderous knock at the door. She jumped in fright and then cautiously went to the door. Surely if whoever it was had knocked there would be no danger. She eased the door open.

Grady Snowden stood on the front porch, looking wet and angry. She relaxed in relief.

"Grady! Whatever are you doing here at this hour?"

"I just heard something I cannot credit."

"Oh?"

"Stu Harper told me your parents have gone to Dallas, leaving you here alone."

"I am not alone."

"Then that Turner boy *is* here!" He looked thunderstruck.

Sarah felt a flash of irritation. Why on earth had Stu run to Grady to tell him?

"Sarah, I cannot allow this."

"You what?" Her eyebrows pitched upward at his peremptory tone.

"You cannot realize what this will do to your reputation."

"Don't talk nonsense. I am perfectly safe here, and I have absolutely no desire to take a ride in the middle of the night in the rain."

"Sarah, be reasonable. You are out here with no protection."

"Luke Turner is here to protect me."

"That's right." Both of them turned at the sound of a third voice. Luke stood at the end of the porch. Lithely he swung over the railing and approached them.

"Hello, Luke," Sarah said calmly, suppressing a desire to laugh. Luke Turner protecting her from Grady Snowden!

"Hello, ma'am. Is he bothering you? Want me to get rid of him?"

Grady looked outraged. Luke looked cheerful and his eyes glittered; Sarah had the feeling he would welcome an opportunity to take out some of his fury of tonight on the hapless Grady.

"No, Luke, thank you. I think Mr. Snowden was just about to leave."

Grady began to splutter angrily.

"You know, Snowden," Luke said, his voice silkily lazy, "I never would have thought you were the type to come rushing out here to a lady's house soon as you knew her parents were gone and she was alone."

Grady's eyes bulged alarmingly and he made strangling noises in his throat. Sarah had to bite her lip to hold back the laughter welling up in her throat.

"Well," Luke continued indulgently, "I can see how it might happen, especially with a girl as pretty as Miss McGowan. So I reckon we won't say anything about it, provided you run along home now."

Grady looked at Sarah. "Sarah, you cannot seriously mean to stay?"

"I do."

"Has he threatened you? Forced you to say this?"

"Why you—" Luke began angrily.

"Luke." Sarah put a restraining hand on his arm. "Really, Grady, don't be absurd. How could he have forced me to say this? We did not even know you were going to come out here."

The lawyer hung there on the porch, uncertain. He could hardly drag Sarah off with him, yet all his instincts were against leaving her there with Luke Turner. Finally, with a disgusted sound he swung off the porch and into his buggy. Luke and Sarah watched him go.

Luke turned to her, grinning. "Did you just lose a beau?"

" 'Fraid so."

He shrugged. "That's one that ain't worth crying over. Now, listen, I want you to lock this door and the back one and then go check every window to make sure it's locked. All right?"

"Oh, for pity's sake."

"No back talk now," he laughed. "I'm in charge of protecting you."

"All right," she laughed, too.

"Ma'am?" He paused and looked out into the darkness. "I'm sorry I got mad a while ago."

"And I'm sorry I said what I did."

"No, it's probably true." He looked back and smiled briefly. "You don't believe in sugaring the medicine, do you?"

"I can always see very clearly what others should do," Sarah laughed softly, and it brought another smile to his face.

He pulled away a little. "Now you lock up, all right? I'm going to stand here and watch to make sure you check every window."

"All right." She stepped back inside and locked the door, then crossed into the kitchen to lock that door. She could hear him checking from the outside to make sure they were locked. Picking up a candle, she went around to each window, even the upstairs ones, to check their locks. At her bedroom window, the last one, she looked down to see Luke standing below in the rain, looking up at her. He had waited and watched to see her light at each window. She waved down at him and he raised one hand and then took off running for the barn. She sat down on the edge of her bed with a little half smile.

The rain stopped during the night and the day dawned bright and cloudless. Sarah hummed happily beneath her breath as she went downstairs to make breakfast. Almost she felt as if she had a home of her own, with a husband out milking the cows and children scurrying around upstairs; it was easy to imagine that, with only herself in the kitchen, slicing bread, slapping sausage into the cast-iron skillet, frying the eggs. When Luke entered, carrying a bucket of milk, she smiled to herself—what would he think if he knew he had been cast in the role of husband in her pretend family!

Luke smiled at her, an infectious, mischievous smile that shifted the lines on his face upward and made deep indentations on either side of his mouth. Dimples, long, deep, masculine dimples; imagine Digger Turner having dimples. She felt like laughing with pure enjoyment of the situation. It suddenly seemed exciting and scandalous to be here alone with Luke Turner, to be involved in a scene that was curiously intimate, as if they were a husband and wife standing together in the kitchen at dawn after a shared night. She felt she would not be surprised, or even indignant, if he gave her a good morning kiss.

He did not, of course, and they sat down to breakfast. The awkwardness of the earlier meals was gone and they ate in easy silence or speculated on her parents' enjoyment of Dallas. After he left, as she cleaned the table, Sarah felt a pang of regret. She had had a glimpse this morning of the life she had cut herself off from for the sake of her love for Stu. To hell with the love or the sex; what she wanted so badly was the companionship, the friendly talking and sharing with someone who was her age and not family, someone who did not know her as a daughter or sister or niece or aunt, but as a person. Suddenly, desperately, she wanted her own house, her own husband, her own children to care for and work for and find joy in. Her future life seemed empty and joyless. She almost wished she had not been angered so last night by Grady's high-handed manner and assumption of authority. She had thrown away her only real prospect of a husband. Then she thought of sitting at the breakfast table with Grady and having him map out her day for her and she grimaced. No, she would not regret missing that. With a sigh she thought of Stu. That was what she would miss. She imagined sitting across the table from Stu, neatly dressed to go to the store, sipping a last cup of coffee. He would lean toward her as she talked, tilting his head in that amused, loving way he did when he listened to Jenny, his eyes alight, his lips quirked in that tender half smile. She felt tears rising in her throat at the thought of it, and she sank into one of the wooden chairs. Why, oh, why, did everything have to be so wrong?

By suppertime, thunderhead clouds were piling up in the west, the sky already growing dark. It looked as though it would storm that night, Sarah thought when she stepped out onto the porch to call Luke. As if to affirm her words, a sudden gust of chill wind whipped around the house and tugged at her skirts. She shivered and quickly ducked back inside; the cold reminded her of a wind coming off of a hailstorm.

"Storm tonight, looks like," Luke echoed her thoughts as he came into the kitchen.

"Yeah. I hope it won't spoil Mama's and Daddy's trip."

Luke sat down to their meal with gusto, declaring, "Stew! My favorite."

"Really?"

"Along with about thirty other things. You and your mother are going to make me fat."

"You could use a little weight." She looked at him, reflecting how much better he looked than he had a month ago. His skin had lost its unhealthy pallor after weeks in the sun, and their cooking had filled him out some. Of course, he still had that rumpled, tattered, uncared-for look, but at least he no longer looked as if he had just gone through a long illness.

"You are eating very precious stew," she said lightly and he looked a question at her. "I nearly cut my thumb off."

He immediately frowned in concern and grabbed her hand to gently inspect her thumb. "I think you'll live," he said and she laughed. "But you ought to wrap it up." He held her hand in one of his, softly touching her thumb with the fingers of his other hand; he wished he could continue to hold her hand so, but he forced himself to release her.

"I did bandage it at first, but it's so hard to do any housework with your thumb wrapped up. The bandage keeps getting wet and coming off; so I took it off." She continued in a bantering tone, "Besides, in our kitchen, that is not much of a wound. My mother has slashed herself so many times she looks like a war veteran."

He smiled and for a moment felt washed with well-being; he could almost believe he belonged here, that he sat at his own table in his own house with his pretty, sweet, humorous wife across from him. They would eat and then retire to the parlor to sit and talk; he would sit in an overstuffed easychair and pull her down into his lap, and she would nestle against him, her head on his shoulder. And later he would take her up to their bed and watch her undress and take down her hair. Determinedly he shook the dream from his mind and attacked his food.

When they had finished, Sarah cleared off the table and brought in the dessert, hot, rich blueberry pie, and cups of coffee. He leaned back in his chair contentedly, feeling pampered. This was what men like Stu Harper or Henry McGowan or Grady Snowden were used to; no doubt they took it all for granted. But Luke Turner did not; no one had ever waited on him like this, not even Julie, as if he was a man like other men, worthy of spoiling. He wanted to stretch like a great lazy cat and pull her into his arms and express his contentment.

Instead, he ate two pieces of pie and complimented her extravagantly on the quality of it, until she giggled and accused him of insincerity. He tried to think of an excuse to linger and talk to her while she washed the dishes, but he could not and finally left for his solitary room in the barn. Now he would go out for his Saturday night, Sarah thought, wishing a little enviously that she could go out and kick over the traces and forget her problems for tonight. She wondered what it was like to be a man and able to do such things, to go drinking and play cards and be rough and noisy. How did it feel? What was it like? She had never even tasted liquor; she could not imagine its taste or the things it did to you. Faintly she could understand a man's desire for a woman; she had felt stirrings herself sometimes, even when the man was a stranger; she could think of several men she had a lurking desire to kiss. But somehow, she never wanted to go further than that.

She went into the living room to do some mending. About nine she went up to bed, first locking the doors and making her rounds of the windows. After she had undressed and gone to bed, a quiet noise downstairs brought her straight up in bed, her heart pounding. After a few moments it came again. Stealthily she slipped out of bed and looked down to see Luke ambling across the yard toward the barn. She went limp with relief. Of course. It was just Luke checking to make sure she had locked the doors. She watched him enter the barn and then the light in his room went out. So he had not gone to town this Saturday night. She smiled; he must take his guard duties seriously indeed.

She was awakened later by a loud crash of thunder. The threatened storm had arrived. She went to the window. It was raining furiously outside. Again the thunder roared and then a flash of lightning blazed across the sky. The brief light revealed the open door into Luke's room; he lounged in the doorway, shirtless, looking up at the house. She wondered if the lightning had shown her equally clearly standing there in her nightgown. The thunder continued to roll and she shivered a little, not from fear, but from anticipation. Thunderstorms excited her; some atavistic yearning in her responded to the wind and rain and noise as an Indian responded to the beating of the drums.

For a crazy moment she wanted to run out into the storm and cavort in the rain until she was drenched. She wondered if Luke would join her if she did, or if he would notice her wet, clinging nightgown. She closed her eyes and leaned against the cool glass of the window, imagining his rough hands on her wet body, his lips buried in hers, his arms pulling her into him, pressing her body against his.

Irritated with herself, she pulled away from the window. As if Luke would want to do that! He had never shown any interest in her; doubtless to him she seemed just an old maid, far too old for him and not at all alluring. *Not*, she reminded herself sternly, that she really wanted him to do anything like that. It was bad enough to think of Stu that way, but to want that from a man she did not love, a man she hardly knew, oh, that was wicked. She buried her face in her pillow and tried to go to sleep.

The storm finally blew past them, but the heavy rain continued all morning, so hard that she did not go to church. Her parents had taken the buggy, and she would have been drenched had she gone in the open wagon. The rain slackened around noon and Stu and Jenny came for Sunday dinner as usual. Stu looked sternly disapproving, but said nothing because Luke was at the table.

"Thank heavens, the rain let up some. I was afraid we would not get to come, it was raining so hard," Jenny fluttered. She looked lovely, her damp hair curling charmingly around her face. Stu's face softened when he looked at her and Luke's eyes reflected his admiration. Sarah felt a stab of jealous anger. So, even Luke, bitter Luke who never so much as glanced at her, was also entranced with Jennifer.

"I pity your parents, having to drive home in this rain. No doubt all the roads are terribly muddy. It may even be that some of the bridges are impassable. I hear that even the Little Elm is almost up to the bridge," Stu said.

"You mean they might be stranded?" Sarah asked in amazement.

"Not by the Little Elm, I'm sure. But I don't know about some of the creeks further away. You know, they have to cross the north fork of the Little Elm as well. I'm afraid they might be delayed."

"Oh," Jennifer cried, "but I was hoping they would get back while we were still here."

"Well, they might, Jen," her husband reassured her.

But the afternoon stretched out and still they did not come. Luke retired to his room in the barn immediately after dinner. Sarah and Jenny cleaned up and then put the children down for a nap while Stu read in Mr. McGowan's easychair. About three o'clock the rain grew heavy again, depressing them all and dragging at their conversation.

After a couple of hours, Stu rose, saying, "Looks like it's letting up a little. I think we had better go, Jenny, before it gets worse again."

Jenny looked doubtfully out the window and then her face brightened. "Oh, here they are. No, wait, that's not they."

Stu and Sarah joined her at the window. Soon the figures grew close enough to be discerned as two men on horseback. A sudden uneasiness struck Sarah, and she ran out onto the porch. Stu and Jenny were close on her heels.

"Why, that's Mr. Hefner, isn't it?" Jenny identified one of the quickly approaching riders.

"And Cal Weatherly."

Sarah gripped the railing of the porch, inexplicably swept with fear, as the men slid off their horses and darted up the steps.

"Well, hello there, Mr. Hef—" Stu began, but Sarah interrupted him, her voice shrill with anxiety.

"What's happened? What's the matter?"

The two men took off their hats under the cover of the porch, revealing drawn, shocked faces.

"The bridge just washed out on the river," Weatherly began.

"The Little Elm?"

"Oh, then Mama and Daddy won't get here tonight," Jennifer said disappointedly.

"No, ma'am." The two men looked uncomfortable. Sarah could have finished their statement for them, except for the fact that air rushed into her throat, swelling, pushing, blocking speech and breath.

"Fact is, Mrs. Harper, Miss McGowan, your Ma and Pa were on the bridge when it collapsed."

"What?" Stu gasped and Jennifer stared at them speechlessly, one hand to her throat, her face suddenly drained of color.

Out of the corner of her eye, Sarah saw Luke approaching, drawn by the unexpected visitors; she noticed he did not wear the hat or slicker. She noticed everything, saw everything with amazing clarity. But somehow her brain seemed disconnected from her body.

"I'm afraid they're drowned. We was at the church, just come to prayer meeting, and we heard it. We got Henry out, but Mrs. McGowan—" his voice trailed off and he looked at his feet.

"Daddy," Sarah said and her own voice startled her, as if it spoke without her knowledge. "He's alive, then?"

"No, ma'am, his neck was broke. The rocks—"

"I must go to them. Where are they?"

"At the bridge, ma'am, you know, on Curry Road. But I think you better not go. We'll bring them back here. You wouldn't want to see—"

She looked at them, blocked by the blank refusal on their faces. She turned to her brother-in-law. "Stu, take me?" Somehow she could not pull herself together enough to realize what to do to get to the bridge.

"Now, Sarah, Jenny, I think Mr. Weatherly's right. You two come on back in the house." He seemed to have recovered a little, enough to propel Sarah and Jennifer toward the front door. "I'll go down there. You need to sit down."

"No!" she said fiercely and pulled away from him. She could think of only one thing: she had to go to them. Pleadingly she looked at Stu, then back to the two men. "Luke!" She turned to look off the porch where he had been.

He stood there, still, his face blank, old. He held out his hand toward her. "Come on."

She pushed past Stu, hearing his voice behind her, "Sarah!" She grabbed the proffered hand and then Luke began to run, pulling her with him through the mud to the barn. Quickly he bridled Mexico, then scrambled onto the horse, not bothering with a saddle. He reached down and swung Sarah up behind him.

"Hold on," he said and she obeyed, wrapping her arms around him and burying her face in his back as if she could block out the world that way.

He dug his heels into the horse's sides and Mexico took off, though clumsily in the slippery mud. It was two miles down to the bridge over the Little Elm at Curry Road, and they were slowed by the muddy road and still-falling rain. By the time they reached the bridge, Sarah was beginning to recover enough that the idea of her parents' death was finally penetrating her brain.

When they stopped, Sarah knew they had reached the bridge and she raised her head to look over Luke's shoulder. The first thing she saw was the remnants of the heavy wooden bridge, and Sarah gasped at the sight. She had crossed that bridge hundreds of times in her life; its absence shocked her and its dangling remains made her parents' deaths suddenly real.

Luke slid off the horse and tied it to a bush, then lifted Sarah down. She leaned gratefully on his supporting arm as they walked toward the knot of people at the river's edge. A man looked up at their approach and his face registered surprise.

"Miss Sarah! You shouldn't be here," he protested, but Sarah walked past him, through the crowd to the inert body that lay there, its face covered by someone's coat.

Her knees gave way and she sank to the ground. Shakily she removed the coat. Her father's face was bruised and cut, his lifeless eyes open and staring.

"Oh, Daddy." Somehow she had not really expected him to look dead. "Oh, Daddy." She held one of his cold, wet hands between her own. "Oh, Daddy."

A woman bent to stroke her hair. "There now, Sary, it's all right."

Sarah seemed not to notice her, but Luke was seized with a desire to push her away from the girl. He wanted to scream at them all to leave her alone with her father. He stepped to one side and stonily watched the search for Mrs. McGowan. A cluster of men held one end of a rope that was looped around a tree for extra support. At the other end of the rope was a man who dived, then bounced back up, treading against the swift rush of the water, then dived again. As Luke watched, the diver gave a signal and swam for the banks. The group pulled him out and conferred with the shivering man who wrapped a coat around himself. The knot of men began to dissolve. One of them walked over to Sarah.

"Miss McGowan?"

She looked up, her eyes dazed, unfocussed.

"I'm afraid it's useless."

"What is?"

"We cannot recover your mother's body. I think that the swift current has probably carried it on downstream."

"You can't recover—" Sarah broke off and stared unseeingly ahead. "But you have to. You can't—you can't leave her in the water. Luke?" She looked up at him. "Make them understand. They have to."

Something broke in him at the wild, desperate look in her eyes, and he squatted beside her, taking her face between his hands. "I'll find her, Sarah. All right? Don't fret, I'll get her out."

"I tell you, it's pointless," the man protested as he followed Luke down to the river's edge.

"I have to," Luke said shortly, pulling off his shoes and stripping down to his underclothes.

The other man shrugged and began to tie the rope around Luke's waist. Luke began close to the bridge and worked downriver, diving only close to either bank. It was pointless to dive in the middle as the other man had done, where the unimpeded current would have carried the body away. Only if she had been caught by the branches or rocks close to shore would her body still be this far up.

Repeatedly he dived, as the evening came and then darkened steadily. The knot of people began to dissolve and drift away. Still he dived. He was young and strong and a good swimmer, but the rapid current often swept him out or flung him against the rocks, and he was soon exhausted by his fight against the flooding water. Only his sheer stubbornness kept him at it; that and the fact that his mind and emotions had separated from his body, so that he moved mechanically, without thought or feeling, the pain in his lungs and muscles never reaching his brain.

The water was murky and heavy with silt, and it was almost impossible to see underneath the surface. That condition was worsened by the cloudy sky and encroaching nightfall. The last few times he broke the surface he almost gave up, but at last, as he clung to a root protruding from the bank, trying to catch his breath, he caught a glimmer of something bright beneath him. Intently he stared down and again glimpsed something shiny. He dived, pushing into the tangle of branches, until his hand touched a soft surface. Instinctively, he jerked his hand away. A dim form floated in the water, the pale round thing above it surely a face. Again the glimmer of gold and he grasped it. Something flat and round and hard, attached to a chain. A locket. He pulled at the mass, but it would not move. Finally he let go of her and burst for the surface to cling to the side and gasp for air. It took four more dives to release the body; he found that her hair was tangled in the branches. On one attempt to pull the body free, he got caught himself and for a moment feared that he, too, might drown, that his burning lungs would explode and suck in the killing water, but at last he tore free and on the next dive was able to extricate Edna McGowan's body and drag it to the surface.

Quickly hands reached out to take his burden and then to pull him out. He knelt, exhausted, on the ground, his lungs aching, his body torn and bruised from the branches and rocks, shivering convulsively in the cool air. He watched two men carry the body, weighed down by the sodden mass of clothes, to where Sarah still knelt by her father. Gravely she reached over to smooth her mother's hair from her face. Someone moved behind her, bent to take her shoulders and lifted her from the ground; he saw that it was Stu. Fools, he thought, they won't even let her have her grief.

"You must be strong," Stu said to her, holding her up. It was the first time he had been able to get her to rise since he had arrived.

"Yes, I know. For Jenny and the children."

"For yourself, as well."

"I know." She found it difficult to think. If only she could lean on Stu as Jenny could, lose herself in his strong arms and let him think for her.

"You shouldn't have come out here. That Turner boy was a fool to bring you."

"I had to come."

They watched as several men picked up the bodies and placed them in the wagon that Stu had driven out.

"Mr. Harper." A man approached them, leading two horses.

"The team on the buggy," Sarah said.

"Yes, ma'am. They managed to swim out all right; fortunately for them the harness broke and the buggy was separated from them. There was a third horse, but it broke two legs. I'm afraid we had to shoot it."

That must have been the brood mare they had gone to Dallas to buy.

Chapter VI

JENNIFER poured two cups of coffee and joined her sister in the parlor. It was midnight now, and the house was quiet. All the people who had come by to bring food, to help, to condole, had gone; Stu, the children, Aunt Betty, and Aunt Clara were asleep upstairs. Only the two sisters were still up, and they sat quietly, their eyes on the two bodies that lay on planks supported on either end by straight-back chairs. The older women had laid them out: rubbed them with a preservative camphor mixture, dressed them, secured their eyelids with silver dollars, folded their hands across their chests. But it was the two daughters who would sit with the bodies through the night.

The two women were weary now, but calm. They had managed to stumble through the horrible evening, had not broken down or yelled or cried. The shock had worn away to some extent, and they had regained the use of mind and tongue. Sarah had even remembered to send Melissa and Penny down to the barn with some food for the weary Luke. The girls said he was asleep and had left it by the bed. Tears started in Sarah's eyes; thank God for Luke. She would have to find some way of thanking him for bringing out her mother's body.

"Do you remember when Daddy bought that awful horse?" Jenny asked.

"The wall-eyed one?" Sarah smiled, and softly they began to reminisce.

After an hour or so, their voices slowed and then stopped; they sat together in the lengthening quiet. Soon Jenny dozed off in her chair and Sarah was alone with her thoughts. She had no desire to be alone with them, they preyed upon her. Never until this moment had she realized how alone she was. She had depended so on her parents, relied on them for companionship and support. Now, without them, she felt cast adrift upon the world. Jennifer had her husband and children, but she had nothing, no one. Today when she had needed help, she had had no one to turn to but the hired hand.

The hired hand. Her mind turned to Luke. It was a brave thing he had done. One of the men had told her how he had dived again and again, refusing to give up, despite the fact that he was worn out and battered and bruised. He could have been killed had the rope given way or had he gotten caught in the undergrowth. Of course, he must have been fond of her parents, her father particularly, because he had given Luke a job when no one else would, had trusted him and helped him. But what he had done was something much more than the mere promptings of fondness. There was a stubborn kind of courage in Luke, and a goodness that no one suspected.

Jennifer stirred and awoke and smiled a gentle apology for falling asleep. Again they began to talk, and Sarah tried to shove her thoughts to the back of her mind, but over and over again, like a drum, they pounded in her brain: *I am so alone. What am I to do?*

Just before dawn their aunts came down to take their places, and wearily the girls pulled themselves upstairs. Sarah entered her room and sank down gratefully on her bed. Thank God that she did not have to sleep in her parents' bed, as Jenny and Stu did. She unbuttoned her dress and slipped off her shoes, but was too tired to do any more. With a little sigh, she lay back against her pillows and was immediately asleep.

She did not awake until mid-morning, when Aunt Betty tapped at her door. Sluggishly she got up and changed clothes, pulling on her one black dress, a heavy woolen dress that was a little too warm for late March. Downstairs she drank a cup of coffee and ate some biscuits left over from breakfast. No one had come over yet, and so she was left blessedly alone. She was not sure how she could get through this day, now that the numbness was leaving her. How could she stand the noise and people pressing in on her? How could she manage to remain calm and polite with them when all she wanted to do was be alone and give way to a frenzy of grief?

Sarah walked to the window above the sink and looked out. It was not raining today, but the sky was gray and dreary. She looked at the mud of the yard. Not good for planting and plowing; they still had to plow the vegetable garden. The road up to the cemetery would be a morass of mud.

Luke Turner crossed her field of vision, walking toward the barn. She wondered if he had come up for breakfast. Knowing Luke, probably not, when he found himself face to face with her aunts and brother-in-law. She fixed him three sandwiches, added a jar of potato salad from the bowl Mrs. McCullough had brought last night, and two pieces of pie and stored them in a basket. That should make up for no breakfast and hold him until this evening. She started to take it out to him when a thought occurred to her and she darted up to her parents' room, returning moments later with a look of satisfaction.

She found him in the hayloft, forking down hay for the livestock. "Luke?" she called, tilting back her head to see him.

"Miss Sarah." He scrambled down the ladder to stand beside her.

"Did you have breakfast?"

He grinned sheepishly. "No, ma'am."

"I thought not. So I brought you a huge lunch."

"Why, thank you, ma'am."

"I—I wanted to thank you, Luke, for what you did yesterday. It meant a great deal to me. I know it was a dangerous, difficult thing to do."

He shrugged, embarrassed.

"Anyway, I want you to know how much I appreciate it. I want you to have this." She extended her right hand; in her palm lay a gold watch and chain.

Luke backed up, making a negative gesture. Stu Harper had visited him last night and thanked him ponderously for the family and offered him a cash reward. If he had not felt so bone weary, Luke would have hit him. And now here she was, with the same opinion of him.

"I didn't do it for that," he cried. "I did it because—because you looked so unhappy and because your father was the only person who was ever kind to me and treated me with some respect. And you did, too, sometimes, or I thought you did."

"Oh, no, please, Luke, I didn't mean it like that. I do respect you and so did Daddy. I could never hope to repay you for what you did; it can't be measured in money. That is a gift. It was Daddy's watch and I know he would want you to have it. It is very dear to me; I wouldn't part with it for any amount of money. But I want to give it to you and Daddy would want to, also. Please, Luke."

Her words stunned him. "Oh, no, ma'am, I couldn't take your father's watch from you."

"Please. It will make me very happy."

Cautiously he picked up the watch; it felt heavy in his hand. Mr. McGowan's watch. His chest swelled and his throat was suddenly full. It was the most precious thing he had ever owned.

"I don't know what to say," he managed, afraid he might cry.

"You don't need to say anything. Just keep it and take care of it."

"I will."

She moved away a little, then turned back to him. "Are you coming to the funeral this afternoon?"

"If you wouldn't mind, I'd like to."

"Good. I'd like for you to come. It's at two o'clock."

She hurried away, and he gazed blankly after her, the watch clutched tightly in his hand.

Sarah discovered she had the strength, or the numbness, or whatever it took to get through the day. She sat calmly through the funeral services in the church, hands folded quietly in her lap. It was one of her family's precepts to meet stress and pain with silent strength. Sarah doubted seriously that she had the strength, but at least she could put up the front.

Her parents' caskets were carried in a wagon to Longhill cemetery, aptly named for it was located on top of a fair-sized rise and approached only by a long, steep road, a road so muddy from the rain that it might mire the hearse's narrow wheels. The mourners were obliged to follow the wagon on foot in order not to get their buggies or surreys stuck in the thick mud. Stu walked between the sisters, a helpful hand under the elbow of each. Their feet sank in the wet earth and they were forced to hold up their skirts and petticoats to walk.

Reverend Carson said a prayer at the graveside, and then slowly the caskets were lowered on ropes into the earth. Stonily Sarah watched as the diggers pulled out the ropes and began shovelling in the dirt. The minister said another prayer, but all through it she could hear only the steady rhythm of the shovels. She looked out at the crowd as they began to break up. She saw Luke Turner standing by himself, a little apart from everyone else. He was dressed in clean work clothes, and his face bore that curious vacant mask he sometimes assumed. At the sight of him, she wanted suddenly to cry. Then she felt the pull of Stu's hand on her arm and blindly she turned away and went with Jennifer and her husband out of the cemetery.

Neighbors, relatives, and friends came in a steady stream all afternoon, bringing dishes of food for the family and expressing sympathy and regret for the loss of their parents. The parlor, kitchen, living room, and front porch were stuffed with people, for Edna and Henry were well-liked and respected and their families large. Even though Sarah knew that the visitors wished only to help and show their sorrow, the press of people frayed her nerves. The noise, the effort of keeping from breaking down, the sheer number of people overwhelmed her. She could not deal with people as Jennifer could. Jennifer gathered strength from people; their sympathy softened her grief and their support gave her back some of her life. But Sarah felt drained by them, defeated and tired by the continual emotional battle of protecting herself from exposing her innermost feelings to the world.

Woodenly Sarah went through the motions, thanking everyone, listening to them gravely, submitting to their hugs and pats and kisses on the cheek. Even after the visitors began to slacken, still she was not left alone. Relatives who would have a long drive home, as well as Stu and Jenny, would spend the night at the house; so at dinner and all through the evening she was surrounded by people.

It was at dinner that Jenny dropped her bombshell. Their cousin Grace asked Sarah what would she do now, and as Sarah stared at her in dismay, Jenny said, "Why, Sarah will come live with us, of course."

"Oh, Jenny, no, I can't," Sarah blurted, and Jenny looked at her in surprise.

"Whyever not?"

Sarah stopped in embarrassment. How could she tell her loving, trusting sister that she was filled with horror at the idea of being forced into living with the husband and children she coveted so much?

"The farm," Sarah said. "What about the farm?"

"We'll sell it, of course," Stu said. "I am sure we would find a buyer."

"But I want to stay here," Sarah replied. "I don't want to live in town. I want to stay."

"Sarah, you aren't thinking straight. How could you handle this farm all by yourself?" Stu reminded her.

"I can take care of the house by myself. I've done it before. And Luke can—"

Grace snorted. "Luke Turner? How long do you think you can count on him to hang around?"

Sarah bit her lip. Of course, Luke was not a permanent fixture; he was only a hired hand and likely to leave at any moment. She would have to find a new hired hand—over and over again. And it really took more than one man to run the farm in the spring and summer. Two hired hands. How could she manage to find and hire and keep two hired hands for all the remaining years of her life? In her exhausted emotional state, the task seemed impossible.

"Besides," Aunt Corrie said, "you could not possibly live here alone with a hired hand, especially Digger Turner. Why, it would be absolutely scandalous."

"Of course she won't," Stu said. "Sarah just hasn't really thought about it."

"But I couldn't impose on you," Sarah said weakly.

"Impose! Don't be silly, Sarah. You know how much we all love you, and, heavens, you're a help, not an imposition."

"But, no, really, I couldn't live on your generosity forever."

Jennifer smiled archly. "Well, it might not be forever, you know. Besides, if you feel that way, you could probably teach at the school. Oh, Sarah, just think how wonderful it will be—all of us together."

Sarah swallowed her feeling of sickness and smiled weakly. *All of us together*.

All through the evening, Sarah moved numbly about, her mind whirling. What was she to do? The idea of spending the rest of her life with Jenny's family terrified her. She knew she could not endure it—to have to live every day so close to what she wanted so badly and could not have. It would be sheer torture, and someday she would be bound to slip and reveal her true feelings, and *that* would split her from them completely. She could not imagine a bleaker future—no home, husband, or children of her own, living always in her sister's shadow, and forever eating out her heart in vain love and jealousy.

Yet there was no escape! Stu and Jenny were right. She could not operate the farm by herself and, of course, she could not count on Luke to stay—or any other hand, for that matter. Even if she could, it would be quite shocking and reprehensible for her, especially at her young age, to live alone on a farm with a hired hand so close by.

She could not go and she could not stay. She felt trapped and frustrated. And through it all she felt the great searing pain of her parents' death.

It was with great relief that she helped Jennifer set up beds for the visiting relatives and then wearily went to her own room and began to prepare for bed. Perhaps tomorrow, when she was not so bone weary, she would be able to think more clearly about what she ought to do. She changed into her nightgown and slipped into bed, but sleep would not come. Her mind continued on its fruitless treadmill long after everyone else in the house had grown still.

Suddenly she remembered Luke—he had not come up for supper and he must be starving by now. It would serve him right, she told herself, for being so standoffish. Then she sighed and got out of bed to look out her window. A light still glowed in Luke's little room. She considered just throwing on her wrapper, then rejected the thought. No, if she was caught slipping out to Luke's room at night, it would be scandalous enough, but if she was wearing only a gown and robe to visit him. . . . With a faint shrug, she pulled off her gown and dressed again, then tip-toed out of her room and down the stairs. She moved about quietly in the dark kitchen, dishing up food from the many pans brought by well-wishers, being careful not to awaken anyone.

Sarah slipped silently out the door with her tray and moved quickly across the moonlit yard to the barn. Her knock at his door was soft.

"Luke?"

Luke Turner rose and opened the door, surprise evident on his face. "Miss Sarah! What on earth?"

"I just realized you hadn't eaten, so I brought this."

He stepped aside for her to enter and closed the door behind her, still amazed at her presence. "You didn't need to do that."

"Well, you should have come up to the house to eat, I'll admit, but I could hardly let you starve."

He ducked his head and smiled tentatively, then took the tray from her. She glanced around the room, noting the whiskey bottle on the table. So he had been sitting out here drinking all evening. She felt she ought to leave, particularly if he was drunk, but she sat down anyway. Somehow there was a certain comfort in sitting in his quiet, undemanding presence.

Luke felt inordinately pleased that Sarah was there. He had spent the evening in a black gloom, thinking of Henry McGowan and his death, and of his own bleak future. Now that his benefactor was gone, he knew his new start in life had vanished. No doubt the two daughters would sell the farm and he would be out of a job. No one else would hire him, and he would be back as before, in his dirty shack, surrounded by hatred, with no more chance to look at Sarah or feel the warmth of her smile. No, worse than before, because now he had tasted the life others led and knew how bitter his own was. He hated himself for thinking of his own problems even in the midst of sorrow for the McGowans, and he had pulled out a bottle of whiskey to try to blot out the whole sorry mess.

He felt the sting of her disapproving thoughts when she

saw the whiskey, and for a moment feared she would leave, but she sat down and he breathed a sigh of relief and attacked the tray with the concentration of a hungry young man. Sarah watched him eat and tried to stop thinking about the dilemma she was in. Think instead of Luke, she told herself; what would he do now? She felt sure nobody but her father would hire him.

"It was kind of you to come to the funeral," she said finally.

"Kind?" Luke stopped eating and moved to sit on the side of his bed. "I respected your father. He was the best man I ever knew."

He looked at Sarah and at the sight of the pure pain and grief in his eyes, she felt all her own unhappiness welling up inside of her, straining at her self-imposed bonds, battering against her until suddenly she burst into tears. All the agony of the past days gushed from her in a storm, and without thinking she flung herself across the room to Luke, blindly seeking comfort.

He cradled her against his chest, rocking her, stroking her hair and back, whispering against her hair, "There, now, girl, let it out. Just let it all come out. I'm here; it's all right."

An incoherent torrent of words mingled with her sobs; he could make out little except that it had something to do with Stu and the farm. Luke continued to rock and croon to her, his arms tight and protective around her. It would do her good to break down, he knew. They were wrong in making her keep it all bottled up inside her. What she needed was a good cry and someone to comfort her.

Finally her sobs subsided and she pulled away from him slightly, attempting a watery little smile. "I—I'm sorry. You must think I'm awful, collapsing on you like this."

"Lord, ma'am, don't worry about that. You needed to cry, and I'm just glad I was here." He wiped away her tears, then gave her his handkerchief to blow her nose. "Now, take a little drink of this." He uncapped the whiskey bottle and extended it toward her.

"Oh, no," she said, shocked. "I couldn't."

"Make you feel better, I promise. Go on."

"But I have never—"

"Just take a little sip. There you go."

Gingerly she raised the bottle to her lips and took a swallow. The liquid spread a fire through her mouth and throat and the bitter taste made her shiver. She coughed and her eyes watered, but Luke commanded her to take another drink. Again she took a small sip, then thrust it back to him. He tilted back his head and took a long pull at the bottle.

"Now, what were you trying to say all that time you were crying? I couldn't understand you."

She shook her head and moved away from him, taking a seat beside him and trying to smooth her hair and clothes. He longed to pull her back into his arms, to kiss and caress her until his own pain and hers were blotted out, erased in joy. Instead, he offered her the bottle and she drank a little more. Sarah looked at him, then down at her hands. Suddenly her problems came tumbling out. What did it matter if Luke knew how wicked she was? He would not, could not, condemn her. Surely he would understand her awful, boiling emotions.

"Oh, Luke, they want to sell the farm: they want me to come live with them. But I can't! I just can't. I'm so alone, I don't know what to do." She paused, uncertain.

He prompted her, "You'd hate to leave the farm. I understand that."

"Oh, yes, I would. I love this place. I've lived here all my life, and I couldn't bear to live in town. I want to keep on raising chickens and watching the crops grow and living out here away from people. But it isn't just that. I could not bear to live in Jenny's house." She stared at her hands and her voice was low, "Oh, Luke, I'm in love with Stu. I have been for years and no doubt will be all my life."

She looked up at him, her eyes swimming with tears. He caught his breath: her apparently brown eyes were really green, flecked with bright gold. Then her words penetrated him, and he felt a stab of anger and envy. Damn Stu Harper—he had everything in the world a man could want and now, added to his excess of blessings was the guilty, adoring, unrequited love of his wife's sister. Lovely, sweet Sarah, wasting her life away on him.

"I couldn't possibly live with them, but I can't even tell Jenny why. Besides, where else can I go? What can I do?"

"Stay here on the farm."

"But how? I couldn't possibly run the place by myself."

"I'll be here—for as long as you want me to stay."

He offered her the bottle and she drank more deeply. A strange, relaxing warmth was spreading through her. She was beginning to calm down. Perhaps—perhaps it could somehow be worked out.

"We could do it, just the two of us," she said thoughtfully. "Only, you wouldn't want to stay here the rest of your life."

"Why not? Where else have I got to go?"

She considered what he said, then sighed regretfully. "No, it wouldn't work. It would be a horrid scandal, me single and living out here with you. I couldn't show my face in town."

Luke frowned, then got up and walked away from her. He stood by the window looking out. Sarah watched him and took another drink. The stuff did not taste as bad now, and the room seemed warm and cozy. Luke was a little blurred, but he too looked very warm and friendly.

"Well," he said, "you could always marry your friend Snowden and let him run your farm."

She giggled at that—imagine Grady behind the plow—and he grinned back at her.

"No," she said lightly, "I would have to marry a farmer."

Ordinarily he would not have revealed his crazy thought, but the liquor had made him light-headed. "Marry me."

She stared at him, trying to absorb what he had said.

"Don't look like that. I swear to God I wouldn't touch you. It would just be for show, so there wouldn't be a scandal. We could have separate bedrooms and live just like we do now. Please believe me."

"I believe you," she said quietly, her huge eyes intent on his face.

"You say you'll love Harper for the rest of your life, so you won't ever be likely to marry for love. So get married for practical reasons to someone who knows how you feel and wouldn't expect any more. I know I'm not much of a person for you to marry—"

"Don't say that!" she said fiercely. "You are the dearest, kindest man ever, to offer to shackle yourself for life to a loveless marriage, just to save me. But I can't let you do that, Luke. You have to think of yourself. You might fall in love and marry a woman you can be happy with, but if you're already married to me, then you're doomed to it. You have your whole life in front of you. This would solve my problems, but there's nothing in it for you."

"Nothing in it for me," he repeated, stunned. "My God, it would be more than I ever dreamed of. To have my own farm to work, my own house, the best of women for my wife." He crossed the room and knelt beside her, taking both her hands in his earnestly. "Sarah, all my life

I've been less than nothing. I've always wanted to have something, to be something besides trash. I love the soil and the dream I've carried is to possess some little part of that soil, to own a piece of land, to be able to work it and love it and care for it. I want to work and to prove that I'm their equal. I want to belong somewhere and have something that belongs to me. Can you understand that?''

''I understand.'' Her voice was gentle and her eyes swam with tears.

''If I married you, I'd have that. Oh, on paper it would be yours, but we'd know it was mine as well. I'd have something better than the freedom to marry—and who would I marry? Tessa? A convicted rapist isn't exactly what you'd call eligible. No, don't hold back for my sake. The only question is you. Are you anxious enough to escape that life with your sister to be Luke Turner's wife?''

Sarah's mind whirled. It was crazy; the whole idea was absurd, this businesslike, loveless marriage. And yet, here was her chance at a life of her own on terms she could accept. It would not be unfair to him, and she would not have to live a lie. He knew she loved another; would be going into it with eyes wide open. He would not expect her love, did not even want it. She felt an unreasonable little flash of resentment at his eager promise not to share a marital bed—was she so undesirable?—but sternly she thrust it from her mind. She could have a life of her own, a husband, a house, a whole being distinct and separate from her sister. She could stay where she wanted to be, do the things she was interested in and accustomed to. Most of all, she could avoid the torment of living so close to Stu.

She took a deep breath, feeling giddy and uncertain and almost happy. "All right," she said. "I'll marry you."

Chapter VII

THE sun pouring through her window awakened her; groggily she stared around the room, trying to pull her wits together. It must be terribly late, judging by the way the sun was coming in. Slowly she sat up and swung her legs over the side, then sat staring at her bare feet dangling above the floor.

Sarah felt awful. Her head ached and her eyes felt swollen and ready to fall from their sockets. Her stomach churned and there was a sour taste in her mouth. So this was a hangover. Grimly she forced herself to her feet and walked to the wash basin to wash her face and brush her teeth. That made her feel slightly better and she was able to proceed to dressing. However, brushing and braiding her hair and pinning it into a coil were almost too much for her tender head, and she sat back down on the bed for a moment.

She must have been mad last night. Imagine sitting out in the barn getting drunk with Luke Turner—and on the night of her parents' funeral! She stifled a moan of shame. How could she have been so disrespectful? As for that crazy plan they had worked out—whatever had possessed them? No doubt Luke had been too drunk to realize what he was saying and was out there regretting it just as she was. She would have to talk to him and get it cleared up.

Gingerly she went downstairs to the kitchen. Her sister turned at her approach and smiled.

"Good morning. Are you ready for some breakfast?" Jennifer asked.

The idea made her slightly ill. "No, just some coffee and maybe a biscuit or toast."

"Coffee's on the stove and I put the biscuits back in the oven to keep warm." She turned back to the sink and resumed her dishwashing.

"It's so late," Sarah said as she slowly gathered her breakfast together. "Why didn't you wake me up?"

"Oh, you were so tired, I couldn't bear to. Anyway, there was no reason for you to get up early. We had more than enough hands to get breakfast."

"Where is everyone?"

"Aunt Corrie and her family have left to go back home, and Gracie and Aunt Clara are outside washing and hanging up clothes."

"I always do that on Wednesday." Sarah felt a spurt of irritation at the way they were taking over her chores.

Jennifer shrugged. "I know, and I do it on Thursday, but Gracie wanted to do it today. And we can hardly turn down the help. We have quite a bit to do."

"What do we have to do?" Sarah asked absently, sipping her coffee and wondering if Luke had already left for the fields or if he was still in the barnyard.

"Well, we have to pack up Mama's and Daddy's things."

"Oh, Jennifer." Sarah's voice broke.

"I know. But it won't get any easier, and we have to do it. And then we have to pack your things and decide what we want to keep and what we want to sell. And get the house all clean and ready to sell."

Sarah felt as if a steel band were wrapped around her chest. She could not; she simply could not bear to do those things. However, she rose and said, "All right. Let's do it then."

All morning they packed her parents' clothes and personal possessions. The band in her chest grew tighter and the ache in her head worse until she felt that she would surely faint. As she worked, the feeling grew in Sarah that she could not leave. Each article she touched seemed to bind her closer to this place. How could she stand to see strangers living here? And how could she stand to live with Jenny, never mistress of her own house, always living by another's plan?

The scheme which had seemed so crazy to her this morning began to grow more appealing. It made sense, really, in a strange sort of way. Luke was a stranger, true, and not the sort she would ever have expected to marry, but he would not be difficult to live with. He knew the evil things about her that no one else did; she would not have to pretend with him or be afraid of disappointing him. They would not be intimate; the situation would really be little different than it was now, except that they would live in the same house. And she would not have to leave her home.

She found herself planning as she worked. Luke could have her parents' room; even cleaned of their possessions, she could not bear to sleep there. They would have to get married soon. It would be improper to marry so quickly after the McGowans' deaths, but it would be even more improper to live here alone together for several months. She would have to talk to Reverend Carson about it at once, perhaps tomorrow. And of course she would have to go meet his father sometime before the wedding. Luke would need a suit, and she doubted he had one. Perhaps she could cut down one of Daddy's old suits for him. That plain silver ring Granny Whitman had left her would do just fine for a wedding band.

She caught herself; whatever was she doing, making plans when she had not yet found out if Luke still wanted to go through with it? It was almost time for lunch. She could take his lunch to him in the fields and ask him if he had changed his mind.

As it turned out, she did not have to ask him. The smile on his face when he saw her was free of any reluctance or doubt. His main concerns seemed to be the wetness of the fields that hampered plowing and whether she had weathered the aftereffects of her drinking.

"Oh, Luke, I feel awful," she confessed. It was a relief to be able to complain about her aches and pains. "My head hurts and my eyes and my stomach. And I'm so ashamed—you must think I'm terrible."

"Terrible? Hardly. You drank some whiskey because you were upset, and it helped you relax and feel better. Where's the harm in that? You hardly qualify as a drunkard."

"I can't imagine why you drink. Do you feel like this whenever you drink?"

"Only sometimes." He grinned. "I wouldn't want to brag, but I do think I can hold my liquor a little better than you."

Sarah looked at him and then said hesitantly, "It—it scares me, your drinking. You won't do it so much, will you? I mean, you know, after—"

"Not if you don't want me to. Just now and then, maybe. I expect I'll be too tired, working these fields by myself, to do any serious drinking anyway."

"Good. I, well, I've been thinking about what we talked about last night."

"Getting married?"

"Yes." Somehow it seemed easier, now that the words had actually been said.

He looked at her. "Have you changed your mind?"

"No. That is, not unless you have."

"I haven't."

"Well, I had been thinking about the wedding."

"Yeah?" He dug around in the lunch basket and brought out a sandwich, then leaned back against the trunk of the tree and ate and listened to her as she talked of clothes and rings and churches and dates. He could not ever remember feeling so peaceful.

Sarah sat with her legs curled under her, enjoying the shade and the smell of spring and Luke's cheerful attention. She felt a million miles away from the morning's sad occupation. Then she broached the subject of visiting his family and the atmosphere suddenly changed. Luke seemed to tighten all over and he stopped eating.

"Don't be silly," he said roughly. "You don't want to meet them."

"Why not?" she said, taken aback at his tone. "Of course, I want to meet them."

"No."

Sarah stared at him in amazement. "You cannot be serious. I can't marry you without at least meeting your father and grandmother."

"I don't see why not."

"It would be very impolite."

"Believe me, they wouldn't know the difference."

"Luke, I just want to meet them and invite them to the wedding. What is so wrong with that?"

"I don't want them at our wedding."

"I don't understand you at all. You don't want your family at your wedding. You don't want me to meet them. Why, I don't think you've ever told them that you were staying here! Why? Why are you so set against them?"

He laughed shortly. "You obviously don't know them."

"Well, I don't know how I ever shall, either, if you continue to act this way."

Luke felt the panic rising in him. He could not let her meet his father and grandmother. One look at them and the place where he had grown up and she would run from marrying him. He was already scared that Sarah's family would talk her out of the marriage. He could not let his own family chase her away.

"Really, Luke, you cannot do this. If you don't want them at your wedding, all right, although it does seem to me that you would at least want Julia there. But surely you could put yourself out enough to take me over there and tell them that we're getting married."

"You don't understand," he said helplessly.

"No, I don't."

"All right, I'll take you." He could not stand the cool remoteness of her tone, even though he knew it was foolish to give in. "You can invite Julie if you want, but it won't do any good. Dobson hates me and he won't let her come."

"How awful," she said sympathetically, and he realized suddenly that she was on his side. After all these years, here was someone who automatically, unquestioningly took his side. She was going to be his wife, and now he was no longer alone. Wives stuck by their husbands, supported them. The idea was dizzying and he clamped it down: there was no reason to expect that of Sarah; she would not truly be his wife, just a partner really, and he must not dream of her acting like a wife.

Sarah had not expected ready acceptance by her family of her impending marriage, and she found she had not been too pessimistic in those expectations. Jennifer stared at her as if she had gone mad.

"But don't you want to live with us?" she asked tearfully. "Will you go so far as that to avoid us?"

"Oh, Jenny, no, don't think that! It's just that I want to remain here on the farm, living as I'm used to. Can't you understand that I cannot live only through you? I must have a life of my own."

"But of course. And living there in town with us, you can see so many eligible young men. Grady Snowden, for instance."

"I have no desire to marry Grady Snowden. And I could not, even if I wanted to, since Stu saw fit to send him out here the other night to rescue me from my immorality.''

''We were just worried about you,'' Jenny wailed. ''And rightly so, since you've come up with this scheme. Sarah, you can't be serious!''

''Oh, can't I?'' Whatever doubts Sarah might have had were killed by Jenny's attack; all her stubbornness rose up to fix her mind very firmly on marrying Luke.

''Sarah, he is shiftless and mean and common and a drunkard. For heaven's sake, honey, he just spent the last five years in prison for rape!''

''Unjustly!''

''How can you be so sure? Sarah, please, you couldn't possibly love him.''

''I did not say I did. But I think it is a very good arrangement for both of us, and I think perhaps I shall be happy.''

''Perhaps! Don't you think that's a pretty flimsy basis for a marriage?''

''Jennifer, please, my mind is set.''

''I can see that. Only I cannot imagine why.''

''Because it is best.''

Jennifer fell silent, deciding to wait until her husband returned that evening from his errands in town and let him dissuade Sarah from this crazy idea.

However, even Stu found he could not budge his sister-in-law. His wife greeted him with a grateful cry and announced that Sarah was planning to marry Digger and that he must stop it.

''What?'' He was obviously stunned. He looked past his wife to Sarah, standing remote and cool in the hallway. ''Sarah, this is not true, is it?''

''It is. I intend to marry Luke.''

He was momentarily speechless, but soon recovered enough to say, ''Why? Why? Has he threatened you? Forced you?''

''No, Stu, of course not,'' Sarah said in exasperation, remembering Grady's almost identical words a few nights ago. ''It's what I want to do.''

''Sarah, the boy is just after your land.''

''That isn't much of a compliment to me, is it?''

''You know I didn't mean—''

''Not that it matters. I mean, he can hardly roll up my land and sneak away with it under his arm, can he? Of course, he would like his own farm, but there are things I want that I'm getting, too. Besides, if I remember correctly from Grady's lectures, community property does not apply to inherited property, so he would not own even half of my land.''

''This all sounds so cold and bloodless,'' Jennifer said, shocked.

''I'm sorry; it's just that I'm tired and unhappy. I told you before that I think I will be happy in this marriage.''

Stu tried a different tack. ''Sarah, you know the farm

is not entirely yours to do with as you please. By your parents' wills, half of it belongs to Jenny."

"They also left us some money," Sarah replied calmly. "I had hoped to purchase Jenny's half, but if you prefer that I not have it, then we can divide the land in half and Luke and I will work only our half."

"Now, Sarah, don't get upset. Stu didn't mean that. Of course we'll do it just as you wish. It's only that we want you to think about it. You'll be sure to see that you're wrong."

"I have thought about it, and I don't believe I am wrong. Now I had better get supper on the table."

As she retired to the kitchen, Stu and his wife looked at each other in consternation. They pursued her, but she foiled them by going out onto the back porch to call Luke to eat. Stu took his wife by the hand and they went to their bedroom for a discussion, which turned out to be perfectly fruitless since neither had any idea of the reasons for Sarah's peculiar behavior.

Luke came in quickly after Sarah's call. Seeing her strained face, he said, "They been giving you a hard time?"

She smiled thinly. "It is a shock to them."

He took her hand and squeezed it to bolster her courage. There was a cold fear in the pit of his stomach that they would talk her out of it.

Dinner was awkward and no one ate much except Cousin Gracie and her family who were blissfully unaware of the wedding plans. After supper, when Gracie and Jennifer trundled the children off to bed, Stu leaned back in his chair and lit his pipe, saying in a fatherly tone, "Sarah, Digger, I would like to have a little talk with you."

Stu forced himself to maintain a calm, rational tone despite the fact that Turner looked at him in that insolent way of his, his pale eyes half closed, arms folded across his chest, his face scornfully amused.

"Now, I don't think that you two have really thought this through. You feel uprooted and so you want to rush into this marriage as if it were some kind of haven. But marriage is not like that. Marriage is a close partnership of two people."

"Spare me the lecture, please," Luke drawled.

Stu plowed on, "The sort of irreconcilable differences between you, differences of age and background, would soon make your marriage impossible. Now, Sarah, you know that you'll be welcome in our house, a vital part of it. As for you, Turner, well, I don't see why we couldn't find you a nice job in my store. Believe me, that would be a much easier way of solving your problems."

"But, Stu, that is not what we want to do. Luke and I want to farm," Sarah protested.

Luke said nothing, just looked at the other man steadily, his eyes suddenly bright and piercing.

His gaze unsettled Stu, who shifted uncomfortably and finally burst out, "Damn it, Turner, you and I both know you're trying to get at Sarah's land. I'll pay you cash to get out of here and never come back."

Suddenly Luke was out of his chair, his fist shooting across the table into Harper's jaw. Harper went over backward with the blow, landing ignominously on the floor on his back, staring up dazed at the ceiling. Sarah jumped to her feet with a gasp, frozen as Luke quickly went around the table and hauled Stu to his feet.

"God damn you, Harper," he said fiercely, "if you wasn't Sarah's brother-in-law, I'd beat the hell out of you for that. You can't buy me, and you can't stop me from marrying Sarah."

He released Harper and plunged out of the room, leaving Sarah and Stu staring after him, stunned. Gracie and Jennifer ran into the room, wanting to know what all the noise was about.

"He hit me! That maniac hit me! Sarah, do you realize now what a mistake it would be to marry him?"

"Oh, Stu, no!" Jenny cried, going to him.

"Marry him? What are you talking about?" Gracie asked, bewildered.

Sarah just stood looking at Stu, torn and uncertain. "I—I am sorry, Stu. He should not have hit you." She took a shaky breath. "But why did you say that to him? It was cruel and unfair. You goaded him into it."

"Sarah! That boy *hit* Stu, and you are standing up for him!" Jennifer's voice was shocked.

"The blame is not entirely his." Sarah felt backed into

a corner, trapped. She was shaken by the unpredictable unleashing of violence in Luke, and she wanted to cry at the sight of Stu's purpling, bruised lip. But she felt compelled to defend her future husband and was also surprised and dismayed at Stu's insulting hostility. He *had* been cruel and unfair, and there was no excuse for it. "He's never done anything to you before! Why did you say that to him?"

"Sarah, it's what he'll do to you that worries me," Stu replied somberly. "You have no idea what someone like Digger could do to you, how he could hurt you. He'll bring the farm to ruin and make your life a misery, drinking and fighting and chasing other women. What are you going to do in a few years when he's saddled you with a passel of kids and leaves you every evening to return the next morning, drunk and in need of bandaging and reeking from some cheap slut's perfume?"

"Stu!" Jennifer said reproachfully as her sister paled and tears sprang into her eyes.

"I'm sorry, but it's better that she faces a few hard truths now rather than live with regret for the rest of her life." He sighed, exasperated, then blurted out, "Good God, Sarah, he just spent five years in prison for rape!"

"Well, he cannot rape me, can he, since I shall be his wife? That would be a legal impossibility, wouldn't it?" Sarah said lightly, fighting her treacherous tears.

Her brother-in-law groaned. "Sarah, you are an innocent young girl. You have no idea of the things he—"

"No! No, I have no idea!" Sarah said, her arms stiff against her rigid body. "Tell me. What exactly are these awful things that he is going to do to me? And also, please tell me why he should do them. Tell me why he should suddenly become a raving monster when up till now he has never been anything but kind and polite. Why, if he is so horrible, did he risk his life just to recover Mama's body for me? Why did he insist on working when his foot was injured, even though he was worn and sick with the pain it caused? Can you tell me that, Stu?" She faced them, her eyes blazing, tears spilling from them, until suddenly she turned and ran out the door and into the yard. Behind her Stu and Jenny stared at each other in dismay.

Blindly she ran toward the fields, knowing only that she had to get away. Luke, who had retired to his room in rage and then stayed there in the sick fear that he had just thrown away his chances, saw her stumbling, tearful progress, and ran to stop her. She felt the strong grip of his hands on her arms, pulling her to a halt, and she looked up to see his pale eyes and ashen hair, blurred by her tears.

"Oh, Luke." Without thinking she flung herself against him, instinctively seeking the hard comfort of his flat, muscled chest and the heavy rhythm of his heart.

"Sarah." He wrapped his arms around her, squeezing her even more tightly against him. "There. It's all right, it's okay." He realized with a pang, part pain, part pleasure, that he should have stayed in the kitchen to take care of her. "I'm sorry. I shouldn't have let you face them by yourself. I never thought."

Gently his hands comforted her, stroking her shining hair and her back, while over her head he looked across the yard at the back door, where Stu now stood. His eyes were bright pools of anger as he stared, his face hard and pale and set; the other man shifted a little uncomfortably beneath his gaze.

"Harper, what did you say to her?" he demanded. "I ought to kill you for making her cry. You're a fine one, aren't you, to tear up a girl whose parents just died?"

"I only told her the truth: that you would use her and throw her over, except as a base to return to when you need sobering or are tired out from your whores or need someone to knock around a little."

The boy's arms tightened convulsively and he began to swear vividly, coldly.

"Luke!" Sarah protested—whether at his harsh grip or his language he was not sure.

"I'm sorry." He relaxed his embrace and she stood loosely within his arms, her head against his chest, thinking hazily how pleasant it was to lean against the reassuring beat of his heart. "Harper, why don't you just leave? Why don't all of you leave before you make her any more unhappy?"

"How dare you order me off this farm!" Stu hissed, starting down the steps.

Turner laughed, almost joyously. "Come on, Harper." His voice was low, taunting. "Of all the things you've got, one thing you don't have is an education in fighting. I'll be happy to teach you."

"Stu!" His wife followed him, concerned, helpless. "Stu, stop it. Sarah—" She appealed for help.

Sarah pulled away from Luke. "Oh, stop it, both of you. For heaven's sakes," her voice was cross, "this is ridiculous."

The two sisters converged, bent on conciliation.

"Yes, you ought to both apologize and let's forget the whole thing." Jennifer laid a delicate restraining hand on her husband's arm.

"Apologize!" Luke declared explosively.

"Yes." Sarah looked at him, her eyes pleading. "Please, Luke. You shouldn't have hit him. You're both in the wrong. We can't let our marriage tear us all apart this way. Please, Luke."

He looked at her. He was not used to being asked. Other people always commanded and then he defied and there was a fight. But here was Sarah, tear-streaked, soft, asking him for something, begging him not to hurt her.

"I apologize for hitting you," he said gruffly.

The other man was silent, but at a look from his wife, mumbled some apology. Luke couldn't hear it and did not care; he was basking in Sarah's glowing look of thanks and approval.

* * *

Sarah found the rest of the community equally unwilling to accept her decision. As the rumors of her impending marriage grew, neighbors and relatives stopped by to express their horror and satisfy their curiosity. Each visit served merely to push Sarah a little farther away from them and closer to Luke, who put no pressure on her but went about his work and shared meals with her in a quiet, reassuringly routine way.

Reverend Carson was struck dumb at Sarah's request that he marry her to Luke Turner a week from Saturday. Sarah suppressed an urge to giggle at his popeyed amazement and an equally strong desire to hit him.

"But, Miss Sarah, my dear, you cannot be serious. So soon after your parents' death?"

"It is no disrespect to my parents, sir, and eminently practical. My cousin Grace cannot remain indefinitely at the farm to chaperone us and Luke and I cannot live for several months close together on the farm without creating a horrendous scandal."

"No, no, of course not. The solution is for you to stay with your sister or your aunt in town."

"I have to remain at the farm. I can hardly expect Luke to handle it all himself."

"You are overwrought. Very understandable, in view of your recent tragedy."

"I am not unhinged," Sarah said crisply, becoming practiced at cutting off her many advisers. "Please, Reverend, I know what I am doing. I would prefer to be married in a church, but if you refuse, I shall content myself with a civil ceremony—or go to the Methodist church in town.''

Mr. Carson gave in at that threat, and Sarah was able to return to the farm with a fixed date for her wedding. Armed with that, she intended to broach the subject of meeting his family to Luke that evening. The opportunity came after supper and dessert when Gracie had left to put her children to bed.

''Luke, Reverend Carson agreed to marry us next Saturday evening—a week from tomorrow.''

He looked at her, immobilized by the idea that it was really going to happen.

''I thought I would send a note to your sister and—'' she paused and took a deep breath, ''I want to meet your father and grandmother.''

Luke said nothing, just clenched his hand until the knuckles turned white.

''Why?'' he said at last, his voice despairing. ''Why can't you just leave it alone?''

''Because they are your family, and they deserve at least to meet your wife, even if you refuse to invite them to your wedding.''

''They don't deserve anything, believe me,'' he said roughly, then shrugged in resignation. ''When do you want to go?''

''Sunday,'' Sarah said and smiled.

* * *

By the time they neared the Turner shack on Sunday, Luke's stomach had twisted into a cold, hard knot, and he sank into a sullen silence. Sarah ignored his sulks and tried to bolster her courage. It was obvious that Luke would provide no support in the coming meeting, and she was by nature shy of strangers.

The wagon topped a hill and directly in front of them lay a house. Sarah barely suppressed a gasp at the sight of the little tarpaper shack with the sagging front porch: surely this could not be Luke's home! She had heard people speak of his shack, but she had not been prepared for this. Beside her, Luke stiffened and avoided looking at her. When they came to a halt, he jumped down from the high wagon seat and did not turn to help her down.

Sarah scrambled down as best she could under the bemused, faintly interested gaze of a slovenly man rocking on the porch. She looked at Luke, who now stood slouched, his hands in his pockets, insolence in every line of his body.

"There he is, the honorable Jacob Turner," he sneered, his voice brittle and thin. "Ain't it grand to get to meet him?"

The man on the porch seemed to lose interest in them and closed his eyes. Luke laughed and called, "Hey, old man, don't pass out yet. I got a lady here that wants to meet you."

Sarah swallowed and firmly advanced on the porch. "How do you do, Mr. Turner? I am Sarah McGowan."

His father looked at her, then rose clumsily and made a mocking little bow to her. "Sarah McGowan, well, la di da. Ain't you a little above your reach, boy, laying respectable farmer's daughters? They'll send you to jail for the rest of your life for this."

Luke reached the porch in three steps and interposed himself between the girl and his father. His eyes were a blue flash of anger as he said, "Shut up, old man, before I shove your teeth down your throat. I am marrying Miss McGowan."

His father burst into a cackle of laughter that sent a shiver through Sarah. Already she was regretting her stubborn insistence on coming. The enmity between father and son, the drunken, leering manner of the older man, the squalid hut all made her feel a little ill.

"Well, my sympathy, girlie, my sympathy," he said at last, after his laughter had subsided. "I don't know if having a daddy for your baby is worth it."

Luke flung open the door and stalked into the house without answering and Sarah reluctantly followed him. The inside of the house was dark and messy; in one corner sat an old woman, her hands twisted together in her lap, her ancient eyes sharp and malevolent.

"Grandma, this is—"

"I heard, I heard. So you found someone fool enough to marry you."

Luke did not make a retort, but said, "Sarah, this is my grandmother."

"Ma'am," Sarah nodded hesitantly.

"This one of your sluts, Digger? Are you bringing one of them into your mother's house?"

"No, Grandma. Her mother and father were Henry and Edna McGowan."

The woman peered at her. "Edna McGowan? I remember her, a bossy little lady, but she was nice to my girl. Come here, child, and I will do you a favor, since your ma was kind to Franny. I'll give you a warning for your own good." Her head swiveled and she shot a malicious look at her grandson as Sarah approached her.

"Don't marry him," she said, "or you'll regret it. He will kill you, just like he killed his ma."

"What?" Sarah glanced at Luke, startled. His face was white and still, etched with lines of pain and contempt.

"Him and that lecherous man out there. My Franny died screaming, birthing him; there hasn't been a day since that I haven't wished he had never been born."

"But, ma'am, it surely is not his fault if his mother died in childbirth," Sarah protested.

"He's never been anything but a shame and a disgrace, a drunken lecher like his father. He'll do the same to you as his father did to my girl, use you for his lust until he kills you."

Sarah's mouth felt dry as dust and she wanted desperately to run out of the house.

"Well, now you see our happy home," Luke said lightly. "Lucky Mama, to have left it so long ago." She looked at him and his eyebrows quirked up. "Unlucky me, to have killed my mother."

"Twenty-three years ago, this May 11th, that's when she died—the day *he* was born," the old woman mused, lost in her hatred.

Sarah felt a consuming anger rise up inside her, hot and acrid. No wonder Luke had lived the life he had, faced with anger from both father and grandmother from the day he was born. Pity welled in her, feeding her anger: poor Luke, he never had a chance, even in his own home. Well, *that* would not be the case from now on.

"Well, I must say," Sarah exclaimed, her angry voice bubbling out, "you certainly have paid tribute to your daughter in a fine way, mistreating her son. I can't think of a word bad enough for you. I used to think Luke was unfair to you, but now I see he was kinder than you deserve. I will leave you here to stew in your own evil and hate, and I hope never to see you again."

Sarah stormed out the door, with Luke on her heels, and passed Jacob Turner without a glance. She climbed onto the wagon, heedless of her entangling skirts, and Luke followed. They rode home in silence, Luke as relaxed as a man on whom a long-threatened doom had finally fallen, and Sarah boiling with hot emotions and words she felt it would be easier on Luke not to express.

Finally he said, his voice remote and toneless, "No

need to spare my feelings, ma'am; I know what they are. Might as well say it's off and get it over with."

"Say what's off?" Sarah said, her mind still occupied with her frustrated anger.

He did not look at her. "The wedding."

The girl stared at him in astonishment and then two angry spots of color flamed in her cheeks. "What do you think I am? Huh? Do you think that I'm like them? Like that old vulture? Is that your opinion of me?"

It was his turn to stare in amazement. "Good God, ma'am, of course not."

"Then please tell me why I should back out because I find out that you've been mistreated all your life!"

He looked away. "Oh, don't you see? They're my blood. What if that's me in thirty years?" His hands clenched around the reins as he struggled to explain his inchoate fears, scared even to say them aloud, fearful of her scorn, fearful of her pity. "What if I'm what everybody says? What if I hurt you? Maybe Harper's right. Sometimes I do things and I don't know why—bad things. I just have to hurt somebody; I can't help it."

Sarah looked at him, frowning in helpless consternation. She did not know how to deal with him. She wanted to reach out and touch his tightened arm or the set face, bloodless and thin and burned out. An image came into her mind of that frightened little boy entering the schoolyard, and she wanted to cry out.

"You can do whatever you want. There's no need for

you to become like your father. You are not like him now; you're strong and brave and—and you won't be alone. I'll be there to help you; I mean, I'll be your wife, won't I? No doubt I will turn out like Mama. Can you imagine her allowing her husband to slide into sloth and drunkenness?''

Suddenly he smiled, shifting the lines of his young-old face. ''No, ma'am, I can't.''

''Sarah,'' she said.

''Sarah,'' he repeated, and they smiled at each other.

The wedding was very small, with only Jenny's family and Gracie's family and her two aunts. Luke's sister was not there, though Sarah had written her an invitation. Luke seemed to expect it and just shrugged.

Reverend Carson ran through the ceremony coldly, disapproval in every line. Sarah gripped Luke's arm tightly and tried to ignore the cold knot of fear in her stomach. It all seemed so remote, so mechanical, so frightening. Luke, standing there in a suit of her father's which she had altered, was a stranger. All her loved ones held themselves aloof. *Oh, Daddy, oh, Mama, I am so alone!* For the rest of her life he was to be her husband. He would live in the same house with her and she would cook his meals and wash his clothes, but never bear his children. Or would he change, as they all said, and force her to bed with him? What if he did revert to kind; what if he became a drunken lout and beat her? What if—

She would have no one to turn to, because she was alienating her family. She was marrying in the face of their warnings; how could she ever ask them for help if their dire predictions turned out to be true?

"You may kiss the bride," the minister said, his voice stiff with disapproval, and Sarah felt the touch of Luke's calloused fingers as he tipped her chin up to briefly brush his lips against hers.

Remotely, as though she watched another person, Sarah registered the fact that at last she had been kissed, and that his lips were warm and dry and firm. It seemed strange and unreal to be that close to Luke Turner, to have him touch her, no matter how briefly. She looked up at his pale blue eyes. He winked at her and squeezed her hand, and she managed to smile back at him, but it did not break the barrier that lay around her.

Her sister hugged her, but Stu did not. The girls, bewildered by the events of the past two weeks, were unsure whether they were excited at this new addition to their lives or unhappy at losing their aunt. Shyly they clung to the back of Jenny's skirts and peered around them at the bright-haired stranger beside Aunt Sarah. Jennifer extended her hand to Luke and murmured that now he must consider himself her brother. Harper did not speak, just looked at him in an aloof, superior way that made Luke put his arm about his bride's waist and pull her close to his side, just to get under Harper's skin.

Sarah's other relatives hurried through their congratulations, as if a little frightened of Luke, and the couple found themselves suddenly free to leave the church. Sarah wanted to throw her arms around Jennifer and cling to her and cry, but she forced herself to merely hug her and the children and then climb up into the wagon. Sarah turned to watch them and wave as they drove off, and her throat began to swell and swell until she thought it would burst. She was separating herself from her family and the man she loved, to live for the rest of her life with this wild stranger, and she felt consumed with guilt and fright and regret.

It occurred to her that her wedding was over, that never for her would there be the lovely ceremony in a filled church, with her in a beautiful white gown, or the happy, joyous reception attended by laughter and music and love. She had committed herself to a life without love or children or closeness, and, oh, too late, she realized her mistake. Tears sprang into her eyes and threatened to overflow onto her cheeks. Secretively she stole a glance at the man beside her. He seemed untouched by any doubt or regret—was it really all so simple for him?

The ride home was made in silence. Luke pulled up beside the front porch and helped her down. She started around toward the side but he caught her hand and pulled her toward the front steps.

"A bride can't go in the back way," he teased. "Don't you know you have to be carried over the threshold?"

Sarah blushed; it seemed out of place to follow the custom, somehow too intimate, but she could think of no reasonable objection. Lightly he swung her up in his arms, and she felt the hard strength of him that belied his slender frame. She reached down and turned the knob, and he carried her in and gently set her down.

He smiled down at her and said, ‘‘Mrs. Turner.’’

Then suddenly he seemed embarrassed and backed out the door. ‘‘Well, I'll go put up the horses and get back to my chores, I guess.’’

She watched him leave, then dragged herself up to her room. She would change into everyday clothes and go down to the kitchen and fix supper, just as she did every day. Loneliness washed over her and she leaned her head against the wall and began to cry.

Chapter VIII

SARAH awoke the next morning to find her fear gone. How silly and hysterical she had been the day before. Of course, Luke was a stranger, but was he really any more so than some boy who had come to call each Sunday for months and sat tongue-tied and held your hand and sneaked a quick kiss as he left? Every woman married a stranger, and at least hers would not be demanding his right to her bed. She had chosen the best course—the only course, really.

Quickly she threw on her clothes and slipped down the shadowy stairs into the kitchen. She lit the stove and put water in the tank to heat, then left to gather the eggs and feed the chickens. When she returned, the water was warm, and she ladled it into a pitcher. Then she carried the pitcher up the stairs and tapped timidly at her parents' door—Luke's door.

''Come in,'' he called, and she entered.

He sat on the side of his bed, dressed, his hair still sleep-tangled. He was tying his work shoes.

''Good morning,'' he said and yawned.

''Good morning. Here's your shaving water.''

He looked at her blankly. ''There's already water in here.'' He indicated the wash basin and pitcher.

''No, silly,'' Sarah laughed. ''This is your shaving water. It's hot.''

He stared at her in astonishment. ''You mean you got up and went downstairs to heat water for me to shave in?''

Now it was Sarah who looked puzzled. ''Of course. Mama always did it for Daddy.''

''Well, thank you.'' He crossed the room to take the pitcher from her and she smiled and left.

''Coffee will be ready when you're done,'' she called over her shoulder as she ran lightly down the stairs.

He dipped a rag in the water and held it against his face to soften his beard. Closing his eyes, he luxuriated in the steamy heat. Imagine that; just imagine that. That lovely girl putting herself out for his comfort. The warmth of the hot rag spread through him, into his bones and deep into his body.

When he finished shaving, he went down into the warm kitchen, alive with the aroma of coffee and bacon. Sarah turned and smiled.

''Want a cup of coffee?''

"Yeah." He watched her pour coffee into a mug for him and thought: she is my wife.

Slowly he sipped the steaming liquid and leaned against the counter lazily to watch her bustle around the kitchen. She was a pleasure to look at, quick, sure, graceful, her body enticingly rounded; he wished he could, like a real husband, enfold that warmth in his arms and kiss her good morning. Sternly he pulled his mind away from such thoughts, set down his cup, and left to do the milking.

When he returned with the brimming pails of milk, Sarah was no longer in the kitchen.

"Luke? In here," she called from the dining room and then stuck her head around the door. "I saw you coming and I put breakfast on the table."

He went into the dining room to find her already seated on one side of the table. His place was set at the head of the table.

"I can't sit there," he protested.

"Why not?"

"But that's your father's place."

"No, that's your place now," she said and added lightly, "the master of the house."

He grinned derisively and said, "Some master." But he seated himself where she had placed him.

Sarah threw herself into work; at least it got her through the day and left her too bone weary at night to get sad or do anything but fall asleep. All the household work now fell on her alone—cleaning, cooking, baking, washing, ironing. And when she was too tired to stand up any longer, there was always mending and sewing to keep her hands occupied. She mended all the tears in Luke's clothing that her hands had been itching to take a needle to ever since she first saw him. She kept his shirts neat and clean and pressed, and found her reward in the way he wore them, tall and straight now, without the old slouch. That was not enough, however. He needed more socks and she set herself to knitting them. She altered a couple of her father's shirts, but the painful memories that task awakened made her abandon it. Then she remembered the new bolts of blue and brown cotton that her mother had bought, and she eagerly pulled them out and began measuring and cutting and sewing two new shirts for her husband.

If Sarah worked hard, it was little compared to the feverish way Luke tackled his work. He did the work of two men, rising before dawn to do his barnyard chores, then working all day in the fields with only a short break for lunch, and not returning to the house to eat until dark had fallen completely, which grew increasingly later as the spring advanced. His skin browned under the sun, and he remained tough and lean, despite the way he wolfed down Sarah's delicious food. But when at night he sank into bed, often he found that his weary muscles would not uncoil and sleep would not come for thinking of the soft, forbidden body that lay asleep across the hall from him. Then the next day he would attack his work with more ferocity, straining to show her and the world she had not chosen foolishly, struggling to wear out the willful, hopeless desire for her.

Saturday nights were the worst for him. He would watch her pull out the copper bathtub into the middle of the kitchen floor and fill it with buckets of water from the cistern, then pour in scalding hot water from the stove to heat it. The luxurious weekly full bath, where one could blissfully soak away dirt and weariness, instead of the daily ablutions at the wash basin that required less time and effort. Luke would go outside while she bathed, wander down to the chinaberry tree and think of her in the kitchen, shut away from his eyes, beautifully naked as she relaxed in the bath. He dreamed of walking back in and taking the washcloth from her surprised hands and kneeling to wash her back, her breasts, her stomach and thighs, until she settled back sensuously, her legs parting, inviting him. But of course, he did not do it; he just waited by the spreading tree and dreamed. Then she would call him, looking deliciously steamy and flushed from her bath, and say his bath was ready. He would undress in the kitchen and then soak in the tub, feeling good and weary and spoiled. It was the first bathtub he had ever been in; he had always scrubbed down in the creek at home.

She pampered him and he revelled in it, hardly able to

believe his good fortune. Hot water in the morning; huge, mouth-watering meals; mended, washed, ironed shirts; clean sheets on his deep feather bed; his room always spotless. She carried in buckets of water for his bath and heated it to just the right temperature. Once he happened to mention his love of doughnuts and that evening found himself greeted by the sweet smell of freshly cooked doughnuts when he returned from the fields. And if he fell asleep sitting on the couch in the evening, she would take off his shoes and pull his feet up onto the couch so that he could doze more comfortably. She spoiled him in hundreds of little ways, in everything except in the one way he wanted most. She did not offer him her body.

Lying in the tub, he would think of her generosity and of the favors she withheld, and he would want her, want any woman to slake the thirst she gave him. He wanted to go out despite his tiredness and aching muscles; go out and get roaring drunk and get into a fight and screw some girl. That would make him feel better, release his pentup desire and frustration, let his aching body relax. Only he could not do that. He could not leave her out here alone; but more than that, he could not expose her so to scandal. He would be damned if he would give all the old gossips a chance to clack their tongues about her and say, "I told you so" and feel sorry for her. The last thing he wanted to do was give her cause to regret marrying him. So he stayed and suffered through his painful-delightful evening and took it out in work the next day.

Two weeks after they were married, one Saturday evening before the bath ritual, Sarah made him remain at the table while she went into another room. After a moment, she came sauntering in, her hands behind her back, looking like a little girl with a big secret.

"What are you up to?" He grinned.

"A surprise," she said and then extended her hands. In one was a blue shirt, in the other a brown.

He stared at them, then looked back up at her. She shook them at him and said, "Well?"

"Where did those come from?"

"I made them," she said in exasperation.

"With all the work you do, you made these for me?"

"Yes. And you could at least look pleased about it, even if you don't like them."

"Oh, I like them," he said and rose to take them out of her hands. "I'm just surprised. What do I say?" Gingerly he touched the material, running his hands down the length of the shirts.

"Thank you?" Sarah suggested lightly.

"Oh, Sally, girl, I do thank you. I never—nobody ever—I mean, all the time it must have taken you."

"Not that long. Anyway, I wanted to. Which do you like better?"

"I don't know." He looked at the shirts, not really seeing them through the mist of emotions that rushed at him. "Both. They're—I—thank you."

She giggled in delight at his evident confusion. "Oh, Luke, you do like them, don't you?"

He laughed with her and said, "Yes," and wished he could gather her into his arms and kiss her.

Sarah felt inordinately pleased about the shirts. His surprise and embarrassment and stunned appreciation made her feel that she had done something grand, not just sewn two ordinary shirts. She would have felt even prouder had she seen the way Luke, after he had taken his bath and retired to his room, tried on the shirts, each time preening before his shaving mirror, bending and twisting, trying to get the full effect.

The next morning he came down to breakfast in one of his old workshirts and saw, to his helpless regret, his wife's expectant face cloud up.

"Why didn't you wear one of my shirts?" she cried.

He jammed his hands in his pockets, feeling in the wrong and unsure why. "Because I've got to do my chores, and then while you're at church, I thought I'd finish planting down by the creek."

"You shouldn't work on Sundays," she said crossly, "and, besides, what does that have to do with it?"

"Why, I can't wear one of those shirts to work in and get it all dirty."

She stared at him. "Since you insist on working every minute of every day, even on Sundays, I would like to know exactly when you think you could wear those shirts, then! They're just ordinary. Why do you think I made them, if not to be worn? I'll make you a nice white shirt for fancy occasions—though where you'll wear them, I don't know, since you won't go to church."

He bit his lip. Sarah's snapping was like having some little dog fly at you; you couldn't fight back but how could you ward it off? He remembered the way Emmy used to chide him for being late, and the way he would kiss her out of it. Couldn't do that to Sarah, of course, but—He smiled at her sheepishly, charmingly.

"Now, Sally girl, don't get in a snit," he teased. "I swear I'll wear them every day and just roll in the dirt in them, if you want me to. I'll wear them until I'm coming through at the elbows. Why, I'll wear them every second; I'll sleep in them. I'll—"

"Oh, stop it!" Sarah burst out, her lips twitching traitorously.

He came toward her, his hands outspread in mock supplication. "Ah, Sally, don't be mad now. I'll cry if you don't forgive me."

"Oh, you!" She slapped his hands away, but could not stop the laughter brimming up from her throat.

She sidestepped him and he followed her, his hands clasped entreatingly. Sarah moved away from him around the kitchen, giggling and commanding him to stop. Suddenly she darted away from him and he plunged after her, and then they were running, tumbling out the back door and down the steps. They raced about the yard and barn with the life and spirit of two young, healthy animals in the spring, laughing, dodging, shouting. She fled and he pursued, caught up in the game, forgetting who they were and where and what lay in the past. To prolong it, he held back his greater speed and strength and let her evade him. He grabbed her wrists, but she twisted away and scampered for the chinaberry tree. And then he ran full speed and caught her from behind, wrapping his arms around her tightly to pin her arms to her side. He lifted her up and twirled around, and she shrieked in laughter. Her hair had come loose and streamed back in his face, soft and sweet smelling; and he felt the lithe firmness of her body held tight against his and her slim waist under his arms. And he realized that he had only to stop and slide his hands up to caress her breasts, had only to turn her around to kiss her laughing, trembling mouth, both of them gasping for air and unwilling to tear their mouths apart to satisfy their lungs. Quickly he released her and stepped back, sucking in air.

Suddenly they felt self-conscious and ill at ease. Sarah tried to smooth her hair back in place, struck with shame and guilt. Here it was Sunday and her parents only dead a month, and she was out playing games in the yard, laughing and yelling like a hoyden. Luke saw the darkening of her eyes and his stomach tightened; she must have realized how closely she had been held by Digger Turner, how near she had come to feeling his tainted touch.

''Breakfast will be getting cold,'' she said awkwardly and they started silently back to the house.

* * *

Church turned out to be the same painful and surprising experience it had been the two Sundays before. When she entered and took her seat, everyone sneaked sidelong, curious glances at her. Sarah's cheeks burned. What did they expect to see on her face? Bruises? Lines of lust and degeneracy? No one nodded, as they once would have, and the pew in which she sat was the last to fill up. After church, people spoke if she spoke first, and Reverend Carson limply took her hand and murmured something. The women looked at her with a hard, avid expression, and something different and almost hungry was in the men's eyes when they turned toward her.

Only Susan Winters, her face sly and eager, was bold enough to talk to her. "Sarah, how are you?"

"Fine, thank you. And you?"

"Is it true you married Digger?"

"I married Luke Turner, yes."

The girl's eyes widened and she wet her lips. "Mama says he—you know. Did he—did he do anything to you?"

"I haven't the slightest idea what you are talking about," Sarah said coldly. She would have liked to have described some outrageous sexual deviation just to teach the girl, but she did not know of any.

"On your wedding night, you know. I mean, what was it like? What did he—what's he like?"

Sarah stared. Suddenly she understood the antipathy,

the curiosity. They wanted him, old and young, guiltily, fearfully, not even admitting it to themselves. There was an aura of sensuality around him, a wicked, forbidden maleness. He was the untiring, immoral ravisher of their hot dreams; and while they decried him, inside they felt a throb of desire. So they were angered and envious because they thought he gave her what they wanted for themselves, and they burned with a fever to know if he was really as they imagined. And to the men, he was the same, a sort of masculinity unrestrained that made them feel weak by comparison, and so they envied and hated him and hunted for the look of a satiated woman on her face.

She felt a blaze of anger at them all. She would have liked to call them down for what they were. Then it flashed into her mind—let them stew in their own sin—and she smiled what she hoped looked like the smile of a woman whose lust had been satisfied.

"Well, I can tell you this: he would never have to resort to rape on any woman," Sarah said, and her throaty laugh carried across the yard.

Without a backward glance, she climbed into the wagon and set the team off at an angry pace. The frown was still on her face thirty minutes later when she pulled into the farmyard.

Luke was standing on the front porch, watching her approach; he was wearing the blue shirt. She pulled up the wagon as he came down the steps toward her. He reached up to lift her down and she leaned down and suddenly her breath caught in her throat and a violent shiver darted through her stomach. His soft fine hair fell loosely about his face, gold and silver against his tan skin, and his eyes, set off by the shirt, were a brilliant blue. How handsome he was! His firm, sinewy hands dug into her waist, and he swung her to the ground.

"Well, how was church?" He smiled down at her.

"Fine." She returned his smile shakily. "You put on the shirt."

"Sunday dinner. That's a special occasion isn't it? Your sister and esteemed brother-in-law, after all."

Sarah scarcely heard him. She realized that what she wanted, quite badly, was for him to kiss her. To feel his lips on hers, his arms around her, the press of his hard, muscled chest against her breasts. She remembered his arms clamped around her this morning, his body pressed against her back.

He moved away from her, grasped the harness of the left mule and led the team toward the barn.

"Oh, Luke," she whispered after him, and pressed her palm against her mouth. So admit it; she was like all the others, secretly wanting him. Oh, how wicked and shameful. That should teach her to be so quick to judge; the same guilty, lustful feelings stirred in her. Of course—how else could she have so easily recognized their desire except that it beat within her, too? How else know of their hot, lustful dreams except that she woke from them also?

Firmly she clasped her hands and tamped down her feelings. Thank heavens Luke had left so quickly, before she had a chance to do something foolish. He thought her a lady; she could not let him discover that she was not, that she wanted him in her bed even though she loved another. She must not let him believe she thought of him the way the others did. Besides, he had no desire for her; he had made it clear that the marital bed was not part of their bargain. She must not embarrass them both and destroy the pleasant friendship between them by trying to make something more between them.

Sternly, she lifted her skirts and hurried into the house to fix Sunday dinner.

The dinner was not an unqualified success, but at least there was no open warfare. Stu and Luke were silent and stiffly polite; Sarah held her breath, dreading some sneer or remark that would set them off, but it did not come. Strangely enough, she felt a little separated from Jenny and Stu; somehow she was becoming, no longer Sarah, but a part of a unit that contained Sarah and Luke. For two weeks she had seen only him; their life had been shared. She lived and worked with him, and though they were still strangers, they were somehow bound. The feeling made her slightly uneasy—she did not *want* to be separated from Jenny and Stu.

After dinner, Luke escaped to the barn and the girls went outside to play. The women cleaned up and then joined Stu on the porch. They sat uncomfortably, unable to come up with anything to say. Sarah and Jenny had gossiped in the kitchen, but they did not gossip around Stu; and he was apparently determined to remain icily aloof. Inwardly Sarah sighed; men could be awfully exasperating sometimes. She wondered where her nieces were. Usually they hung about her skirts, begging for a story. To break the awkward tableau, Sarah stood up and walked to the end of the porch to scan the farmyard. She saw the girls sitting on the corral fence, Luke's blue shirt and flaxen hair bright spots of color between them.

Smiling, she returned to her seat and Jenny said, "Where are they?"

"Down at the corral with Luke."

Stu frowned at her words, and Sarah felt a spurt of anger. She had an image of him telling the girls not to hang around Luke, poisoning them against him. It wasn't fair! Why couldn't anyone else see Luke as he really was?

It was not long before Stu stood and said it was time to leave. Jenny called the girls, and soon they came tearing around the porch in a flurry of petticoats and pigtails.

"Mommy! Daddy! Aunt Sarah!" they cried, extending their hands. "Look what Uncle Luke made for us!"

Sarah bent to examine the simple little carved figures in their hands. In Penny's palm lay a comic dog crouching with his front paws on his nose, and Missy's was a cat, arched and spitting.

"Why, how darling!" Jennifer cried, and Sarah knew Luke had taken a huge leap forward in her favor. "Sarah, aren't they cute?"

The females of the family all giggled, their heads together, entranced by the cunningly whittled animals. Stu scowled, feeling a pang of jealousy at this invasion of his flock.

"And he told us the best story!" Penny exclaimed, blue eyes wide in wonder. "About the Indian brave Satchemach, and the raid he made on the Apache ponies!"

"And the time he saved his sister from the buffalo herd," Melissa chimed in. "And he said next time he was going to tell us about how he ran a race with the Iron Horse."

"Well, how splendid!" Sarah laughed. "You certainly seem to have had a nice time with Uncle Luke."

"Uh-huh!" Penny enthused. "He knows all kinds of things. He threw his knife for us, and he promised he would teach us how to hunt rabbits and squirrels and deer."

Jenny and Sarah burst into laughter. "Oh, dear, you are going to keep him busy," Jenny said, pulling the children toward the surrey.

After they left, Sarah went in search of her husband. He was no longer by the corral, but up at the stump chopping wood. His shirt was off, hanging on the lowest limb of the elm tree. He smiled at her, but did not grab for his shirt; she guessed he had gotten used to her—or the weather had gotten too hot for modesty.

"You seem to have charmed Penny and Melissa."

He laughed ruefully and shook his head. "Those two keep you hopping. I never heard so many questions in my life."

"I understand you told them stories, about Satchemach, the Indian brave."

"Hell, I had to do something to get them to stop the questions." He rested the head of the axe on the stump and leaned slightly on the handle, squinting at her in the sun. "Stealing ponies from the Apaches was really stealing old man Gilstrap's watermelons."

She laughed, and he, after adjusting his gloves and wiping the sweat from his forehead, went back to cutting wood. Sarah sat down beneath the elm and leaned against the trunk, content to sit and watch the beautiful symmetry of his movement as he arched back and up, then flung his axe down to bite into the log. He split each piece neatly, then tossed it on the pile and set another in its place to be split. His motions were precise, economical, and steady.

There were doubtless many things she ought to be doing, but Sarah decided not to think about them. She preferred to sit here lazily and dream and watch Luke work. After a while, he put the axe down on the cutting stump and flopped down on the cool ground beside her.

She could feel the heat from his body, see the sweat glistening on his skin. He lay with his arms behind his head and his eyes closed, his chest rising and falling rapidly.

"Am I a bad influence?"

"Mm," he answered and nodded. "Shirker."

"Luke—" Sarah said, an entreating note in her voice that made him open his eyes and look at her. "Could we go into town Saturday?"

He looked at her and then away. "Why?"

He did not want to take her to town; they had never been together in public, and it knotted his stomach to think of her seeing the way other people acted toward him or, even worse, to think of her being subjected to the same treatment just because she was with him. Of course, it had to be faced sometime. They couldn't hole up here alone forever. But he wasn't ready.

"To get the mail. It's been ages since we picked it up and there must be a whole bunch of Saturday Evening Posts there by now. I've been reading a serial in it, a mystery, and I'm anxious to find out what's happened. Please, Luke, let's go." She pleaded prettily, her head to one side, her eyes wide.

It occurred to him that she was asking his permission, and he blinked, disconcerted. She had given him control over her, and it was a heady sensation. He wanted to prolong it, to have her tease and flirt and cajole him into getting her way, so he said, "I need to work on Saturday."

"You work too hard. At the rate you are going, you'll drop from exhaustion. Please, Luke. Wouldn't it be fun?" She touched his bare arm lightly and smiled into his eyes. "I'll make you a batch of doughnuts."

He grinned. "I give in." And now, were they any other couple, he should be rewarded with a kiss. But they were not any other couple and the kiss did not come. He sat up to rid himself of her hand on his arm; even that slight touch could make his loins tighten in excitement.

"I'll start planting your garden tomorrow. How many rows do you want of everything?"

She realized then that she really did not know; her mother had always been responsible for that. She thought for a moment, trying to picture previous gardens, and began to guess, hoping she was right. From a discussion of the garden they slid into the topic of Luke's plans for the farm. It was pleasant listening to him theorize on how he might cut down on the cows' grazing meadow in order to raise more hay for the winter; then he could make a profit buying, fattening and selling cows in the winter. Maybe he would even cut down on the corn; and he was thinking of adding peach and cherry trees in front of the house.

"Mainly," he confessed with a boyish grin, " 'cause I'm awful fond of peach cobbler."

"They'll be pretty, too. Oh, Luke, let's get some flower seeds, too. I'd like to plant some around the porch."

"You know what I'd like?" Luke said shyly.

"What?"

"Honeysuckle. You know, climbing up one of those things—"

"Trellis," she prompted.

"Yeah. Maybe on the south end of the porch. It would shade the porch, too."

"Oh, Luke, I think that would be wonderful. And the smell—can you imagine how heavenly it would be out on the porch on a summer evening? Oh, let's do it!"

They got excited about the house then and began to plan—painting the trim, maybe next year, and expanding the porch and maybe sometime even trying to grow a real lawn in front of it. And around back, Sarah confessed what she had always dreamed of having was a cool little grape arbor. Luke promised that she would have it someday. Dreamily they drifted into silence, and softly, easily, Luke slid into sleep, his head pillowed by his arms. Sarah propped herself on one elbow and watched him. Asleep, he showed his tiredness, his skin marked with lines of exhaustion. Already he was deeply asleep, his hands and arms sprawled and boneless. She wanted to take him in her arms and cradle him like a child, as if that would make his rest more strengthening. The idea was silly and it made her smile, but she contributed to his sleep by remaining at his side, so that her departure would not awaken him. It made her feel quite useful and protective, doing nothing.

* * *

Sarah sat straight on the high wagon seat, her face happy beneath the wide-brimmed bonnet that shielded her from the sun. She was flushed with elation at her first trip to town in weeks. Besides the copies of the magazine to be pored over, Sarah had in mind looking for something she had not mentioned to Luke: a birthday present for him. She remembered his grandmother's bitter recital of his birth date, May 11, and that was only a week away. She was not at all sure what she was going to get, but she was excited at the prospect of hunting.

Beside her, Luke drove the team without her cheerful expectations. Already his stomach was clenching in anticipation. He didn't want her to see; he just didn't want her to see. He could take it; he was used to it. But to have her see what everyone thought of him—he wasn't sure he could bear it. What if she realized that the others were right? What if she saw how she was wasting herself on a no-account? What if suddenly there was that familiar revulsion in her eyes?

They stopped first at the post office to pick up the mail. Luke felt every eye in the place on them, and it was an effort not to turn and run. Sarah, too, felt the stares and uneasily glanced over at her husband. He seemed a stranger suddenly, his face an insolent mask, his eyes opaquely unreadable. She felt somehow abandoned. Quickly she asked for her mail and left, not pausing to chat with the obviously curious postmaster.

"Let's go to Stu's store," she said once they were outside, and he shrugged, hunching his shoulders.

They walked along the plank sidewalk to Harper's Store, the object of countless gazes. Mrs. Parker, the banker's wife, passed them with barely a nod and blatantly held back her skirts to give Luke as wide a berth as possible. Sarah's cheeks flamed with embarrassment and hot, bitter anger. How dare they! How dare they look at Luke like that, as if he were dirt beneath their feet! She squared her shoulders and set her jaw; she'd show them.

She sailed into the store on her righteous indignation, coolly ignoring all who stared and barely nodding at those who mumbled a greeting. Luke followed uneasily in her wake, slouching and silent. Sarah went straight back through the store to speak to Stu. Her husband's mouth twisted into a parody of a grin—naturally she would go running to Stu.

"I'm going on to the feed store," he said cutting abruptly into their conversation. A faint look of relief touched her eyes at his statement, and Luke's stomach tightened when he saw it—how glad she was to be rid of him.

Sarah remained chatting with Stu about his children until Luke left the store, then began her search for a present. Thank heavens he had decided to go to the feed store; she had been wondering how she would get rid of him so she could find his birthday gift. She wandered through the store, looking at and rejecting one thing after another until she wound up by the knife counter. It was then that she remembered his beautiful whittling and knew she had found just what she wanted. Carefully she chose a small knife with a glittering, razor-sharp blade and carved handle.

Highly pleased with herself, she proceeded to make her more ordinary purchases: thread, a bowl to replace the one she had dropped, flour, sugar, salt, coffee, cornmeal. It was while she stood fingering a bolt of cloth, wondering whether she ought to buy some to make new curtains for Luke's room, that she heard the pounding of a boy's boots on the sidewalk outside and heard him call, "Hey, Johnny, come on, there's a fight down at the feed store!"

Luke! Instinctively her hand flew to her throat and she looked back toward the counter. Stu had heard, also, and he came out from behind his counter, giving her a look that plainly said, "I told you." His movement freed her from her momentary paralysis and she started to the door.

"No," Stu said and laid his hand on her arm, "I'll go get him. There's no need for you to see it."

Sarah pulled her arm away and swept past him out the door, hardly noticing her rudeness because the knot of fear in her stomach overwhelmed all else. She hurried down the sidewalk to the feed store, the beat of her heart increasing the rhythm of her footsteps until she was almost running.

There was a knot of men on the sidewalk and street in

front of Warner's Feed Store. She pushed her way through them, using her elbows in a most unladylike way. When she had worked her way to the front of the group, she saw them and stopped abruptly. Luke and an oafish-looking boy circled each other warily in the street. The boy's left eye was puffed and darkening and his nose was swollen. She realized sickly that the damage had been done by Luke's fist.

"Oh, Luke," she whispered and put her hand to her mouth to suppress the wild nausea. Her husband was a stranger to her. His eyes burned fiercely and his face was alight with an animal excitement; blood trickled down from one corner of his mouth and spotted his new blue shirt. She had never seen him look like that, so wild, so bad, so filled with blood lust, and it sickened her.

Suddenly Luke darted in, surprising his heavier opponent, and felled him with one blow to the chin. Luke stumbled back and then stood still, sucking in air and letting the rush of blood and excitement and fear in his head subside a little. Then he looked up and saw a woman on the sidewalk and realized it was his wife. She stood with one hand pressed against her lips, and above her hand, her eyes were huge and dark with horror and disgust.

Luke swallowed hard and wiped his forehead with the back of his hand. All his elation was gone. He tried to pull his thoughts together and say something, but he could not.

He had not really been looking for a fight, although he had felt sick and tight from the tension of being in town with her. He had driven the wagon down to the feed store and gone in, all the while remembering over and over the way she had wanted to get rid of him back there at Harper's store, so she could be with the man she loved. Luke damned her and he damned Stu, and, as always when he felt shut out, he was alive to every barb. There were a bunch of farmers in the feed store, and they all stared at him as he bought the seed he needed for Sarah's garden. There were whispered comments as he got his purchases and a few men trailed out after him when he began to load the wagon. Someone laughed and said something about marrying a farm.

Then William Garrett, a well-to-do farmer from out by Choctaw, said, "Yeah, but think of poor Sarah McGowan. That's an expensive price to pay just to have a name for your baby."

Luke had swung on him, choking with fury. "My wife's name is Turner, not McGowan, and I'll thank you to keep her name out of your filthy mouth!"

Garrett's son, a big hulking farmboy, laughed and said, "Lucky girl, she's a Turner now. And no doubt she'll have the usual Turner baby—two months early."

He had burst out in guffaws at his humor and therefore did not see the blow coming that sent him sailing off the sidewalk into the dusty street. Garrett was strong and big, but slow and inexperienced in fighting, and Luke made quick work of him.

But then he had looked up to see his wife, and he felt embarrassed and afraid. Explanations did no good; he had discovered that long ago. Besides, he could hardly reveal to her the slight on her name that had launched him into the fight. So he just stood, not quite looking at her, waiting for her to begin to berate him.

In that, he misjudged his wife. The horror that swelled in her at the unleashing of his violence was not something to cause her to berate Luke. Rather, she had seen a glimpse into his character that frightened her; the only thing she really wanted to do was run from him. Moreover, Sarah was never one to make a public scene. In fact, she was becoming aware of the group of men observing her, and she felt quite embarrassed and anxious to extricate herself.

"Sarah." She heard Stu's concerned voice behind her and his hand touched her back. "Come on with me. I'll take you home."

She could not suppress the thrill she felt at his touch and his protectiveness, and she almost turned to go with him. But something rose up inside to stop her before she moved. She was her father's daughter: you did not condemn a man without knowing the facts. And she was her mother's daughter: whatever one felt in private, loyalty was all important, and a husband and wife must present a solid front in public.

So it was that, to both Luke's and Stu's astonishment, she stepped from Stu's hand into the street where her husband was. She pulled her handkerchief from her reticule and wiped the blood from his mouth.

"Have you hurt yourself?" she asked, surprising herself with the calm in her voice.

"No."

"Good. Have you gotten everything here?"

"Yes."

"Then shall we leave?"

He nodded mutely and helped her into the wagon. They drove away, leaving Stu gaping after them in the street.

Chapter IX

SARAH tried to put Luke's outburst of violence out of her mind—after all, there was nothing she could do about it now—but all day Sunday her mind kept straying back to it, like a tongue seeking out a sore tooth. She could not understand it, could not reconcile the Luke she had seen in the dusty street, his face stamped with blood lust, with the one she knew here at home, the quiet, hardworking Luke who had never even raised his voice against her.

She felt that he avoided her Sunday, staying out in the fields even longer than usual and hardly speaking to her at their meals, not meeting her eyes. She would have liked to talk to him, try to discover what moved him to act like that, but she knew she would get nothing out of him in the mood he was in. It was not that he was surly, just so removed and so eager to avoid any discussion.

"Why, he's hiding," she said to herself in amazement. Running and hiding from her, like a child hides until his parent's wrath has cooled down. Imagine that—the tough, wild Luke Turner afraid of his wife's anger. She smiled softly. Scared, kind, mean, angry: what a puzzle he was. Would she ever understand him? Mentally she shrugged; well, she had a whole lifetime to figure him out.

For the present, it was best, she felt, to let the matter slide from her mind, to concentrate on the day-to-day workings of her life. Time would straighten things out; someday she would come to understand Luke; someday all the violence would be gone from him. Look at how much he had changed from the slouching, defiant, scared young man who had come to work for her father. But right now, spring was here and Luke's birthday almost upon them, and she had too many things to do to spend her time idly wondering about Luke.

Besides her regular work, every spare minute was spent in making a white dress shirt for Luke. After she had cut and sewn it, she embroidered the collar, cuffs, and front with white thread. The delicate stitchery was almost invisible against the white material, but gave it a soft richness and subdued beauty. The work strained her eyes and took much needed time from her housework, but she had promised herself to give Luke the birthday he had never had.

The morning of his birthday she woke with an excitement that was totally absent in Luke. His birthday had never been anything except the anniversary of his mother's death. When he was a child, he had sometimes longed for the birthdays other kids had, but as he got older he managed to wipe out that sort of useless wishing until now his birthdays came and went almost without his noticing them.

In fact, he did not realize that it was May 11 until, when he came downstairs, Sarah said to him, "Happy Birthday."

Luke looked at her in surprise and then looked down at the floor in embarrassment. He did not know how to respond and he felt a fool. How had she known? Why remember? It pleased him that she bothered, and yet it made him feel anew the difference between them. So he bolted down his breakfast and made his escape to the fields. It never occurred to him that that had not ended the matter of his birthday.

But after supper that evening, Sarah went into the kitchen and returned with a chocolate cake blazing with candles. Luke stared in amazement.

"It's beautiful," he said. "But why—"

"It's your birthday cake, silly. Go on—make a wish and blow out the candles."

He looked at her and felt a sudden tearing pain and for a moment his whole being ached for her to love him. An entire life in one wish. She was watching him expectantly, so he smiled and blew out the candles. Sarah laughed and clasped her hands together, as if he had done something clever. Then she disappeared again, this time to return with two gaily wrapped packages.

"Here," she said, holding them out to him and, when he did not move to take them, went on in mild exasperation, "they're your presents, your birthday gifts."

Gingerly he took them from her, hardly daring to touch them. His fingers shook as he unwrapped first the knife, then the shirt. Softly he ran his roughened fingers over the fragile embroidery and lingered on the carving of the knife's handle.

"I never—" he began, but the sudden huge knot in his throat made it impossible to go on.

He looked at her; for an instant Sarah saw the sparkle of a tear in his eye and she hurt for all his hard, lonely past. Gently she put her hand on his and convulsively his fingers tightened around hers and she felt a sudden, overwhelming burst of happiness.

A few days later Sarah was standing at the cabinet kneading bread when she heard the sound of wagon wheels and then the snort and jingle of horses in harness. Wiping off her floured hands on her apron, she stepped out on the back porch to see who had come to see her on a workday.

A wagon had pulled up in front of the house and a stranger leaped down off the seat.

"Howdy!" he called, seeing Sarah, and waved at her.

"Hello." Sarah came down the back steps toward him, her eyes on the wagon.

It was loaded with boxes and tools and furniture. A woman sat on the wagon seat, with a small child in her lap. Behind her, two bigger children perched on top of the load. As Sarah watched, a second wagon pulled up beside the first, similarly loaded, and with two teenaged boys on the seat.

"Jake Crowley, ma'am," the man on the ground said. "And this is my wife, Mary Etta. And these are our children."

"Pleased to meet you. My name is Sarah Turner. My husband Luke is out in the fields. You folks moving?"

"Sure am. We're from up 'round Honey Grove. I've bought the Jamison place."

"The old Jamison place!" Sarah echoed, delighted. "Why, then, we're neighbors."

"Well, I'm right pleased to hear that, ma'am. Truth is, we were beginning to think we were lost, and we stopped here to ask you how to get to our new place."

"Why, we'd be happy to show you. But first, you must come in and rest a little and get acquainted." She took in the woman's tired, dusty appearance. "Maybe you'd like to wash up a little."

Mrs. Crowley beamed. "Why, thank you, Mrs. Turner."

"And how about some nice cold lemonade?"

That brought an enthusiastic response from the children, who immediately began to scramble down from the wagon. It was not long before they were washed up and the lemonade drunk and the children out playing in the yard while Mr. Crowley watered the animals. Sarah and Mrs. Crowley were free to sit down for a friendly little chat.

Once she was refreshed, Mrs. Crowley was a cheerful, talkative woman, and it was not long before Sarah knew all about her children and her former home and her husband's migrating instincts. The two women liked each other immediately, despite the fact that Mrs. Crowley was probably ten years older than Sarah. Farm and home were common topics, and they faced life with a similar good humor. They even discovered that both belonged to the same church.

"Why, good," Mrs. Crowley exclaimed. "You and Mr. Turner will have to come with us to church, then. Won't that be fun?"

It took Sarah a moment to realize who Mr. Turner was, then she said, a little embarrassed, "I would love to, Mrs. Crowley, but I'm afraid my husband is not really a churchgoing man."

The other woman made a sympathetic noise. "My Pa was the same way. You had to drag him to get him to church. But he was a good man, nevertheless."

"Oh, so is Luke," Sarah hastened to assure her. "It's just the way he was brought up—his family wasn't religious." Mentally Sarah grinned—what an understatement!

"Ah." The older woman nodded sagely.

"You all must stay and eat with us," Sarah said. "Why, it's practically noon. No point in going over to your new house until you've eaten. And I'd like you to meet Luke. I'll just run down and fetch him."

Mrs. Crowley protested a little, but quickly gave in. The idea made sense and, moreover, was what she wanted. "But now you must let me help," she said.

They worked efficiently together, and though she prepared a much larger meal than usual, it seemed to be done with less effort, what with the help and the conversation. It reminded Sarah of the way she and her mother used to work together, and she felt a treacherous prickling behind her eyelids.

"I'll just go on down and get Luke," she said, "if you would watch the peas. It's getting late, and he must be wondering where I am."

"Why, sure, and I'll round up that family of mine."

Luke had, indeed, begun to wonder about her lateness and had started back toward the house by the time Sarah arrived.

"Did something happen? I was beginning to worry." His voice and face were anxious.

"Oh, no, no," she said breathlessly, and he noted the flush in her cheeks and the excited sparkle in her eyes. "Neighbors. We've got new neighbors."

"Who?" His face closed and his tone turned suspicious.

"Their name is Crowley. Come on. I want you to meet them." She took his arm and pulled him along with her, and he fell in willingly at her touch.

"They've bought the old Jamison place. Won't that be nice? They're really good people. They're from Honey Grove."

Luke relaxed a little. They weren't from around here; that meant they would not know about him. Imagine that—starting out new with somebody. Somebody who didn't know his father or Earl or the things he had done. How was he to act with somebody like that?

He smiled down at Sarah as she chattered about the Crowleys. She was so happy about her new neighbors. One thing he knew, he must do his best not to turn them against him, for her sake. He had cut her off from everyone else she knew. He must not separate her from these new friends. The idea scared him; he had no idea what a person did to make other people—respectable people—like him.

"Don't you think it would be nice if you took them over and showed them where the Jamison place is? After lunch, I mean."

"Sure, if you want me to." He felt his palms begin to sweat; what if he failed her—again.

Mary Etta Crowley, standing at the back door, watched Sarah and Luke approach and she smiled at the way his bright head was bent attentively to her. What a nice-looking young couple they were. He was lean and browned and handsome, with that fine hair falling carelessly across his forehead, and she was a soft, pretty little thing, with a sweet smile and lovely big eyes. Sarah looked up and saw her on the porch and waved to her; Mary Etta waved back and moved down into the yard to join her husband and children.

Sarah introduced Luke to the Crowleys, and he forced himself to look them in the eye and not mumble his hellos. But he felt awkward and was glad of the excuse that he needed to go wash up, so that he could get away. By the time he was through, they were all seated at the table, and as he sat down he felt another moment of panic. Grace. They were like Sarah's family, the kind who said grace before meals. It was his place to say it—it would seem strange for Sarah to do it—but he had never said a prayer in his life.

Words stuck in his throat and he shot a glance of appeal at Sarah, who saw his dilemma and came quickly to his rescue. "Would you like to say grace for us today, Mr. Crowley?" she asked, her tone making it an honor extended to a guest.

For the first time he could remember, Luke joined in with a heartfelt "Amen" at the end of the prayer.

There was complete silence for a few minutes as everyone dug hungrily into their food. But then the eating slowed down, and Luke knew that conversation was approaching. He felt scared and ridiculous.

"Nice place you got here," Mr. Crowley said finally.

"Thank you."

"And Luke does it all by himself, too," Sarah added, and Luke warmed to hear the pride in her voice.

"Is that right? Well, this is quite a load for a young couple like yourselves. Least I got my two boys here to help me, for what they're worth. How many acres you got here, Mr. Turner?"

"Hundred and twenty," Luke said and then suddenly found himself launching into the number of acres he had in cotton, the number in corn, and how much in hay, the progress of his crops, the weather and its effect. Before he knew it, Sarah and Mrs. Crowley were clearing the dishes from the table and he realized that he had carried on a lengthy conversation with ease.

Then he volunteered to guide them over to the Jamison place, and the men went outside to hitch up the wagons again while Mrs. Crowley helped Sarah wash the dishes.

"You two are newlyweds, aren't you," the older woman said with such a knowing smile that Sarah blushed.

"Yes. How did you know?"

Mrs. Crowley laughed. "I've seen the way you two look at each other. Think I don't know young love when I see it?"

Sarah just smiled and looked away. She could hardly tell the woman that she was wrong, that theirs was a loveless, material marriage, entered into by both for the farm and for security. She hated to think how shocked Mrs. Crowley would be if she knew.

Soon the dishes were done and the horses harnessed, and Sarah stood on the back porch, watching the Crowleys leave and waving. It sent a pang of sadness through her for her new-found friend to be leaving already. And how long would she remain Sarah's friend? Soon they would meet other people and those people would tell the Crowleys about Luke and their hasty marriage. Would Mrs. Crowley still be her friend then? Sarah was shaken by a wave of anger: for the first time Luke had been taken at face value and measured by what he was instead of by reputation, and he had been liked. She could tell that Mr. Crowley thought him a fine, hardworking young man. But everyone would be only too anxious to tell them about Luke's past, and then, no doubt, Crowley would despise him. Why did people have to be so cruel? Why couldn't they let Luke be happy? Tears sprang into her eyes and she rushed back into the house to drive away her thoughts with work.

An hour later, much to her surprise, Sarah again heard the sound of wagons in the yard. She went rushing out into the yard to find that Mrs. Crowley and the children had returned with Luke.

"What happened?" she asked, worried. "Is something the matter?"

"The house," Luke said succinctly.

"What?"

"The Jamison place is in bad shape. We'll have to do some work on it before it'll be fit to live in. So Mr.

Crowley and Joe Bob are going to stay over there and work on it, and I brought Mrs. Crowley and the kids back. I asked them to stay with us until they get their house fixed up."

"Well, of course. Why, that will be real nice—for us, anyway. I know I'll love having the company. But I know you must be awful disappointed, Mrs. Crowley."

The other woman was philosophical. "Can't expect things to be perfect. We might have known an old house like that would need some work on it. I just hope we won't be too great an inconvenience to you."

"Heavens, no. Come on in. I'll just run on up and get the bedrooms in shape." It was then that it occurred to Sarah how bizarre it would seem to Mrs. Crowley to find that she and Luke slept in separate bedrooms. Sarah just could not bear to explain their marriage of convenience to her.

So now, breathing a silent prayer that Luke would not be shocked and disgusted at her boldness, she darted up the stairs to Luke's room. Quickly she grabbed his clothes and personal articles and threw them into her room. Their sleeping in her room instead of the master bedroom might seem a bit odd, but Luke had fewer things to move. By the time Mrs. Crowley reached the top of the stairs, Sarah had stripped Luke's room of all traces of his habitation.

"Now, you're going to have to let me help you, or I'll feel like we're imposing," Mrs. Crowley said.

"Of course," Sarah said, taking fresh sheets from the linen closet. She was glad to have her help, now that there was nothing embarrassing for her to discover.

The two women worked together cheerfully, opening up and preparing the extra bedrooms and getting supper ready. The men came in late and set to their food with gusto, and afterwards they retired to the porch to rock and talk while the women cleaned up, so Sarah was unable to get Luke alone to explain her actions to him.

When she and Mary Etta finished in the kitchen and joined the men on the porch, Sarah said casually, "I put Mr. and Mrs. Crowley in Mama's and Daddy's old room and the girls in Jenny's room and the boys in the guestroom."

Luke looked at her, but his face was unreadable. Sarah wondered what he thought and wished she could explain it to him. But surely he must see the problem. And she had to tell him now, before he went up to bed in the wrong room.

"Sounds good," Luke said, hoping he had hidden the shock that went through him at her words. Of course, it would look strange to the Crowleys, their sleeping apart, and so they must sleep in the same room. But Good God, to sleep with Sarah! To be beside her soft body all night long, to be so close to those enticing curves concealed only by a nightgown. What pleasure; what torture. He swallowed and tried to turn his thoughts to what Jake Crowley was saying, but relentlessly his mind crept back to the image of Sarah lying beside him, relaxed in sleep. He wished everyone would stop talking and go to bed—and yet, how was he to endure it? Lost in thought, it took a moment for him to realize what had been said, when at last Mr. Crowley did stretch widely and admitted that he was ready for bed. When his words did penetrate, Luke's heart began to pound and unconsciously he clenched and unclenched his fists. Slowly he fell in behind the others as they trailed through the door and up the stairs to their rooms.

Sarah had lit kerosene lamps in all the bedrooms, and the upstairs had a warm, cozy glow, but Luke felt none of it, only the extreme heat in his hands and the freezing cold in his stomach. Mrs. Crowley herded the children to their rooms and Mr. Crowley disappeared into Luke's room, and Luke found himself awkwardly following Sarah into her room. He closed the door behind him and stopped there at the edge of the room. Sarah, as uncomfortable as he, crossed over to the foot of her bed and studied the bedpost.

"I—I moved you in here because—well, the Crowleys would have thought it odd, don't you think? I didn't quite know what to do. Somehow I could not seem to explain it to Mrs. Crowley."

"Yeah, I understand." He jammed his hands into his pockets and hunched his shoulders.

"I—I hope you don't think badly of me."

"Me? Think badly of you?" Luke's voice rose in astonishment.

"Yes. I—I mean," Sarah floundered. Why had she said anything about it? Of course he had not thought anything about it; he thought she was sweet and good—he would not suspect her of bad intentions. It was only because she knew her own wicked thoughts that she felt her actions were suspicious. Angry with herself, she bit her lip and traced a design on the bedpost with her thumb.

Luke stared at her, wondering what she meant by that remark. Did she actually think he would be so lowminded, so—so stupid as to interpret the move as an invitation to bed her? He had no doubts on that score: let him touch her and she would probably turn green with disgust; he would be lucky if she didn't scream.

"Don't worry," he said roughly. "I promise I won't 'presume'."

"I know," she said, her voice low and choked.

He realized then how mortified she was by the whole situation. To have to lie in the same bed with him, to undress with him in the room, to let him see her in nothing but her gown. She must feel humiliated and degraded.

"I, uh, I think I'll just go down and check the barn. You go on to bed."

"All right. Good night." Then in a muffled voice she said, "Thank you."

Luke was so kind, she thought after he left. He must have realized the embarrassment she would feel undressing in front of a man. He was always so sensitive to one's feelings. She hummed to herself as she washed her face and changed into her nightgown. Suddenly the world seemed so nice and almost exciting; she guessed that it was having visitors.

Sarah crawled into bed and curled up, but she found she could not sleep, and she realized that she was on edge, waiting for Luke to come to bed. Well, that was only natural; it was hard to sleep when there was an uncomfortable situation waiting to be resolved. After a while, she heard the door ease open and softly close, and she knew her husband had returned. She restrained her impulse to turn and look at him and instead kept her back to him. After all, he too would no doubt welcome the chance to undress without someone watching.

Luke had walked around outside, trying to persuade himself that sleeping with his wife without touching her was not the most refined torture, but one look at Sarah's form beneath the sheets convinced him anew that it was. The lines of her body molded the sheet to them, and her luxuriant hair, released from the confinement of her braid, lay in profusion across her pillow. Luke swallowed, fighting the constriction in his throat. Never had he wanted anything as much as he wanted now to caress her. For a moment he stood without moving, looking at her, watching the gentle rise and fall of her chest, seeing the long shadows cast on her cheek by her eyelashes that gave her face a delicate, vulnerable look. He could hear his own breath, coming quick and rasping, and the sound shook him—he was an animal, a beast driven solely by his own hunger.

He closed his eyes and clenched his fists, fighting for control. Desire for her raced along his veins and lit his nerves, so hard and strong that to refuse it racked him with pain. Yet a great tenderness welled in him at the sight of her so innocent and trusting in her sleep. He could not let anything hurt her; he had to protect her from pain and unhappiness. The conflicting emotions struggled within him, and he felt as if he were being torn apart.

"Luke?" Sarah said softly, wondering why he was standing there so long without doing anything. "Is something the matter?"

He jumped at her voice. Good God, she was awake. "No, I—I was just—it was too dark. I couldn't see anything at first."

"Shall I light the lamp?"

"No, it's all right now." Hastily he knelt and fumbled at his shoelaces; his fingers were trembling. He got a knot in the laces and cursed quietly.

"Luke?" Sarah sat up, struck a match and lit the kerosene lamp. Replacing the chimney of the lamp, she said, "What is it?"

"Nothing. I just pulled a knot in these goddamn shoe laces—oh, I'm sorry, Sarah, I didn't mean to swear." He tugged desperately at the laces; it seemed as if all his frustrations had become centered in that little knot, which perversely got tighter the more he worked at it.

Sarah laughed and hopped out of bed. "Men! Honestly, men are more helpless than babies."

She came and knelt beside him and, shoving his hands aside, began to untangle the knot. Luke straightened, his senses reeling at her nearness. He could see the movement of her breasts through her nightgown as she worked, see the darker circle of her nipple. And standing above her, he could see down the open neck of her gown to the soft, creamy smooth swell of her breasts.

"There!" she exclaimed triumphantly and stood.

"Thank you," he managed to say, although his mouth was dry as dust.

She walked back around the bed to turn off the lamp, and his eyes followed the gentle sway of her hips and lingered over the clean outline of her legs. She turned the wick down and the room melted into darkness. Luke unbuttoned his shirt and pulled it off, then unbuckled his belt and began to unbutton his trousers. He always slept naked, but that was unthinkable now, of course; he hoped his underwear would be sufficient covering.

Sarah lay in the dark, listening to him undress; the scrape of metal as he unfastened his belt buckle sent a strange tremor through her. Suddenly she wished that she and Luke were really and truly married, that they loved each other and that when he got into bed, she could roll over and snuggle up in his arms. And he would—what? Well, he would kiss her and she would kiss him back, and it wouldn't feel at all like the peck on the lips that Grady Snowden had given her. And then—then—her mind could go no farther. It was too wicked, and besides, she was a little unclear as to precisely what would happen.

The sheet was drawn back and the bed sank under the weight of Luke's body. Their bodies did not touch, but she was intensely aware of his presence.

"Good night, Luke," she whispered.

"Good night." His voice when he answered was strangely hoarse.

"Are you all right? You sound odd."

Luke clenched his teeth and said shortly, "Yes, I'm fine."

Feeling vaguely dissatisfied, Sarah turned back on her side; she forced her eyes closed, but it was a long time before she could fall asleep. Beside her, Luke lay wide awake staring at the ceiling, his whole body taut, until long after he heard Sarah's breathing slip into the slow, shallow breaths of sleep.

The Crowleys stayed with them for four more days. With the children to help around the house, Mrs. Crowley and Sarah were freed to help with the hoeing. Luke spent his days breaking the Crowley's fields for them. They were late to begin planting, and time was of the essence, so he began the field work while the Crowley men repaired the house. Luke basked in the warm gratitude and friendship of the Crowleys; they thought him an excellent young man and a very good neighbor. No one had ever treated him as they had, and there were times when Luke found himself believing he was the man they thought him.

But he faced the nights with mingled dread and anticipation. He slept fitfully, if at all, and his nerves and muscles were wound up tight. He awoke feeling more tired than when he went to bed, and blue shadows formed beneath his eyes. Sarah worried that he was working too hard and was falling ill, and at night she plagued him by questioning and admonishing him and putting her hand to his forehead to feel for fever.

"You shouldn't work so hard," she would say, leaning across the bed to peer into his eyes, and he would breathe in the dizzying smell of her and long to touch the luscious skin so close to him.

It was all he could do to keep his gaze off her breasts swaying full and unrestrained beneath her gown. Once her breasts accidentally grazed his arms as she put her her hand to his forehead, and his skin flamed at the touch. Her concern pleased him and he enjoyed her touch, but sometimes he felt that she would run him mad with frustrated longing.

The second night they slept together, she fell asleep quickly, trustingly, and soon rolled over in her sleep and cuddled up against him. He hardly dared breathe for fear of awakening her. Cautiously he slipped his arm beneath her head to hold her to him, and then he lay there, savoring the warmth and feel and scent of her. The way she lay against him, it was easy to pretend she loved and trusted him, that she felt towards him as a wife felt towards a husband. He closed his eyes and imagined her waking up, looking up at him and smiling, reaching over to kiss him. He thought of her soft lips beneath his, of her mouth opening to him, that sweet, pure mouth accepting, loving. Slowly he would take her, slowly and tenderly, awaking her innocent, untutored body.

Almost involuntarily his hand came to rest on her hip and slid softly down her leg. Back up it came, moving to her flat stomach and up to her breast; he caressed her breast beneath her gown, feeling the hardening nipple through the thin cloth. His mind told him to stop, pointing out that he was torturing himself to no avail, that he was taking advantage of Sarah, violating her privacy. But he could not stop himself. Gently he brushed his lips against her hair, then her closed eyelids, then trailed down to her lips. Some last shred of sense kept him from strengthening his kisses and so waking her, but he could not keep himself from kissing the velvet skin of her throat, his mouth drifting down to the rounded tops of her breasts.

Sarah stirred in his arms and with a groan Luke jerked away from her. For a long moment he felt that it would be impossible to exist anymore, that he must surely splinter and the pieces fly apart. He got out of bed and walked over to the window and looked out, letting the soft night breeze caress his body, and gradually he began to calm down.

"I can't stand it," he whispered to himself, but he knew that he would. He had to, or else leave all this—the farm, the house, Sarah. And *that*, he knew, he could not bear at all.

He remained at the window a long time, and when he finally came back to bed, his face was lined deep with exhaustion. He climbed into bed and slipped his arm around Sarah, feeling her again snuggle up to him. And at last he slept.

Sarah awoke the next morning to find herself lying with her head resting on Luke's shoulder, one arm thrown across his hard chest, and their legs intertwined. She blushed and glanced up to see if he was aware of their embarrassing position. He was deeply asleep and she was thankful for that. Funny, how warm and safe she felt in his arms. Cautiously she disentangled their bodies, being careful not to awaken him. Once free, she sighed a little and looked back at Luke's recumbent form.

How thin he was; his ribs showed through the tough brown skin of his chest. His face, relaxed in sleep, was worn beyond his years. For a moment, Sarah wanted to fold him in her arms, like a mother protecting her child from the world. She smiled at her protective urge. It had been only a moment before that she had felt safe and protected by him. Perhaps that was what marriage was like. Quietly, she slipped out of bed to dress and go start breakfast.

Somehow Luke managed to survive the following two nights, though again Sarah would roll over against him once she had fallen asleep, and he would have to endure the feel of her body pressed against his. He accepted her into his arms, but he refrained from touching her, and was greatly relieved to hear the Crowleys say they would be leaving since it meant he would no longer have to face that nightly ordeal.

Sarah went with the Crowleys to help Mrs. Crowley clean the long-vacant house, and she stayed over for the night. Luke discovered how miserably vacant the house seemed without her presence. And though she had left him a filling cold meal, he found it gloomy and tasteless without her warm smile and pleasant chatter. He went to bed feeling dissatisfied and his arms ached for the feel of her soft round body.

Chapter X

THE house seemed lonely to Sarah with Mrs. Crowley gone. She missed having someone to talk to as she worked, and she missed the assistance. Luke helped Mr. Crowley plow every afternoon and usually came home late, and he took to disappearing into the barn as soon as supper was over. His desertion made her curious—and a little hurt; but most of all, she just plain missed him. What's more, she found she missed him at night in her bed. She could not exactly put her finger on it, but somehow there was a certain excitement lacking.

By the time a week had passed with Luke's almost constant absence, Sarah was feeling rather glum and sorry for herself. She was standing at the sink washing the dishes, pondering what had made Luke so suddenly averse to her company, when he came in the back door.

There was a glow to his face and a barely suppressed excitement in his stance that made Sarah straighten instinctively; something was up.

"What's the matter?" she said, and he smiled and extended the hand he had been holding behind his back.

"I made you a present," he said, "with the knife you gave me."

"What? Why, thank you," she exclaimed, astonished, and took the object.

It was a wood carving, a man and a woman standing side by side, the man's arm around the woman's shoulder. The couple were vibrant, their faces alight with life and humor. They were clearly her mother and father. Sarah clutched the carving, staring at it.

"Oh, Luke," she said, her voice choked with emotion. "Oh, Luke, how beautiful."

She looked up at him, her face shining. Luke smiled and looked at the floor. Her happiness filled him with an almost unbearable joy; he felt immensely powerful to have given her something that gave her pleasure.

"Oh, thank you, thank you. You're so sweet, so good. Oh, Luke!" In a burst of emotion she flung her arms around his neck and kissed him. It was a light, brief kiss; she barely pressed her lips to his. But without thinking, Luke's arms went around her and pulled her to him, and he kissed her long and deeply, his lips playing on hers, opening them. Sarah had never felt anything like that before, and when suddenly he stopped, she fell back a step, her hand going to her mouth, and stared at him wide-eyed. He stared back, as surprised as she, but then full realization of what he had done hit him and he turned pale. She must think he was horrible now—and she had been so pleased with him before.

"I'm sorry," he muttered and, ducking his head, almost ran from the room.

Shakily Sarah leaned against a cabinet. Luke had kissed her! Imagine that. Of course, he must have thought her awfully forward, to have kissed him back as she did. Even so, it was unlike Luke. He had never done anything to indicate that he even found her attractive. But the way he had kissed her just now, his mouth fierce and demanding, his arms crushing her to him—surely that was passion. She smiled a little to herself. Was it possible that Luke felt some affection for her?

Surely not. The qualities that were her mainstay, the attributes that had attracted Grady—calmness, steadiness, the ability to work hard and manage a house well—that could not be the sort of thing that attracted Luke or invited that kiss. He would want someone with looks, someone enticing. Like that overblown Emma Whitehead, she thought spitefully. He had always hung around her before he went to prison. Sarah pictured Luke in her mind: that shock of pale, wind-tossed hair, the blue eyes bright and startling against his brown skin, his hard muscular body. Why, any girl would take him; she knew that even the pious ones had a secret yen for him.

Except that he was married. Sarah straightened, struck by the thought. It would not make any difference in his being able to get a woman; Luke was illicit anyway, married or not. But might it not make a difference to Luke? Though few would have believed it, he had his principles. Perhaps he was too kind to embarrass her publicly by having an affair. Maybe he was even morally against it. So he avoided other women, and his natural passion had no outlet. It would not be surprising then if she began to appear attractive to him. Not a very flattering idea, but it made sense.

But what was she to do about it? It would not be difficult, she thought, remembering his kiss and the way it sent a tingle all through her, to let him take her if he wanted to. Yet somehow it seemed sinful, even though they were married, for them to sleep together when they did not love each other, just coming together out of sheer animal lust. She supposed she ought not to encourage him; but on the other hand, she was his wife and by God's laws and man's, she could not refuse him.

Sarah smiled to herself: just having the opportunity to be in this dilemma warmed her. It was exciting to think of someone wanting her, just desiring her, not respecting her admirable qualities—or taking her as second best to her sister. She went upstairs to her room and looked at herself in her mirror. There was a glow to her face and her eyes sparkled. I am pretty, she thought; I may not be beautiful like Jenny, but I am pretty. And Luke wants me.

She had the wicked feeling that she would say yes to Luke if he asked her to share his bed.

"Wicked or not," she said to her reflection, "I don't care, I just don't care."

Luke was scared by his loss of control; he did not know what her reaction was, but he knew it must be bad. No doubt it had frightened her or disgusted her or made her hate him or maybe all those things. He dreaded her coldly ignoring him or giving him a tongue-lashing or sidling away from him.

To his surprise, she did none of those things. She acted a bit shy and blushed when she first saw him the next morning, but apart from that she acted as if all were normal. And he found that she grew daily more distracting, playing havoc with his vows to retain control. When she smiled that sweet, shy smile, looking up at him through her thick lashes, a quiver would dart through him. And when she brought his dessert to him and stood so close to him pouring his coffee, it was all he could do not to turn and rest his head against her breasts. Once she put her hand on his arm as she told him something, and he hoped that she could not feel the way he tensed at the touch of her hand on his skin. She seemed even prettier than usual, more sparkling, quicker to laugh. There were times when he could have sworn that she was flirting with him.

At night he lay awake thinking about her, seeing again in his mind every gesture, every smile, hearing again her words and laughter. He would recreate scenes from the day, but turning them into what he wanted to have happened. In his mind she came to him, arms outspread, and he took her in his arms. He kissed her and she did not protest, but opened her mouth to his probing tongue. He would imagine that she undressed for him, let him take her to his bed, let his eager hands caress and explore her body. Gently, tenderly he would arouse her, bringing her inexperienced body to the shuddering heights of passion.

But these waking dreams left him only more unsatisfied, hungrier for her, and less able to control his desire. He feared that some time he would break and, unable to restrain himself, force her into his bed. At times his fears and longings drove him almost to despair. Every way seemed impossible. He could not rape her; he could not leave; he could not continue to live this way. Yet somehow he managed to hang on, trying to get through each day.

Almost two weeks later, the oldest Crowley boy came riding up to the house to invite them to a party at his family's place. The party was to celebrate their new home and their recently planted crop. Sarah accepted gladly and spent the rest of the week looking forward to Saturday evening. Since only the Crowleys and Luke and Sarah would be there, Luke did not fear the party. In fact, he was as eager as Sarah to go, feeling that such a break in the usual routine might allow him to rid himself of some of his pent-up emotions.

By the time Saturday came, the air was electric with their barely suppressed excitement. Luke took his bath quickly, his mind for once not on Sarah's bath to follow, but on the party ahead.

After his bath, Luke went upstairs to dress. He put on the white dress shirt Sarah had made for him, running his fingers gently over the delicate embroidery work she had done on the collar and front—tiny flowers and curls and leaves in white thread, so that they hardly showed but gave the shirt a rich look. When he thought of the time and care that had gone into it, he marvelled that she would have done that for him. My God, he thought, what would she have done for Stu Harper? The thought made him scowl and resume his dressing angrily.

The shirt required cuff links, and he had none, so he searched the room for a pair of Mr. McGowan's. Finding none, he went downstairs, still in his stocking feet, to ask Sarah where they were. At the bottom of the stairs he stopped abruptly. The door into the kitchen was almost closed, but had come open an inch or two, and through the wide crack he could see Sarah sitting in the tub in the middle of the kitchen, still taking her bath.

His heart began to pound violently and he stood stock-still, looking at her. His quiet approach had not disturbed her, and she leaned back lazily against the tub, soaking, her white, slender body open to his gaze.

Hungrily his eyes slid over her, lingering on her full soft breasts. He knew he should leave, felt himself wicked to spy on her like this, but he could not force himself to move. It required all his control just to keep from bursting in upon her. The mere sight of her naked sent desire flooding through him and his restraint made him tremble. Then she stood and stepped out to towel off and Luke almost groaned aloud. He longed to take the towel from her and dry her caressingly. Almost he could feel the velvet skin beneath his hands and lips.

Desperately he swallowed and wiped his sweating palms against his trousers. She must not come out to find him lurking on the stairs; the thought of her outrage gave him the strength to turn and move cautiously back up the stairs. Once back in his room, he sank into a chair and fought to regain control of his breath and racing pulse. How long, he wondered, could he stand it? He thought of his long celibate years in prison, then that one night with a woman, followed by months without release. And now this: to be tortured day and night by the nearness of Sarah, knowing he could not take her and yet unable to relieve himself with another woman for fear of embarrassing her before the town. Must he spend the rest of his life as pure as a priest?

It took Luke some time to calm down enough to knock on Sarah's door and ask about the cufflinks. Even then, as he finished dressing, his blood still ran like fire in his veins, and he was afraid that the slightest thing would set him off.

He went out to hitch up the team, then returned to the living room to wait for his wife. When at last she came hurrying down the stairs and into the room, he rose in admiration.

"You're beautiful," he breathed.

His wife giggled and twirled around for him to view her. "Do you mean it? Do I look all right?"

Sarah was dressed in an apple green party dress that turned her hazel eyes green and emphasized her slender waist. She had dressed her hair differently, in a full, soft pompadour that gently framed her face. Her cheeks were flushed prettily with excitement, and she radiated a happy glow.

"Do I mean it!" he repeated in amazement. "My God—Mrs. Turner, you are so pretty, it hurts."

"Well, Mr. Turner, you look awfully nice yourself," Sarah replied, reaching out to take his arm. "Come on. I'm ready for a party."

The Crowleys were obviously ready for a party, too. Their house was all lit up and so clean and neat and changed inside that Sarah exclaimed over it again and again. The Crowleys were spruced up, too, and plainly excited. All of them, Crowleys and Turners, had been working to the limit of their endurance recently and the release of a party made them all a little giddy.

Mrs. Crowley showed Sarah around the refurbished house and Sarah was satisfyingly impressed. The men disappeared to look at the barn and corrals and lingered an uncommonly long time.

"What on earth is keeping them?" Sarah wondered as she and the older woman set the food on the table.

Mary Etta Crowley laughed. "Well, I think they're doing more down there than just talking."

"What do you mean?" Sarah asked, intrigued.

"It's my guess Jake has got a little corn liquor down there for refreshment." She stopped as a new thought struck her and she looked at Sarah a little uneasily. "You don't mind, do you? Generally, my Jacob is a good, sober man, but every now and then a man has got to kick up his heels, if you know what I mean."

Sarah wasn't quite sure what to think. Luke had promised her before they married not to drink, and he hadn't. But the way Mrs. Crowley put it—surely it couldn't do any harm.

"Why, I don't know. I never thought about it. Luke's never drunk anything since we've been married."

"That's a good man you've got there. But he needs to relax a little. He works so hard, he's always coiled up tight as a spring."

"I know; you're right."

When Luke came in she could smell a trace of whiskey on him, but she could also sense a relaxation in him, the loosening of nerve and muscle, and she could not fault his drinking.

Their dinner was hearty, and afterwards they rested by playing parlor games. At first Luke felt uncomfortable, not knowing the games, but Sarah explained them to him, whispering with her head close to his and her hand upon his arm, and for that he would have endured any amount of parlor games.

Soon the games palled and Jake and Luke slipped out to the barn again while the women cleaned up the dinner dishes. The men reappeared and Jake, his eyes twinkling, pulled a fiddle from the closet and pronounced it time for a little dancing. Sarah clapped her hands in excitement and flashed a smile at Luke that made his heart jump.

The chairs in the parlor were pushed back and Crowley tuned up his fiddle. He burst into a fast raucous square dance and Luke whisked Sarah out onto the floor, followed by Mrs. Crowley and Burt, one of her teenaged sons. Jake seemed indefatigable, and he played for hours. Sarah danced with each of the boys and Luke took the floor with Mary Etta and even with the little girls. But mostly he danced with Sarah, and she drifted happily in his arms. Sarah had never danced much, but Luke was an excellent dancer, quick and light and sure, and with him Sarah floated through the steps. She had never seen him like this, having fun, happy and elated and among friends. His face was flushed and his eyes glittered, and he laughed and joked and teased the girls. And when they waltzed, he pulled Sarah to him, his arm firm around her, and guided her so easily around the floor she almost felt as if they moved as one person. She could feel the heat of his body and the hardness of his chest and hear the quick, loud thud of his heart. She leaned against him, losing herself in the music and the movement and the warmth of him and felt regret every time the waltz ended and the mood was broken.

The two men made several side trips to the barn and by the time Sarah and Luke left for home, Luke was rather unsteady on his feet. However, he managed to help her into the wagon and clamber up himself and direct the horses homeward. As they drove along, he threw an arm around her and pulled her close to him.

"Sally," he said, his voice filled with alcohol importance, "I am a happy man."

"Good," she said, snuggling against him and smiling at his tone.

"I have everything a man could want—a farm, a house, and the sweetest, most beautiful woman in the world." He paused, then said in a different tone. "Are you my woman?"

Something in his use of the word sent an odd shiver through her. "I am your wife," she returned uncertainly.

"Ah, but are you my woman?" he said and bent his head to nuzzle her hair. "Do you know what it means to be a woman? My woman?" he breathed close to her ear and shivers of excitement darted through her. "Sally, you're so beautiful. Do you know what you do to me? Let me love you. Let me make you a woman."

"Luke, you are drunk," she said shakily. She was excited and yet scared—he was so different from usual, so strong, so suddenly demanding, as though the liquor had unleashed the power and wildness normally kept under such tight control. Sarah was not at all sure that this Luke would not hurt her.

"You are right," he said agreeably, as his arm slid lower until his fingers touched her breast. Her flesh tingled beneath his touch. "I want you." His voice was a husky whisper in her ear. "I want to take you to my bed and undress you and make love to you. Oh, Sarah, please; please let me. I lie awake at night and think about you, about your lips and hair and breasts, the feel of your skin, the color of your nipples—so soft now, so hard when I touch them."

"Luke, please!" Sarah exclaimed, shocked at his words, and she pushed at him.

A little to her surprise, he pulled away from her. He leaned back and spread his arms wide, looking up at the sky. "What a hard, cold wife she is. Can you believe this? Denies me her bed, calls me a drunkard, pushes me from her."

Sarah had to smile at his conversational tone addressed to thin air. She reached down and picked up the dropped reins and clicked to the horses to go faster.

Luke closed his eyes and felt the light breeze ruffle his

hair and caress his face and let the movement of the team carry him along. He felt good and free and happy. He had the nagging fear that he would regret it all tomorrow, but tonight he could not help himself, did not want to help himself. The night was lovely; the stars were lovely; and loveliest of all was the woman beside him.

They pulled into the yard of their house and Luke jumped down to unhitch the team. Sarah soon realized that she would have to help him. When they had accomplished that and set the horses loose in the corral, suddenly Luke pulled her to him and began to waltz about the yard. She laughed and went along with him, enjoying the rush of the air against her, the velvet blackness of the sky and the shimmer of the moonlight, the feel of his hard body against hers. They spun, laughing giddily, until suddenly he stopped and kissed her.

His kiss was long and hard, like before, but this time his tongue plunged into her mouth, and she gasped with shock. When he released her, she stumbled back a step and looked up at him. The moonlight streamed across his face, turning his hair white and his face strange and waxen; his blue eyes glittered opaquely. He was a stranger to her, and when he reached out to touch her breast, she turned and fled toward the house. For a moment he stood, and then ran after her. He caught her just inside the door. He gripped her arms so hard it hurt and again he pulled her to him and kissed her in the same frightening way. He pushed her against the wall, his body pressing into her, and he kissed her until she could hardly breathe. His hands plunged into her hair and he tugged it loose; hairpins went flying and tears sprang into her eyes at the pain. Yet it sent tremors through her when he buried his face in her hair.

Luke stepped back, panting, and looked at her, and though she had never seen passion before, she recognized it now in his face. He pulled her to him again, but this time bent and lifted her in his arms and carried her from the room. She clung to him, scared and eager.

"Luke, please don't hurt me," she whispered in a tiny voice.

But he seemed not to hear her, just bore her inexorably up the stairs to her room. He kicked the door to behind him and carried her to her bed, where he laid her down, then straddled her. Sarah lay looking up at Luke, frightened, yet dizzily excited. His hands roamed her body freely, cupping her breasts, caressing her waist, unbuttoning her dress and unlacing her petticoats to unveil her breasts.

"You are beautiful," he breathed, his voice husky and low with desire, and he quickly unbuttoned his shirt and pulled it off, then stood to remove the rest of his clothes.

Sarah watched in fascination as he undressed, blushing at the sight of his lean brown frame and the swollen shaft of his manhood. When he came to her, she stood to facilitate his disrobing her. She could feel the eager trembling in his hands as he pulled her clothes from her.

At last he kissed her, fusing their two naked bodies together, his lips and tongue making her mouth his own. He kissed her mouth, her face, her ears, her throat, until she was breathless. Then he pushed her down onto the bed and covered her body with his. His passion raged out of control and his hands swept over her almost roughly as his mouth played over her breasts, his tongue arousing and hardening her nipples.

Luke murmured to her in broken whispers, but she could not understand him. His hand slid between her legs and she was embarrassed that he should feel the warm wetness that had inexplicably come there. But he seemed not to mind for his hard fingers explored her most private parts, even reaching inside her. She gasped and tried to pull away at that touch, but his arms were like iron around her.

"Oh, God," he groaned. "My virgin, my sweet, beautiful virgin."

His stiff shaft probed her tender flesh, pushing into her, hard and huge, hurting her, and she tried desperately to pull away.

"No, please, Luke, stop," she begged, but he was so on fire that the words did not really reach his brain, and he held her tight and plunged into her. Sarah felt as if she was being torn in two, and she struggled against him, flailing at him with her hands, but he pinned her arms to the bed and stopped her cries with his mouth. Again and again he entered her sore flesh, pumping harder and harder, thrusting into her as though he could meld the two of them together. And now Sarah clung to him, feeling through the pain some deep satisfaction at his filling her. He shuddered and relaxed against her.

"Sarah. Oh, God, Sarah."

He fell asleep with his body still pressing against hers.

Chapter XI

SHE awoke tangled in Luke's arms and legs; she blushed when she recalled the night before, then smiled to herself. How strange she felt—so light, so jumpy and excited, embarrassed that a man had seen her naked and touched her so intimately, and yet rather giggly and pleased in her embarrassment. Leisurely she went over the events of the last night, reliving each touch, each look, each sound. Oh, the sounds—she closed her eyes in pleasure, thinking of Luke's harsh, ragged breaths, his groans, his saying of her name.

Careful not to awaken Luke, she shifted from his embrace so that she could look at him. He slept as boneless and content, his face as relaxed, as a baby. There was no sign on it now of pain or tiredness or passion. She thought of him as he had looked last night, his eyes bright and hot, his lips heavy with sensuality, and the thought made her hug herself with mingled excitement and anticipation and fear. How would he look when he awoke? What would he do and say? And how ought she to respond? She wondered whether he was pleased with her and whether he would take her again tonight. And most of all, she wondered whether she had enjoyed it herself and whether she wanted him to repeat it. It was all so wildly new and unknown and frightening. He had seemed like a stranger, he had hurt her, he had violated her modesty. Yet never had she felt anything as pleasurable as his hands and mouth on her skin, never had her senses been stirred like that.

The longer Sarah lay in bed thinking, the shyer she grew, until at last she felt she could not bear to meet Luke's gaze when he awoke. So she crept from the bed and quietly dressed, then retreated downstairs to the kitchen.

Luke awoke some time later, with a queasy feeling in his stomach and a headache burning behind his eyes. Goddamn hangover, he thought foggily, and tried to orient himself. Then all too clearly his memory came flooding back in on him, and he buried his head in the pillow with a groan. Oh, my God, what had he done! He had taken Sarah—his sweet, beloved Sarah—by force. After all his promises to her, knowing she loved another, knowing she did not want him, in a fit of drunken lust, he had forced her. Raped her. He remembered her protests in the kitchen, her vain struggles to push him away;

he had ignored them, carried her upstairs and pinned her to the bed, overcome her with brute strength. After that she had not struggled—gentle Sarah, she would not fight her husband—but he could not deceive himself that she had enjoyed it. His memories were hazy from the alcohol and his own driving passion that obscured all else, but he remembered quite clearly her cry of pain when he entered her. For all his early experience, Luke had never lain with a virgin, and though he knew there was inevitably some hurt, he could not believe that it should have been so much. And because he loved Sarah, any pain of hers seemed to him greater than it was. He castigated himself for his brutality, his animalism; intent only on his own need, he had not been gentle enough with her.

She must despise him, he knew, must hate and fear him. She would feel she could never again trust him and must each night fear another attack from him. His stomach wrenched and he swallowed against the bitter bile in his throat. Rapist. That was what they had accused him of being; how bitterly ironic it was that with the false reputation he had lived with for years, he had finally raped a woman and that woman was the only one he had ever loved.

Shakily he rose and began to dress. He could not bear to face her, but he could not remain hiding in here forever. He had learned long ago to take his punishment. No doubt she would cry or storm at him and order him from her life. For a moment he hesitated; dear God, let her do anything but that—he could endure anything but never seeing her again.

Sarah was in the kitchen fixing breakfast, her back to him, and he entered the room so quietly she did not hear him. Luke stopped, watching her, thinking that she did not turn toward him because she hated him and refused to speak to him. Luke's stomach tightened; he would have to be the first to speak.

"I'm sorry. It won't happen again. I promise," he said, and his voice came out harsh and loud from the effort.

Sarah jumped and whirled to face him. His face was hard and set, the pale eyes unreadable; in his anguish, he looked as stern as death, and it set Sarah's heart pounding with fright. Her mouth was too dry to speak; she could only stare at him.

"It was the whiskey; I was crazy drunk. I swear I'll never take another drink. I swear to God, Sarah, I'll never touch you again!"

She continued to look at him, unable to speak for the thoughts and emotions tearing at her. Luke wanted to cry out that she was killing him with her silence, but he choked it back. If that was to be his punishment, then he must take it; it was better than he deserved.

He looked away from her and said, "I'm going to the fields now." He paused for a moment, praying she would not tell him to leave the farm.

"All right," Sarah managed to force out, and was surprised to hear how calm her voice sounded.

Relief flooded him, and he hurried out the back door without looking at her again. Sarah stood stock still, tears biting at her eyelids. How angry, how hard his voice had been! He must despise her, the way he had talked. "I swear I'll never touch you again," he had said. What had happened last night had happened only because he was drunk. He did not desire her, that was evident. She must have disgusted him last night, giving herself so easily to him. He did not care for her or even want her.

Sarah's stomach tightened and scalding tears slipped from her eyes. What an awful sinful person she was. She should not have enjoyed any of what had happened last night. She should not have been so curious about love-making, so ready to discover. No doubt she had encouraged him, just as she had been doing ever since he kissed her. It had all been her fault, and now Luke despised her. Now he knew what a low, wicked person she was. She began to sob in earnest; now she had even lost Luke.

The day got no better as it wore on; if anything, it got worse. Stu and Jenny and the children came out for Sunday dinner and, for once, Sarah wished her sister's family were not there. The girls' chatter grated on her nerves, and their parents angered her. Luke did not join them, and Stu looked so smugly vindicated and Jenny so pitying that Sarah wanted to scream. Yet after they left and Sarah dragged through a long, lonely evening waiting for Luke, she almost wanted them back.

Alternately, she worried that Luke had injured himself, then was convinced he had abandoned her. Dark came and still he had not come. Reluctantly Sarah went upstairs, then dawdled preparing for bed. At last, she blew out her lamp, but stationed herself by the window to watch. Moments later, her husband came across the yard and into the house. She scurried to the bed and lay there, heart pounding, some demon in her brain praying that he would come into her room. But she heard his steps go into his bedroom and the door close behind him, and she called herself ten kinds of a fool. She realized then that he had probably been lurking outside somewhere, watching and waiting until she turned out the lights so he could return without risking running into her. He could not stand the sight of her. Quietly she choked her tears. Dear God, how was she to stand this for the rest of her life?

The days dragged by. Hunger forced Luke to come to the meals, but they both sat stiff and silent, avoiding each other's eyes. In the evenings, Luke always found some excuse to go outside. Sarah was relieved to see him go—his presence would have been too painful—but it hurt her. He could not even stand to be around her, she disgusted him so much, she thought, and it made her want to cry.

At first Luke felt so ashamed, so dirty, he could hardly

bear to be close to her; he could not even think of that night or of the things he had done to her. But before long, memories began to slip in to tease and torture him. He would remember her naked body and the way it felt beneath his hands, remember the hot sweetness of her mouth and the glory of her breasts. And he yearned to have that again, even as he hated himself for what he had done. Once he had thought that if he could just have her one time, it would be enough to satisfy his need, but he discovered that the taste of her only made him hungrier. Now as he lay alone at night, he knew precisely what it was he was missing, and he wanted her more than ever.

Every time he looked at her, he stripped her in his mind; he clenched his hands to keep from reaching out and touching her. It was all he could do to restrain himself, and the longing grew worse daily. At night he dreamed hot, lascivious dreams in which Sarah crawled all over him in wanton abandon, and he would awaken sweating and trembling like a hard-run horse, his manhood stiff and throbbing. Once he had to bite his hand until it bled to keep from going to her bed and taking her again.

Why did it always have to be this way for him? Why must it always be his lot to want and never have, to hunger and never be filled? It seemed as though it must be written somewhere that no matter where Luke Turner went or what he did or how well he behaved himself, happiness would forever be beyond his reach. Here he was, with a pretty, kind, accepting girl for a wife, one who was a perfect mate in almost every way, and he had come to love her deeply. Yet to express his love was to defile her, to take pleasure in her was to rape her. His touch was abhorrent to her because she loved another man.

For the first time, anger at Sarah tore through him. Damn her! What right did she have to deny him her bed? All he wanted was his marital rights, whereas she coveted her sister's husband! Was it so awful a thing for him to make love to her, to kiss and caress her? Only because he was Luke Turner. Digger Turner—it would make a nice woman's skin crawl to feel his touch, no matter how kind she might be to him otherwise. After all, he was dirt, wasn't he? And for all her sweetness, for all the charitable things she had done for him, when it came to the most essential thing, he was poor white trash to her, not good enough to be joined with a lady.

His lips curved in a bitter smile. No doubt she hungered after "nice" sex with that paragon, Stu Harper—why, that staid storekeeper could never show her a fraction of the pleasure that trashy Luke Turner could. Other women ached for his touch; they shuddered and moaned in ecstasy beneath him. But not a lady like her, of course—she would prefer the safe, pale, bloodless lovemaking of a Stu Harper.

He flung the sheet aside and rose from his bed, impelled by some furious desire to prove himself. He would show her; she was his wife, and he would take her. Again and again he would force her to accept him, until, somehow, his body would fill her mind and heart, too. He would rape her, take her, force her until finally he drove Harper out of her thoughts, until at last she knew his touch and could not live without it.

Quickly he went down the hall to her floor, but he halted outside her room, drawn up short by the sounds coming from behind the closed door. Sarah was crying. Suddenly his anger melted from him. His breathing slowed and his fists unclenched; the red haze of fury cleared from his brain. No doubt she was crying because of him, because of the brutal thing he had done to her. And here he was, about to storm into her room and rape her again. He drew a shaky hand across his face.

What if he had hurt her? What if he had not regained control of himself? He had acted just as he used to—blind with anger, crazy with frustration, lashing out at the world for hurting him. And all it had ever done was prove to them that they were right about him.

Once he had calmed down, Luke started to return to his room, but then turned back. He knew she would want no comfort from him; yet, he was unable to bear the sound of her unhappiness. Finally he called her name softly. He received no answer. Tentatively he pushed open the door. Sarah lay in bed, her face buried in her pillow, her body wracked with sobs. His love for her pushed all else aside, and he went to her and pulled her into his arms.

"There now, Sarah; shh, Sally. Sally, my love, there now, I'm here," he murmured, stroking her back and hair.

"Oh, Luke," she breathed and threw her arms around him. She had been crying because he did not want her, because he avoided and ignored her, and now here he was, caressing and comforting her.

Her sobs subsided until finally she lay still against him. As she quieted, he became aware of her body against his, of the thin nightgown that lay between his skin and hers. Her hair smelled of honeysuckle and he rubbed his cheek against it and lightly kissed her head. He could feel her soft breasts pressed against his chest, feel the nipples harden, and the breath caught in his throat. So good, so sweet—and how easy to take her now, weak and in need of comfort as she was. His hand slid down her back to rest upon her buttocks.

Sarah felt the movement of his hands and lips, and excitement leaped in her. Now he would kiss her, now he would caress her legs and slide his hand inside her gown. It would happen again. But he did not move, and she leaned her head back to look at him. His face was flushed, his breath heavy, and his eyes were dark with desire; there was the same look to his face that had been there that other night, before he kissed her and carried her upstairs. He wanted her again, she knew it; he wanted her badly.

But he let her go, almost pushed her away from him, and rose.

"Are you all right?" His voice was angry and gruff.

"Yes." Why was he rejecting her? Why was he so dead set against her? For a moment, she was on the verge of throwing herself at him and begging him to return to her bed, but she managed to control the impulse.

Luke closed his eyes and took a deep breath. She was crying because of the wreck he had made of her life, because of the brutal, irreparable harm he had done to her. He would be damned in hell before he would seize upon this moment and damage her further.

After that night she began to tease him. It seemed to him that she took every opportunity to stir him sexually, to stoke the fires of his passion. He knew that her actions must be innocent, that it was only his ever-present lust that made the things she did seem intentionally provocative. But at times he felt that she did them on purpose—to punish him for what he had done. Why else would she find so many excuses to brush her body against him? Or so often accidentally reveal some part of her anatomy?

One evening Sarah climbed into the cherry tree to pick cherries and called to Luke to help her down. Stuck up there in the tree, she showed a great deal of her shapely legs. And when he reached up to help her down, she turned a little so that his hand touched her breast, sending waves of desire through him.

Sometimes when he came in from the fields and sat down at the supper table, Sarah would bring his food to him and he would see that her dress was unbuttoned several buttons down. When she leaned down to put the food on the table, he could see the creamy swell of her breasts.

If she was trying to punish him, she was certainly doing a good job of it. Sometimes he felt as though he might go mad with desire for her. Did she think he was made of steel, that he could withstand such torture? Luke ached to rip the clothes from her and assuage his raging passion. He cursed himself for wanting her and cursed her for not desiring him; most of all, he cursed the fate that had made this impossible marriage his lot in life. But no matter how angry he grew, or how hot with desire, he could not bring himself to seek Sarah's bed. At the last moment, he would always check himself; he loved her too much to cause her such pain.

His only recourse was to avoid her entirely. He had to see her at mealtimes, but other than that he steered clear of her. No longer did he linger at the table after a meal, talking to her. Nor did he sit with her on the back porch of an evening, watching dusk fall and the bright stars emerge. He worked sun-up to sun-down in the fields, and after supper he always found some task to occupy him in the barn or tool shed. He would tend to the animals or mend harnesses, clean the farm equipment, repair the corral fence—anything he could find to keep busy until finally her bedroom light would go out and he could creep up the stairs to his room.

But even then, sometimes she would not leave him in peace.

One night she called to him and when he went into her room, he found her standing there, her hair unbound and flowing loosely down her back.

"Can you unbutton this dress for me, please? I can't reach some of the buttons."

With hands that shook, he went to work at the buttons, his clumsiness prolonging the ordeal. The upper buttons were hidden by her hair, and he had to put his hands on the heavy silken mass and hold it out of the way. When at last he finished and started to leave, she picked up her brush and began to pull it through her hair. Slowly, sensuously, rhythmically she ran the brush through her hair, and he could not leave but hung in the doorway watching her, hypnotized. He could think of nothing but his desire to shove his hands into her hair and slide them through it. By the time she finished brushing and gave her head a little shake to put her hair in place, his legs were so weak he was surprised he didn't sink to the floor. Then she turned away, embarrassed by her own forwardness and what she interpreted as his lack of response, and her movement broke his trance, allowed him to flee to his room.

He felt tormented, driven to the brink by her teasing. Didn't she realize how she tortured him, how close she drove him to a repetition of that night? Damn it—must she punish him forever for that one time when he had slipped! She seemed to expect him to have some sort of superhuman strength, that he must take such assaults on his senses over and over without giving in to his emotions.

Like a prisoner he paced his room, swearing softly, bitterly beneath his breath. Maybe the men she was used to—cold fish like Harper or Grady Snowden—could take that sort of treatment. But not him. Not him. With an inarticulate cry of rage, he slammed his fist into the wall.

He had to have her. He did not think he could bear it any longer. But even as he asked himself how he could go on like this, his iron control made him unfasten his clothes and crawl into his bed.

After Luke left, Sarah sighed unhappily and pulled off her dress and petticoat. As she undressed and put on her nightgown, her mind ran over and over his actions.

Luke wanted her; he must—she had seen that stark longing in his eyes. Then why had he told her he would never touch her again? Why did he avoid her so assiduously? Why, oh, why had he worn that look of deep disgust with her?

The weather was hot, arid, and Sarah felt clammy with sweat. She went to the window to stand and let the slight breeze cool her body. It was late, she knew, and tomorrow she would regret her sleeplessness, but right now she could not bear to return to her bed to toss and turn in the heat. She pulled her nightgown away from her damp body and shook it slightly. If only she could stop thinking, stop *feeling*!

She leaned her head against the window frame and looked out at the darkened barn. Not that long ago, she remembered, she had stood so, looking out into the rain, and had seen Luke there at the barn door, looking up at her. With a sigh, she left the window and flopped back onto her bed.

Just three weeks ago, he had been here in this bed with her. Sarah smiled faintly and closed her eyes; softly she touched her breasts through her thin cotton gown. She remembered the way he had caressed her breasts, gently circling her nipples with his fingers until they stood up hard and proud. Dreamily she traced the path of his fingers, then ran her hands down her body as he had done. How hard and calloused his hands had felt against her skin, and yet how gently they had touched her. She remembered his breath, hot and smelling of whiskey, on her cheek and neck, and then the feel of his lips against hers, devouring, opening, his tongue probing her mouth while his hands roamed her body.

"Oh, Luke," she moaned softly, and then sat up, shaken out of her dream.

Whatever was she doing! Lying there like a wanton, lusting after a man she did not love, a man who had made it plain that he did not want her, despite that one night of drunken desire.

She no longer understood herself. It had been so strange and frightening—and how he had hurt her there at the end. Yet ever since, she had been jittery and excited, waiting, hoping, dreading, wanting it to happen again. It was a strange feeling, nothing like what she felt for Stu. Just an odd, dissatisfied, restless feeling that made her want to pace her room at night and left her unable to sleep.

Why had he stayed away from her? Was she so ugly, so undesirable? It was said that he had slept with many girls—could they all have been so much more attractive than she? Or was it that her shy awkwardness had repelled him? It had not seemed to at the time. She closed her eyes with pleasure as she remembered his kisses and the soft endearments he had murmured to her.

And hadn't she seen that same hungry look on his face the other night when he held her while she cried? Then why had he not come to her again? Surely even as inexperienced as she was, she must be better than no woman at all. Surely, with all the lovemaking he had done in the past, he didn't prefer to remain celibate.

No, it must be that he thought her a pure girl, one who would not enjoy that, especially since he knew she loved another. That had to be it: he was disgusted with her because she enjoyed it, because she let him have her body without protest. And no doubt he was disgusted with himself for taking a virgin, a good girl. And he would not take her now because he had control over himself again. Everyone called him a sinner, but he was a man of honor, she knew. He would not violate her, thinking her to be a pure woman. Moreover, he would not put her to another test where her moral fiber might fail again.

Sarah bit her thumbnail thoughtfully. There had to be a way out of this. If only he could be made to feel that he had a duty to bed her, a moral right. He had taken pleasure in her. Surely she wasn't mistaken about that. Yet if he knew she wanted to lie with him, no doubt he would be repelled. But if she had a reason, a duty, and if she pretended not to enjoy those exciting, scary things he did to her, then perhaps he would—suddenly, she smiled and snapped her fingers, then went quickly from her room before she had a chance to think and delay.

"Luke?" Softly the door opened and Sarah slid inside.

"Yes?" Luke was instantly awake.

"Are you asleep?"

"No." He watched her, his pulses beginning to pound. She crossed the room to stand at the foot of his bed, and the bright moonlight streamed across her, revealing the outlines of her firm, rounded body beneath her nightgown. He clenched his fists to keep from grabbing her and pulling her into his bed.

"I wanted to talk to you."

"All right."

She stopped, suddenly at a loss for words. What if he refused her? How could she bear the humiliation?

"I—I've been thinking about the other night," she began haltingly.

He closed his eyes in pain. "Sarah, I told you I was sorry, you have no idea how sorry. I swear it will never happen again. I won't ever get crazy drunk like that again."

"But didn't you—I mean—" Her knees felt weak, and she sat down on the side of the bed. "But did you dislike it?"

"I don't know what you want," he said, his voice tortured. "I dislike myself for doing it."

She kept her eyes fastened on the wall and said in a still voice, "What I mean is, do you ever want to do that with me when you're not drunk?"

He couldn't believe it. What was she trying to do to him? Coming in his room at night and sitting on his bed, wearing only a thin nightgown, and asking him if he ever wanted her. Surely she must realize how he ached to take her in his arms!

"Yes."

"Then you would not be completely averse to doing that again?"

The muscles in his throat tightened and he could not answer. What was her game? Was she trying to break him?

"You see," she went on hastily, "I've been thinking,

you know, about our agreement, and if we kept to that, why, then there would never be any children, would there?''

''No.'' His voice was unsteady.

''And I would like to have children, wouldn't you?''

''Yes.'' He could hardly believe what he was hearing. Surely she could not really be offering herself to him.

''Anyway, I just thought that if sometime you wanted to, you know—I would like to have a child, and we could—not that I mean tonight necessarily, but if you ever felt like that—'' She trailed off miserably, her face flushed with embarrassment.

''If I ever felt like that,'' he murmured in amusement, then in one swift movement reached down to her and pulled her up in the bed toward him.

Gently he wrapped his arms around her and kissed her, a long, soft, undemanding kiss. She felt the smooth hardness of his bare skin against her chest and she began to tremble.

''Sarah, Sarah, oh, my Sally.'' His voice was a sigh. Weeks of frustration and pain flowed out of him.

She clenched her teeth and tensed against her trembling. Don't let him know, she thought, how he stirs you. Don't let him suspect your wantonness. But softly he won her from her purpose, stroking her body, finding all the hidden spots where his touch aroused her. His lips moved over her face and neck and then down to her breasts, his mouth soft and warm and almost unbearably pleasurable. He pulled her nightgown off over her head and for a moment he lay still, looking at her naked body gleaming pale in the moonlight.

She was so beautiful; and she was giving herself to him. Everything he had ever wanted and never dreamed he could have, and she was offering it to him. It made him almost dizzy with desire and he wanted to take her immediately, thrust himself into her and satisfy his hunger. But he could not do that; she was shy and virginal, and he must take it slowly, must be careful to soothe her, arouse her, let her taste the pleasure of it. So he held himself back and caressed her body until he thought he would burst with longing. His fingertips drifted over the flat plain of her stomach, and slipped in between her legs, teasing them open.

A moan escaped her at his touch, and the sound of her pleasure excited him past bearing. He pulled his hand away and rolled over on top of her. Sarah felt him slide into her, this time with only a twinge of pain, and at last that restless feeling was satisfied. He moved inside her, riding his passion, past reason or restraint. Instinctively she wrapped her arms and legs around him, but she buried her face in his shoulder so that he would not hear her shameless noises of pleasure. At last he shuddered and relaxed against her, then rolled off. Sarah bit her lip; she was reluctant to have him leave her.

Luke put his arm beneath her head and she cuddled up against him, her head in the curve of his shoulder and one hand on his chest. His skin was cool and moist with sweat, his breath still ragged and uneven. Sarah revelled in a happiness she had never felt before, feeling all at once a tingling of her skin and a heady power at his response to her and a deep satisfaction at giving him so much pleasure.

"Heaven," he said, his hand drifting across her; his voice was strangely broken. "Your body is heaven. Sally, you are beautiful."

Sarah blushed and said nothing, hoping for more.

His hand came to rest on her abdomen. "A child—my child. Do you really want to have my child?" There was wonder and amazement in his voice.

"Oh, yes," she replied, realizing suddenly that in fact she did very much want to have his child.

"I'll work on it." He laughed softly and nuzzled her hair. "Believe me, I'll work on it."

Luke awoke feeling more content and at peace than he could ever remember feeling. For a moment he simply lay there with his eyes still closed, luxuriating in the sun streaming in the window and across the bed and in the smoothness of the sheets and in the quiet ease of his body. The hunger that had tormented him for months was gone. She was his—the legs, the lips, the breasts, the smooth flat belly; he knew her, had taken her, and her body had pulled from him all his pain and need and bitterness. Dear God, she was lovely.

He had never had a woman before who had not had another man. But Sarah had never felt the touch of any other man; no one else had ever seen her fresh young body. He alone possessed her, and the thought sent a quiver of desire through him. She had given herself to him; he was not violating her, yet he had the freedom of her body. She had given him his marital rights; now he was her husband in fact, as well as word. And none of those bastards, not Stu Harper or Jimmy Banks or any of them, would ever know the sweetness of her. Only Luke Turner would; only he had the right.

When he dressed and went down the stairs, he found Sarah in the kitchen. She was scrambling eggs and humming merrily. Luke smiled—she was happy, humming like a well-satisfied woman. She looked up at him and smiled shyly, then blushed for the thoughts that went through her head upon seeing him.

"Good morning." Her voice was soft and a little breathless.

"Good morning." He pulled her into his arms and kissed her gently. And for that moment, it would have been hard to find in the world two people any happier.

Both of them threw themselves into their work with a will. The early crops were ripening, the onions and cucumbers and tomatoes and melons. The cherry tree was already producing, and the berries and wild plums were almost gone. Sarah had more than enough canning and pickling and preserving to do, while Luke was kept busy picking the food crops and weeding the acres of commercial crops.

But they were young and healthy and it seemed now that they had enough enthusiasm and energy to take on the world. Each day Sarah worked until she felt she would drop from exhaustion, but when she saw Luke returning from the fields, his shirt off and his lean brown torso glistening with sweat, she would feel a leap of excitement and be filled with eager energy.

At first Luke tried his best to confine himself to nighttime, in-the-bed lovemaking. After all, she had asked for a baby, not for extracurricular kisses and gropings. He did not want to embarrass her or disgust her. They would sit after supper and wait for bedtime to come, the tension building in them until when at last they went to bed, they could hardly tear their clothes off rapidly enough, so hungry were they for each other.

But he found that the more he had of her the more he wanted her. Before long, he was kissing her before they went up to bed, and then caressing her, and moving back farther and farther from bedtime until soon they were spending the majority of the evening stretched out on the couch, kissing and stroking each other, delightfully tormenting themselves with their clothed bodies. Nor could he long refrain from kissing or hugging her at any time of the day.

Did all women feel as she did, Sarah wondered? Was

it only her? Was it just that Luke was special? She wondered if he had had this effect on Tess Jackson, and if so, she wondered how the girl could ever have brought herself to lie and send him to jail. Sarah rather felt that she would lie to keep him out of jail.

No doubt she was immoral to feel this way, to get so much pleasure with a man that she did not love. Love was what was supposed to make it right and good. But, frankly, she did not see how it could be any more wonderful with Stu. She smiled to herself—somehow she could not see staid, proper Stu taking his wife in impatient passion. Only Luke. Only Luke. But then, no doubt a proper girl would not have enjoyed having that done to her. It really was quite wicked, but she didn't care; she was happy, and she just didn't care.

One day Jenny and the girls came out to help Sarah with the canning, and Jennifer noticed the change in her sister. She looked softer, prettier, happier. That tinge of sadness that had always been in her eyes was gone; now they glowed. The reason for the change could only be Luke. They were obviously in love, Jennifer knew; she could see it in the way they looked at each other and the way they found so many occasions to touch. Whenever Sarah spoke of Luke and the things he had done to the farm, her tone was full of pride and warmth.

Even though she had not wanted Sarah to marry him, had never thought him good enough for her sister, Jennifer had to admit that she had been wrong. It didn't matter that he wasn't good enough—after all, who could possibly be good enough for Sarah? It didn't matter that he had a bad reputation, that he had been wild and mean and loose or even that he had been in jail. All that really mattered was that he obviously worshipped Sarah and that he made her happier than Jennifer had ever seen her. That made up for everything else, and Jenny was now his friend.

Sarah found to her surprise that she was even closer to her sister than before. She had thought that her new relationship with Luke might put a barrier between them, but instead she felt more similar to Jenny. Sarah felt more secure, more confident, no longer envious of her sister; she was now desired and satisfied, with a husband and home of her own, and children of her own in the future. Moreover, marriage was a common ground for them, since she now also knew the secrets and pleasures of marriage, was no longer an outsider. They could put their heads together and giggle over men and their funny ways.

"Stu is so silly—he thinks I shouldn't know anything about what men talk about or what bedroom kind of talk means," Jenny laughed. "The other day I overheard him and Morris Langley and Bo Wellman talking. I was in the kitchen making coffee and they were on the back porch, and of course, they didn't realize that I could hear what they said. Anyway, they were talking about Georgia and Martin Hampton. And Stu said something about how Georgia is always riding horses. Then Bo said, 'Yeah, I hear she rides Martin as well.' And they all laughed, and Stu said, 'You can bet she never goes any way but in the saddle.' "

"What does that mean?"

"I don't know. I asked Stu about it later, and he blushed. He actually blushed! And he said, 'Jennifer, don't say something like that. A woman like you doesn't need to know about such things.' He would not tell me! Can you imagine? As if I were still an unmarried girl of eighteen!"

"Well, I shall ask Luke. I am certain he will tell me," Sarah said, unconscious of the complete confidence in him that sounded in her voice.

That night, after they had gone to bed, she related the incident to Luke.

"What did Stu say?" he asked.

"He wouldn't tell Jenny. He said it was something she should not know."

Luke laughed aloud. "What an idiot!"

"Well, what does it mean?" Sarah pressed him, hardly noticing the aspersion on Stu.

"I imagine they meant that Georgia Hampton prefers to be on top in sex."

"On top!" Sarah exclaimed in amazement. "But how—"

Luke's laugh was soft and tinged with desire. "Come here, and I'll show you."

Sarah hesitated for a moment, then giggled and went willingly into his arms. Gently he guided her, teaching her to caress and arouse him, to straddle him and ease herself down upon his stiff love shaft. She closed her eyes at the surge of pleasure, then began to move on him, rising and falling, sliding sweetly up and down. She watched his face, loving the passion playing across his features. He covered her breasts with his hands, softly massaging them, then slid his fingertips all over her body.

When finally her legs grew tired, he wrapped his arms around her and rolled over, still locked together, and began to stroke within her in the more usual way. Sarah felt an odd sensation building up in her, something she had never quite felt before in her pleasure. It was as if something was growing in her, some grand and glorious thing that built into such a crescendo that she felt she must die if she did not reach the final note. And then suddenly it crashed upon her, shaking her to the depths and sending shock waves of pleasure out into her body. Within her, Luke too exploded in his passion, and they clung together, each one's pleasure multiplying the other's until at last the torrent subsided and they lay against each other in peaceful exhaustion.

After that night, Luke began to explore new paths with Sarah, to open up to her all the many varied wonders of sex. He taught her to please him with her mouth and tongue and even, despite her initial dismay, aroused her and brought her to the peak with his mouth. He tried different positions with her and was surprised and gratified at her responsiveness.

Sarah went about dazed with pleasure; she really had not known such things existed. Sometimes he pampered her, undressing her gently, even kneeling to remove her shoes and brushing out her hair in long, electric strokes. At other times he drove himself into her hard and fast, as if he would touch the very center of her. But whatever form his passion took, it made her breathless and throbbing with desire, and more and more often, he released that desire into a flood of pleasure. She was shaken, amazed—but always eager for his touch.

Luke's confidence soared. He could bring her to delight; she would wrap her arms and legs around him and shudder in sweet abandon. As June slipped away night after pleasurable night, Luke grew more sure of himself. Sure, the weather was hot and the rain seemed to have stopped coming. Sure, lots of people disliked him and sneered at him. But now, somehow, he was beginning to feel that he could handle it. Somehow it did not seem so frightening anymore.

Chapter XII

THE Fourth of July burst upon them bright and airless; July was promising to be hot and dry, after the flooding of the spring. But the weather did not concern Luke and Sarah Turner today. It looked as though it would not rain on the fireworks and dance this evening, and that was enough for them.

It made Luke smile to see Sarah so excited—she was practically floating off the ground. They were to ride with the Crowleys into town, eat lunch at Jenny's, and then watch the parade and hear the speeches with the Crowleys and Harpers. The day would be topped off with a huge picnic at the park, followed by the annual dance and fireworks display. The Crowleys would drive home, but Luke and Sarah would spend the night at Jenny's and stay on for a big Sunday dinner with family and friends.

Although Luke was excited about the festivities today,

he secretly dreaded that night and Sunday. He and Harper never got along and he did not relish facing all those inquisitive, unfriendly faces tomorrow at noon.

Sarah had none of her husband's qualms about the upcoming events; she was looking forward to seeing Jenny and the girls and watching the fireworks and dancing with her husband again. Her face glowed and she gaily exchanged loud pleasantries with Mrs. Crowley back and forth between the wagons. Now and then she would squeeze Luke's arm and grin at him in her happiness, and that made the idea of dinner tomorrow bearable for him.

As it turned out, the day was not bad at all. The women kept Stu and Luke separated so that the day would not be spoiled. Both men were blissfully ignorant of their scheme and marked the unexpected compatibility down to their own forbearance. Luke found the speeches dull and thought even worse of the one made by Grady Snowden. But he found himself caught in the excitement of the parade and thoroughly enjoyed the picnic and dance in the park afterwards.

For once in his life, Luke did not feel conspicuous and disliked in a crowd. Surrounded as he was by the Harper and Crowley families, people gave him little more than a second glance. Though the faces turned toward him were curious and not kind, at least they were no longer stamped with distaste and distrust. At least no one stepped back from him as if he might contaminate them.

And no longer did he feel the need to do something wild and violent to get back at them. The woman he loved was beside him and he could put his arm around her and let the warmth and strength of her flow into him. They danced almost every dance, until they were exhausted. The people in the dance pavilion looked at them in surprise: Sarah McGowan looked blissfully in love with Digger Turner, and he seemed almost tame! It was rather disappointing to everyone to see that their dire predictions did not seem to be coming true.

When the dancing finished, the fireworks started, and, looking at them, Luke felt as if he too could burst apart in wild, high streaks of color, so full was he of love and excitement. It made him want desperately to make love to Sarah, to celebrate the beautiful, surging love inside him, and he chafed at the delay of the leisurely stroll back to the Harpers' house. Sarah dawdled at the door to their room, talking to her sister, until he was on fire for her, hot and impatient in his desire.

When she stepped inside the room, he pulled her to him and kissed her hard, his fingers fumbling at the buttons on her dress. Sarah was startled by his sudden, forceful passion and instinctively brought her hands up against his chest to hold him back.

"Luke!" she protested, softly laughing.

"Sally, Sally," he murmured, his breath hot against her neck, and slipped his hands inside her dress to roam over her breasts.

He tugged her clothes from her, all the while kissing and caressing her until a soft moan of pleasure rose from her throat. He pushed her back until they fell onto the bed, and the great creak of the bed springs snapped Sarah out of the trance of pleasure Luke was working on her. She realized suddenly that Stu and Jenny's bedroom was next to theirs; only a wall separated the two beds. Stu and Jenny must have heard the noise; they would hear all the noises of their passion if Luke continued. She blushed with embarrassment; imagine revealing to her sister and brother-in-law her own unbridled passion. How would she be able to face them tomorrow at breakfast without blushing?

She pushed in vain at her husband's shoulders. He was adrift in his passion, his mouth roaming over her breasts as he pulled her clothing away from her body.

"No, Luke, really, please. Don't; you must stop," she whispered anxiously, but he hardly heard her. She tugged at him and her voice was almost fierce as she explained, "No, Luke, don't! Please—what if Stu and Jenny hear us?"

That remark penetrated his brain and he drew back from her. Goddamn it! No matter what he had—the farm, freedom, Sarah's delight in his lovemaking—there was always that to destroy it. She loved Stu Harper. Luke could bring her to the heights of passion, but still she loved Stu, would always love Stu. Even now, in the midst of his lovemaking, her thoughts were of Stu. She was afraid he might hear them, ashamed that he might hear her passion for her husband. No doubt he was always in her mind when they made love; perhaps she even pretended that it was Stu caressing and exciting her, not Luke.

"Damn you," he hissed, his voice harsh in his pain, and he hurled himself away from her. Sarah stared at him, stunned.

"Oh, Stu might hear us, is that it?" Luke mimicked viciously. "And we wouldn't want that. Heavens, no! How horrible for him to think you let Digger Turner put his filthy hands on you. Well, go ahead then—enjoy your fidelity to your sister's husband. Sleep alone like a virgin in his house. I'm getting out!"

He whirled and raced from the room. Sarah rose, saying "Luke?" in bewilderment. Too late she ran after him; already he had clattered down the stairs and out the front door.

"Luke." Sarah stared after him, gripping the railing of the stairs for support. "Oh, no."

After a few moments, she stirred and turned back into the bedroom. All night she lay awake, tossing and turning and agonizing over Luke's departure. She could not understand why he had left so abruptly, so hatefully. Why had he lashed out at her like that? Where had he gone? And, when, oh, when was he going to return?

By the time the sun rose, Sarah was red-eyed and pale from lack of sleep, and Luke had not yet returned. She could not imagine how she was to face Jenny and Stu or what she could say to them. They would never understand Luke's behavior; she did not, so how could she expect them to? They would be so disapproving—and just when Jenny had gotten to liking Luke! Now that would be all ruined. For the first time she could remember she felt really angry with Luke. Why had he had to act like this at her sister's house? And with all those people coming for dinner. Now there was a pretty kettle of fish. What was she to tell all those relatives and friends? They did not like her husband to begin with, and now his absence at the gathering would really put him in disgrace.

Finally, she worked up her courage enough to dress and sally forth to explain to Stu and Jenny. She had thought up a weak story to tell them about something Luke had forgotten to do at the farm and had rushed home for. She did not expect them to believe it and she could tell by their faces that they did not. She endured the morning in their quiet disapproval, feeling it so much for Luke that she almost felt as if she were the one they disapproved of. Even though she was angry with Luke, she wanted to protect him from their wrath, and she found her two-sided emotion very wearing. And when the dinner guests began to arrive, she found it even worse. Besides the disapproval toward her husband, there was also a streak of malicious delight at her discomfiture. It was as if they were all a little gleeful to see their expectations panning out. *That* would teach her to ignore their warnings.

For the sake of pride, she lasted it out until some of the guests had departed before she took her leave. After all, she would not let it appear that she was running away. But once Stu had harnessed the horses for her, she sprang into the wagon and clucked loudly to the team, spurring them on to move faster. She could hardly wait to reach the safety of home. Stu offered to follow her home, finding it unthinkable that she should venture the miles by herself. However, she felt she could not endure his company all that way; he would go on and on about Luke, and she would have to defend him, when all she really wanted to do was cry. Steadfastly she resisted his offers of accompaniment and set the team toward home as fast as they would go.

When she reached the farmhouse, it was obvious that Luke had been there; by the sink sat a plate with the remnants of a cold bachelor dinner. So at least he had returned home; at least he had not left for good. No doubt he was out in the fields working it off, as always. And no doubt he would skulk around out there until she had gone to bed so as to avoid a scene.

Well, for once that was not going to happen; she had made up her mind. As the afternoon slipped into shadows, she worked on her mending and stoked the fires of her anger. Finally she went upstairs and put out the light, then sat in the dark waiting for her husband to return.

Before long he came up the stairs, just as she had known he would, walking softly so as not to awaken her.

"I'm not asleep," she said, and he jumped.

"Sarah! What are you doing up?"

"Waiting to talk to you."

"What about?" He looked away from her. By now he felt a fool for lashing out at her like that last night. He knew she loved Stu; she had never pretended otherwise, even though she slept with him. It was stupid, he realized, to get angry because she loved another and did not want him to hear the sounds of her lovemaking with another man.

"What about!" she repeated in astonishment. "About why you left like that last night! Whatever possessed you? I can't understand it."

Luke crossed his arms protectively; at last it was coming, the berating from Sarah he had always expected and never received.

"If you had tried, you could not have done anything more likely to make all those people dislike you. They all came, thinking you are shiftless and irresponsible, and instead of staying there and letting them see you for the good person you really are, you run off, which convinces them that you are just like they thought."

He stared in surprise; he had expected her to castigate him for insulting the guests or her family or her, but he never expected her to be angry because he had not given them a chance to see how nice he was.

"They hate me anyway," he said defensively.

"But if only they knew you, they would feel differently. They would like you, just like the Crowleys do, if only you would give them the chance."

"Not likely."

"You don't know. You won't even try! All you ever do is run!"

"I'm no coward! I don't ever run."

"Oh, not from a fist fight, maybe; not from physical punishment. But every time you get in a situation that scares you, you run. If you think I'm mad or if you've done something you think is shameful, you leave the house as early as you can and hide out in the fields all day."

"That's not true!"

"It is! The way you fight, the way you try to look tough and uncaring, the way you act 'bad,' all of those are running. You are scared of people and what they are going to do to you and what they are going to say about you. So you try your best to keep them away from you. You run from them. You run from letting them see you as you really are."

"Shut up!" he cried, and slammed his fist into the wall.

Sarah's insides clenched at the show of violence, but she stood her ground. "You left the house last night so you would not have to face those people today. You ran from them."

He stood unmoving, taut as a bowstring, and Sarah feared that she might have gone too far, that he might snap with the strain. Cautiously, she went forward and reached out to touch his arm. He jerked away from her.

"Please, Luke." Her voice filled with tears. "At least don't run from me. It scares me to be all alone without you. I need you."

Suddenly the tension drained from him and he reached out and pulled her into his arms, holding her so tightly she could hardly breathe.

"I'm sorry, Sarah," he said, his voice muffled in her hair. "I'm sorry. I swear I'll never leave you alone again."

July continued hot and arid. It had rained very little since the floods of the spring, but in July the lack of moisture was heightened by the intense heat. Each day the sun rose like fire, reddened by the dust hanging in the air, and set each night in the same way. And in between the day lay heavy and scorching.

"It feels," Sarah told her husband, "like someone put a huge clear cover over us all and then sucked all the air out."

As if the heat were not bad enough, Sarah began to often feel sick. When she got up she felt slightly nauseous until she had forced down a little breakfast, and sometimes in the afternoon she would feel dizzy and would have to sit down to keep from fainting. At first she attributed her sickness to the heat, but its regularity made her decide instead that she must have some dread illness. It was not until one day when she realized how long it had been since her last monthly, that it finally dawned on her that she was pregnant.

The thought jolted her, and she quickly sat down. Pregnant. It was hard to believe. She could not really be pregnant, not her, not Sarah. Such joyous things were reserved for others, like Jenny, not her. Slowly the realization of it seeped in, and she grinned to herself. A baby—a beautiful little blond-headed, blue-eyed baby. She closed her eyes and thought of Luke coming in from the fields and being swamped by a clan of little tow-heads, saw them laughing and jumping and swinging on him, saw his own gilt head bent to converse with them.

She wanted to leap up and run out to Luke immediately and share this happiness with him. Except—a thought stopped her dead in her tracks—once she told him, she would no longer have an excuse to lie with him. She had told him she wanted it only to bear children; he thought her a good, pure person who would not want sex just for the pleasure of it. If she told him she was pregnant, then he would expect her to stop sleeping with him. She could hardly bear the thought of giving that up until they could work on another child. Neither could she bear to see his disillusionment if she let him know how much she wanted him.

The only solution was to avoid telling him. She could not put it off forever; before long, her condition would begin to show. But at least she could delay it for a while. At least she could shorten her future period of abstinence a little.

So she did not tell him. However, she continually worried about it. She was almost bursting with a longing to share the joy with him and also torn with guilt at hiding this happiness from him. Yet the thought of the consequences made her suppress these emotions.

At any other time, Luke would have noticed the change in her, both physical and emotional, but just then he was too concerned with his failing crops to notice much of anything. The drought was stunting his crops, slowly strangling them. And now the blast of the July sun was literally scorching them. Slowly the more tender crops shrivelled and turned brown. Before long, he knew, the others would follow suit.

He racked his brain trying to find some way to stave off the seemingly inevitable death, and came up with a way to use the creek that ran twisting through their land. First he dammed the little creek, then hoed trenches down the rows of his crops, all running back to the main trench leading to the creek. He opened the trench into the creek and the water collected there flowed out and irrigated his crops.

His scheme gave his plants a few more days of life than those of less innovative farmers. But the creek was very low and soon dried up completely and once again the drought began to work on the fields. And there was nothing Lúke could do but watch his crops slowly brown and die in the sun.

Chapter
XIII

TIREDLY Luke undressed and crawled into bed. Every bone in his body ached wearily. The drought was beating him—with all the work and sweat and heart he had put in it, the weather was whipping him. Tried and failed. Tested and found wanting.

He rolled over on his side away from Sarah; he could not bear to look at that pretty, trusting face. She had believed in him, and he had let her down. A sun-scorched crop dying daily on the vine, that was all he had to show for all his toil. As always, his brightest hopes had turned to ashes in his hands. For the first time in a long while, his lonely, black despair closed around him, shutting out Sarah, smothering him.

Sarah sensed his unhappiness. She knew how bitterly disappointing it must be to see his beloved crops wither and die before his eyes, although she did not really understand that their death represented a personal failure to Luke. However, she was rather unsure as to what to do to ease his depression.

Softly she ran her hands over his hard back, her fingers tracing his bones and the funny little ridges here and there on his back. Her gentle touch penetrated the black fog of his feeling, and his throat closed with emotion.

"Luke, what are those little scars? Did they—did they do that to you in prison?"

He swallowed hard to maintain control. He could not tell her about them and yet he felt a tremendous desire to pour out to her all his past hurt and let her ease it.

"No," he said, his voice rough with restrained pain. "Those are from a belt buckle. Dad used to strap me with his belt when he was drunk. Only sometimes he swung the wrong end and the metal would—"

He stopped because the tears welled up inside him and all the old hate and fear and pain boiled in him until he felt he must explode if he went on. Sarah's hand halted on his back; she was too horrified to speak or even move. Luke was rigid with tension from holding back his pain, every muscle tensed to force it all back down inside him. He couldn't let it go, couldn't fly all apart in front of her.

Then Sarah moved closer and softly kissed his scars. Somehow the gentle tenderness of her touch broke his resistance and suddenly, helplessly, he began to cry. Scalding tears flowed down his face and his body was racked with desperate sobs. Sarah wrapped her arms around him, and he turned into her, and they clung together, their arms tight and hard around each other. At last his sobs quieted, and he began to speak, his words bursting forth as if torn from him.

He told her of his past, of all the pains and sorrows, the beatings, the fights, the anger, the humiliations, all the horrors of his loveless childhood. Tears of empathy sprang into Sarah's eyes at his words, and she clutched him tightly, fiercely, as if she could protect him from his past, drain the black emotions from him with her touch.

Finally his voice trailed off and he lay against her, numb and exhausted from the emotional upheaval. There was a strange quiet in him now, a peace he had never experienced. Sarah's arms were soothing, healing.

"I've never had anything good in my life till you," he said. "I've never been worth a red cent."

"Don't say that!" she said and squeezed him tighter. "You are a fine, brave, wonderful man. They are the ones who are despicable, everybody who did those things to you. Awful, horrid people. All you ever needed was a little encouragement, and no one ever gave you anything but pain."

"Except you," he said, his voice drowsy. "Except you."

She caressed his hair and gradually his taut body relaxed, and just as he slid into sleep, he said, so softly Sarah was not sure she had heard correctly, "I love you."

* * *

The next morning Luke drifted awake, lazily peaceful. He remembered the night before and flushed with embarrassment. What a fool he had made of himself—imagine telling Sarah all those painful, shameful things. Imagine breaking down like that in front of her and crying like a kid, like a girl. She must think him pathetic.

Cautiously he looked over his shoulder. Sarah was out of bed and sitting at her dressing table, braiding her hair. She paused and glanced up and saw him in the mirror. A radiant smile broke across her face.

"Good morning," she said, her voice warm and light, as always.

He could not help but smile back and roll over so he could watch her more easily. It was amazing—there was no hint of contempt in her manner. If anything, there seemed to be more liking for him than before. Funny, he did not even feel so bad himself. He felt better, sort of purified; as if Sarah had pulled all the bad feelings from him last night.

I said them, and they're gone, and she doesn't hate me, Luke thought, and almost laughed out loud. Even the drought did not seem so hopeless now. Some years were bad and the farmers lost, but next year he might make it up. Farming was not a sure thing for anyone; he wasn't the only one to suffer. Besides, maybe he was not yet licked. If he could hold out for a while longer, the rain might come to his rescue. If he could just save the crops a few more days. There was always hope.

"The river," he said aloud, and Sarah turned toward him.

"What?"

"I could haul water from the river for the crops."

"How?"

"Take the wagon down there, loaded with all the barrels and buckets we have, pull up water from the river, then bring it back here and water the crops."

"But, Luke, that would take forever! Think of how much water that would be for all those crops."

"I know. But I could try, Sally. If I don't try, I might as well just give up and die."

Sarah looked at him for a moment and then smiled. Luke would never quit; there was iron in him, a tough unbreakable spirit. Knowing, as she did now, all the harshness of his past, she could see clearly the courage in him. He never gave up and went bad like Earl, despite everything. He had clung on stubbornly and tried over and over and faced them all down. She felt a warm rush of pride and admiration for him and gratitude that he was her husband.

"I'll go with you," she said.

"No, it's too hard for you."

"Please, Luke. You'll need help; you know you will. Those barrels are heavy. Please—I want to be of some use. Think how much quicker it would go if there were two of us working."

He smiled at her. She made sense, and he was flattered by her eagerness to help him. "All right."

The day was hot and airless, and even the early morning ride to the river drained the moisture from them. The sight of the river reminded Sarah of that Sunday, which now seemed so long ago, when she and Luke had gone there to retrieve her parents' bodies. The water, then so wild and overflowing, now was placid and shallow, shimmering languidly in the sun. She remembered how Luke had searched the rushing river for her mother's body, risking his life to dive again and again into the murky water. Even then he had protected her, helped her. Poor Mother. She wondered if her mother knew how wrong she had been about Luke, if she saw now how well he looked after her. For a moment her eyes clouded with tears at the thought of her mother, but then she turned to Luke and smiled.

All day they worked as if possessed, dipping buckets into the sluggish water and hauling the water to the barrels sitting in the wagon, then driving back to the farm to unload the water and pour it into the irrigation rows they had dug before for the creek water. Once that was done, they would start for the river again to repeat the process. It was exhausting work, and they kept at it steadily all day long, pausing only to consume a quick cold lunch. By the time they finished loading the last wagon load of water for the day, Sarah felt numb with tiredness and drenched with sweat.

Luke took her hand and led her down the river bank to a group of shade trees around a slight bend in the river. It was a quiet, secluded spot, sheltered by the trees, and Sarah sank down gratefully onto the ground. For a while they sat and rested, listening to the gentle lapping of the river and watching the play of the dying sun on the water.

"It's so beautiful," Sarah said with a tired sigh. "I'd love to just jump right in it and wash away all this grime."

Luke smiled briefly and then said teasingly, "Why not?"

"With all my clothes on? No thanks."

His eyes sparkled and he said, "Then take off your clothes first."

"What!" Sarah exclaimed, a little shocked—and yet a little intrigued by the idea.

"Why not? Who's to see? Close to the bank, the bend hides it from the road."

"But, Luke, right out in the open—" She looked at him, her eyes beginning to reflect the mischief in his.

He rose, grinning, and began to undress. Sarah felt excitement rising in her throat and suddenly stood up to peel off her clothes as well, feeling headily reckless. Like giggling children, they ran naked into the water, screaming with glee as the water enveloped them. Sarah doused herself well, letting the water swirl away the dirt and sweat and tiredness. She undid her hair, unbraiding it and combing it through with her fingers, and ducked underneath the water to wet it.

They cavorted like children, laughing and splashing water at each other. Sarah felt free, wild, unrestrained, and when at last Luke stood still and reached his hand out to her to pull her close, she went eagerly into his arms. He kissed her, and they wrapped together in a tangle of arms and Sarah's loose, long hair. His hands slid over her slick, wet body, drawing wonder all anew from it. And there, in the heat of the dying afternoon, amidst the water that had carried her parents to their deaths, he put his life into her, and the river gently swirled around them and flowed away.

Chapter XIV

DAY followed sweltering day, with never a break in the dry heat. Luke and Sarah worked from dawn to dusk carrying water from the river to irrigate the crops. It was exhausting, numbing toil, but still they fought on, until finally the level of the river got so low they dared not take out more, or there might not be enough left for drinking.

After that, there was nothing to do but watch helplessly as the sun baked the life out of the farm. Probably a third of the corn was dead already, and only immediate rain would save the rest. The frustrated waiting wore on Luke, and one morning he could stand it no longer.

"Let's go into town," he said at breakfast.

Sarah stared at him. "But it's Thursday."

He shrugged. "What does it matter? There's nothing I can do here except watch the corn shrivel. Besides,

Mexico needs to be reshod. We'll take the wagon and get some supplies. Come on, it'll be a break, at least."

Sarah agreed. She knew he had felt better about losing the crops ever since that night he had told her about the beatings. He no longer seemed to take it as an indication of his general failure at life. But still, it was killing to his soul to have to watch his crops wilt in the blazing sun. It would probably do him good to get away from it for a while.

When they first reached town they stopped at Jennifer's and had a glass of lemonade and talked and played with the children. Little Jonathan was actively crawling around and pulling himself up to stand now. Sarah stroked his silky head and thought about the life growing in her own stomach. She was convinced now that she was pregnant; even Luke had make a joking comment the other night about her thickening waist. Soon it would be obvious, and she would have to tell him. Oh, how badly she wanted a plump, soft baby like this, a blue-eyed, silver-haired child of Luke's. And yet, how awful if he then expected her to leave his bed.

After lunch they went on to Stu's store to buy supplies. Luke and Stu loaded the wagon and Sarah decided to drive it back home and start supper while Luke remained in town to have the horse shod. Luke walked back inside the store to pay the bill, but Stu stayed a moment to help Sarah into the wagon.

Luke turned and watched them; he saw Sarah turn her

head toward Stu and smile, saw the way Stu flashed his charming smile and solicitously put his hand under her arm. Damn him, he thought, the familiar jealousy gnawing at his vitals, he tries to make her love him. He wants her admiration and he doesn't care what that hopeless love does to her.

His anger, his jealousy, the pain of his love for Sarah, the frustration of his crops burning in the sun all boiled up in Luke. When Stu returned to the store, Luke's emotions broke from his control and he snarled, "Can't you leave her alone?"

"What?" Stu turned toward him, startled.

"Goddamn it, you must see what you do to Sarah! She loves you, and it kills her. But you do everything you can to keep her loving you."

Stu stared him, open-mouthed, and Luke flared, "Don't you care? You're so damned selfish, all you care about is your own satisfaction. You never think about the fact that if she didn't see you so much, if you didn't try so hard to be so God almighty charming, she might get to where she didn't love you anymore. To where she was happy with her own home and her own family and not forever hungering after something she can't have."

"You are crazy!" Harper retorted, stunned by Luke's words. "Sarah loves her sister. She would never—"

"Of course she 'would never,' " Luke said, his voice heavy with sarcasm. "That's what cuts her up. That's why it's so cruel of you to encourage her love."

"You're insane. I don't believe you."

"You are a blind, selfish fool," Luke said bitterly. "But I'll give you a warning. I'm tired of you messing with Sarah. Leave her alone. Just leave her alone."

The young man slammed out the door, leaving Stu staring after him in shock. Never before had anyone spoken to him like that, and he found it hard to comprehend. The boy had practically threatened him there at the end. Imagine that—someone threatening him! And Sarah in love with him—ridiculous. Sarah was a tender, innocent girl; she would never consider loving her sister's husband. It was just Digger Turner's own lewd mind that interpreted her feelings and actions in that way. Luke was a jealous maniac who had no understanding of higher emotions.

All afresh it struck Harper how wrong it was, Sarah's having to live with that scum. His very presence degraded her. No doubt he forced himself upon her constantly. He envisioned all too clearly Sarah lying passive beneath Turner's hot passion. No doubt he berated her about his jealous fantasies. He probably threatened her, too. Poor Sarah, out there on the farm, lonely and afraid, too embarrassed and too fearful of Luke's wrath to return to her family.

Stu rubbed his jaw thoughtfully. Of course, that must be it. Sarah just did not realize that he and Jenny would accept her gladly despite her unfortunate marriage. She must not know that he would protect her from Luke, that the whole town would. That was it; otherwise, she would not have remained there.

Well, obviously it was up to him to save her from this disaster. He must go out to the farm while Luke was occupied at the blacksmith's and convince Sarah to leave. He would explain how they would welcome her, how they would surround her with protection. Once she realized, once she understood, she would be eager to leave.

Quickly he went home to harness the surrey and follow Sarah. He arrived at the farm shortly after Sarah did, much to her amazement.

"Stu?" She came to the kitchen door, alarmed. "What's the matter? Did something happen? Is Jenny all right? The girls?"

"Yes, yes, of course," Stu said and came inside, slightly annoyed at her misinterpretation.

"Luke! Oh, no, what happened!"

"Nothing is wrong with *him*," her brother-in-law snapped, now fully irritated by her concern over the villain of his plot.

"Then what is it?" she asked, puzzled.

"It's you, Sarah."

"Me? What on earth—"

"Sarah, I've come to take you home."

"Home? What are you talking about? I am home."

"No, I mean to Jenny's and my house. Sarah, there's no need to pretend; we won't turn you away. I know you must think that because of your marriage to him, we no longer want you, but that's not true.''

Sarah stared at him, so amazed that she could not speak.

Her brother-in-law, misinterpreting her silence, went on, ''Don't be afraid, Sarah. I won't let him near you. You'll be perfectly safe.''

Suddenly Sarah began to laugh—it was so utterly ridiculous. As if she was scared of Luke! As if she had any desire to leave him! She had everything she could possibly want, and here Stu was, offering her sympathy.

Stu stared at her in complete confusion. What on earth was she laughing about? The stunned bewilderment on his face only made Sarah laugh harder. He sighed and shoved his hands in his pockets, exasperated.

''I swear to God, I don't understand you, Sarah! What is so all-fired funny?''

''Oh, Stu, I'm sorry,'' Sarah gasped, trying to force down her laughter. ''I didn't mean to laugh. It's just that it's so silly. Why should I want to leave Luke? Why on earth would I need your protection from him? The only problems I have are the heat and the drought, and I don't think you can do too much about them.''

''But, Sarah, Luke Turner—''

''Hush! I won't hear a word against him, even from you. He is a fine person, a gentle, good man, and he's never been anything but kind to me. He's the dearest, nicest, handsomest man around, and—''

"You can't—you can't mean to say that you are in love with him!"

Sarah stared at him, hanging on the thought. In love with Luke. *In love with Luke*. Suddenly it surged through her—but of course, how obvious: she loved Luke. For so long she had had her mind set on loving Stu that she had stubbornly refused to see the truth. Her every waking thought, her every feeling, was for Luke; she yearned for his body and his touch, felt truly satisfied only in his arms. Of course, she loved him; there really was no one else in the world for her.

She smiled and radiance flooded her face. "Yes," she breathed. "Yes, I love Luke."

Stu could only gape at her, utterly astounded. Sarah had to giggle. Poor Stu—looking at him now, Sarah wondered how she could ever have imagined herself so in love with him. She realized suddenly that much of her love had been just because he was Jenny's husband. He had been a part of what she had most wanted all her life: to be like her sister. What she had desired was not so much Stu, but the love and adoration that Jennifer always received and she did not. Stu had simply been an embodiment of all that was forbidden. She put her hand on his arm and stood on tip-toe to place a brief, sisterly peck on his lips, a good-bye gesture to all her foolish girlhood dreams that had no place in her reality.

By the time Luke finished waiting for Mexico to be shod, he had cooled down and regretted his words to

Harper. No doubt Harper would repeat them like an idiot to his wife or maybe even to Sarah herself. Let Sarah catch wind of the fact that he had revealed her secret to the very one she most wished it kept secret from, and she would hate him forever.

Besides, even if Harper did not repeat what he had told him, it had been stupid to reveal Sarah's feelings. Now Harper would think about it, and the more he thought about it, the more it would interest him, until he might grow to want to test Luke's theory, to use Sarah's love. And then Sarah would be lost to Luke.

As he rode back to the farm, Luke grew more and more depressed. When he saw the Harpers' surrey, despair washed over him. So Harper was already out here—dear God, was Sarah already lost to him? With leaden feet, he walked to the house and up the back steps. He reached for the door and froze in the movement. Stu and Sarah stood in the kitchen, talking. Although he could not hear Sarah's soft words, he saw the glow of love on her face as she stared up at Stu. He saw her put her hand on his arm and then reach to kiss him.

With an inarticulate sound, Luke broke and ran. Sarah heard the sound and turned, startled. She saw a bright flash and it took a moment for her to realize that Luke had been there, then another moment to realize that he had seen the kiss. No doubt he had misinterpreted. Of course, he must have, knowing as he did how she had felt about Stu. He had seen it and had run, as he always did, hurt and angry and scared.

"Luke," she said and started for the door.

Stu grabbed her arm. "Let him go, Sarah. He's not worth it."

"Let go of me," she snapped, twisting from his grasp, and ran for the door.

However, by the time she got there, he was gone from sight. She clenched her fists and blinked to keep back the tears. Why had he had to arrive at just that moment, to see that innocent kiss and assume from it that she was giving her love to Stu, when in reality she had just discovered that she loved Luke! It was so unfair, so wrong!

Angrily she bit her lip. She had to find Luke; she simply had to. She must explain to him that she loved him, not Stu; that she wanted a life and home with him; that she carried his child; that she wanted more than anything else to make him happy. She had to find him—what if he was so upset this time that he never came back? She must follow him, but where could he have gone? This was his home and she was the only person who cared for him.

He must have returned to his father's shack; it was the only home he had ever known besides this one. Unless—he had completely given up on her and the town and left for parts unknown. Resolutely she pushed the idea from her mind; she must not think that, absolutely must not.

She had to reach him and make everything right. She could not let herself think of any other possibility. Determinedly she set off toward the Turner place.

"Sarah, wait!" her brother-in-law called after her. "What are you doing? Where are you going?"

"To the Turner place."

"Have you gone daft? You are going there by yourself? No, you can't."

"And why not? They are my husband's family. What harm can come to me there?" she said with false bravado, for in truth the people frightened her. "I have to find Luke. He thinks—oh, he has everything wrong, and I have to explain to him. I have to tell him how I—" She broke off and began walking away.

Stu sighed in exasperation and followed her. "All right, then; get in my surrey and I'll take you."

She paused, tempted by the idea of Stu's protection, but she shook her head. "No, I don't think so. It would only make Luke madder to see you with me."

Purposefully she strode off and Stu grimaced and kicked angrily at a stone, then sat down on the porch steps. Obviously she would not let him accompany her, but he could not just leave, with her unprotected like that.

Sarah walked quickly over the fields, now and then breaking into a run. And all the time her brain pounded in time with her feet: she must find him, she must find him.

When she reached the shack, it looked ominously quiet. There was no sign of Luke, and her heart began to skitter with fright. Cautiously she approached and stepped up onto the porch. Still no one appeared and she went inside. The old lady dozed in the corner, her snore a rhythmic purr in the silence. Sarah tiptoed past her into the kitchen, then the bedroom. Nothing. Her shoulders slumped in despair and she turned and left. She had been wrong; there was no telling where he was now, she could do nothing except go home and wait and hope for his return.

Blinded by her tears, she almost did not see the man standing beyond the porch. When she did, her heart lifted for a moment, then plummetted when she recognized that it was not Luke.

"Well, hello, little lady," he said, his voice a sneer, and she frowned. Who was that? He seemed somehow familiar. "So the little wife is out looking for him, huh? Now, why would he be staying out on you? I always knew my little brother was a fool."

"Earl!" she exclaimed. "What on earth are you doing here?"

"My home, ain't it?" he said, the same sarcastic tinge to his voice.

"Yes, but the sheriff—"

He laughed. "Ah, are you worried? I *am* touched." He moved closer, and Sarah felt trapped there on the porch.

Funny how he resembled Luke in some ways—the

coloring, a certain tone in his voice—and yet he was so essentially different. He seemed so coarse, so dirty, so evil somehow; it made her feel queasy to see the similarities, like a distortion of Luke.

It took all her courage to move forward. He did not move, just loomed there at the top of the steps, and she had to sidle past him to leave the porch. As she did, he grabbed her waist, and her stomach jumped in fright.

"Say now, no need to be so haughty. Don't I get to kiss the bride?"

He grasped her shoulders and pulled her to him. She twisted her face away, but roughly he turned her head and kissed her hard, ruthlessly on the mouth. In terror, she lashed out at him, kicking and struggling so fiercely that he released her in surprise, and she ran, screaming. He recovered quickly and came after her, catching her from behind.

"Let go! Let me go!" she cried, flailing her arms and legs vainly. "My God, what are you doing? I am your brother's wife!"

He merely laughed in reply and hurled her down onto the ground. She fell so hard, it knocked the breath from her, and she was too stunned even to move before he had dropped on top of her. His weight pressed down upon her, and his breath was hot against her neck. She closed her eyes in fright and despair.

Then suddenly, miraculously he was gone from her. Dazedly she opened her eyes and struggled to sit up. Earl was several feet away, rolling over and over in the dirt with a man. Luke! Though Earl was larger, he was on the losing end of the fight. Luke attacked him like a demon, his fists pounding into the other man relentlessly.

"Luke!" Sarah called weakly, and staggered to her feet.

Her husband was straddling Earl now, his fingers digging into his brother's throat, his face a mask of fury. Sarah rushed to him and tugged at him.

"Luke! Please, no, you're going to kill him! Luke, he's your brother!"

Finally her voice penetrated his brain; he looked up at her and the crazed expression left his face. He looked down at his hands as if they belonged to someone else and quickly pulled them from Earl's throat.

"Sarah." He stood up and she flung herself into his arms.

"Oh, Luke," she sobbed into his chest.

He pulled her away, leaving Earl gasping for air on the ground behind them. "Come on. Let's go home."

It was some time before Sarah could regain her composure enough to speak. But at last she raised her head and wiped the tears from her face.

"How did you know? Where did you come from?" she said shakily.

"Harper told me where you had gone, and I followed you. When I got close, I heard you scream, so I ran and there you were. I could kill that son of a bitch! He's lucky I didn't.''

''But how—'' Sarah said, puzzled. ''Where did you see Stu?''

''At the house. He was still there when I came back. See, I ran away, hurt and mad, saying to myself that I'd leave and let you have him, if that was what you wanted so bad. But then I slowed down and I thought about what you said that time after the picnic, that I was just too scared to face up to things, that I always ran. And I knew you were right, I was just running hurt and scared. I realized what a mess I was leaving you in. There you would be, with a farm and no one to work it, and everyone scorning you because your husband ran out on you. You couldn't have Stu any more than you could before. I couldn't fool myself that I was helping you; I was just running from you and—and everything.

''So I decided that I wasn't going to run anymore, that I was going to face up to life and accept it the way it is. I know you love Stu, and I know you don't love me—God knows I'm not worth it. But you can never have him, and you need a husband. I can take care of you and provide for you; we can have lots of kids and be a family, a real family. I don't think I ever admitted it before, Sarah, 'cause I was ashamed of myself and afraid of what you would say, but—I love you. I love everything about you: the way your eyes change color, your laugh, your walk, your kindness, the soft way you moan when I make love to you.

"I'm scared of that—of loving you, of the pain that can mean to me, of laying my soul out so maybe you could cut it to ribbons. But I'm not running anymore; that way I lose everything."

Luke looked straight ahead, afraid to see the reaction on her face. Sarah took his hand and held it; she was unable to speak. All her newly discovered feelings swirled around in her until finally they burst from her in joyous laughter.

Luke's jaw hardened. "God, Sarah, don't laugh at me."

"Oh, no, no, you don't understand!" She pulled him to a stop. "I wasn't laughing at what you said. I was laughing with happiness. I was laughing at how silly I've been and how beautifully everything has turned out.

"Oh, Luke, don't you see?" She pulled at his arm, forcing him to face her. He looked down at her, his face open, his eyes dark with love and pain and fear. "Luke, I love you."

He stared at her in stunned surprise. At last, he spoke, his voice low and almost rasping, "Don't tease me, Sarah."

"I'm not teasing you! Luke, I love you. I love you!"

Some final, painful restraint in him broke, and he reached out and pulled her to him, wrapping his arms around her as though she were life itself.

"Oh, Sarah," he murmured, his voice cracking, and buried his face in her hair.

She clung to him as tightly. Home at last; safe and warm and loved. In all her life she had never felt the swell of love she felt now.

"Sarah, I can't believe—" Reluctantly he released her and stepped back a little to scan her face for truth. "Why? How?"

"Why!" she repeated in amazement. "How can you even ask? You're so kind, so hardworking, so good and strong. And you're so—" She smiled and glanced at him a little shyly. "So handsome and—and I love what you do to me in bed."

He chuckled. "Oh, Sarah, do you honestly mean it? Sometimes I'm afraid I must disgust you, that you only endure me for the sake of a child."

"Good heavens, no! In fact, I'm quite certain that I'm in the family way; I have thought so for over a month. But I didn't tell you because then my excuse would be gone and I feared you would stop."

"A baby! You're carrying my child? Oh, Sally—" He picked her up and swung her around in his happiness, then paused and looked down at her. "Good God in heaven, Sally, why would I have stopped?"

"I thought, perhaps, you held too fine an opinion of me, that you would think me too good to do that just for pleasure."

"I do think you're good; I think you're the finest

woman that ever lived. But nothing could make me happier than your wanting me and enjoying my touch.'' He looked down at her for a moment, like an artist gazing at the work that culminated his efforts and that he had never hoped to achieve. ''Sally, oh, Sally, I can't believe this has happened.'' Gently he traced the lines of her face with his fingers. ''That you should be carrying my child—a beautiful little girl, just like you.''

Sarah giggled. ''I was thinking more of a little blond, blue-eyed boy.''

Suddenly he caught her to him. ''Sarah, I love you. I could die I'm so happy.''

''It's going to be good. From now on, whatever happens, we'll be together. Nothing can be too bad, if we have that.''

''Sarah, look.'' Luke stiffened, his gaze suddenly riveted on something behind her.

She whirled to look, and there, on the horizon, clouds were building, dark, heavy clouds, skimming low across the sky. ''They're moving. Oh, Luke, they're moving toward us.''

A cool breeze suddenly fanned them, lifting Sarah's hair and tugging at her skirts.

''That wind's coming off rain,'' Luke said.

Sarah laughed with glee. ''Luke, it's going to rain!'

He grabbed her hand and pulled her along with him and they hurried toward home, running eagerly back to the farm.

The rushing wind grew stronger, pushing against them and carrying the dark thunderheads swiftly towards them. Lightning flashed jaggedly, and there was a low rumble of thunder. The sky darkened above them, and even as Luke and Sarah ran, fat drops of rain began to splash down on them. Thunder and lightning cracked again, and, as if on cue, rain began to come down in torrents.

By the time they reached their house, both were soaked through, but neither of them cared. Luke turned his face up to the pouring rain and lifted his hands, revelling in the feel of the water on his skin. Saved! Their crops were saved! He had managed to keep enough life in the crops so that, with this rain, they would revive. Other farmers had not irrigated their land, had given up their crops to the relentless dust and heat, and those brown stalks would not be helped by this late, generous rain. But Luke's plants would swell and grow greener. He had succeeded where others had failed—he, Luke Turner! In a wild outpouring of exultation, he picked Sarah up and whirled her around and around in the drenching rain. She laughed and clung to him, feeling giddy and secure at the same time.

At last, happily exhausted, they went into the kitchen. They stripped off their wet clothes, hung them before the stove and towelled vigorously at their wet hair. Finally, warm and dry, Sarah stretched contentedly. Luke's eyes lit up with appreciation, and she laughed softly. Gently, without speaking, they came together. Luke kissed her, a long, deep kiss, and Sarah felt as if her soul were rising up to meet him. They separated long enough to go upstairs to the bedroom.

"Luke, look!" Sarah gasped when they stepped inside the bedroom. She pointed out the window.

They walked to the window and looked out at the sky. The swiftly moving storm had passed as quickly as it had come. The farm lay glittering and clean in its wake, and over it all lay the smell of rain and freshly watered earth. On the horizon, as bright and shimmering as a promise, rose a rainbow, its iridescent bands of blue and pink and gold arching across the clearing sky and trailing off into infinity.

"A rainbow—it means hope," Sarah breathed.

Luke wrapped his arms around her and gazed at the sight. Hope. It meant more than that—all the glorious green promise of new life. He bent his head and kissed his wife.